MW00939681

Strangers and Pilgrims Series
Book Two

THE CONTINUING SAGA

A PLACE FOR FARMER AND EMILE

Written By

John and Patty Probst

A Place for Farmer and Emile
By John and Patty Probst

Printed in the United States of America

ISBN 1-60034-655-3

Unless otherwise indicated, Bible quotations are taken from the King James Version.

Cover illustration by Yakovetic

www.xulonpress.com

Angie,

God crosses our paths with others, always with a purpose and reason. Never loose sight of the Big Picture — forever in Heaven.

Blessings!

John + Patty

Jan. 2013

We humbly give all the Praise and Glory to a loving God, who not only called us to this mission with a message, but also gave us the stories for this series and the incredible images contained therein.

We dedicate this book to Pat Walmisley for her tireless labor of love, transcribing our longhand scribbles into something readable.

To Joni Nicholas for endless hours of editing in the midst of caring for her husband, three small children and going to school.

Also to daughters Connie and Wendy whose interest and enthusiasm was a consistant spark of encouragement to keep us going on this mission.

FOREWORD

In my Father's House are many mansions: If it were not so, I would have told you. I go to prepare a place for you. And if I go and prepare a place for you, I will come again, and receive you unto myself; that where I am, there you may be also.

John 14:2 & 3 KJV

Sing the wondrous love of Jesus
Sing His mercy and His grace
In the mansions bright and blessed
He'll prepare for us a place

CONTENTS

PROLOGUE

From the time man was cast from the beautiful Garden of Eden into a harsh and unforgiving world, the question has been asked, when man and woman dies – will they live again?

It soon became apparent to Adam and Eve that what once seemed timeless, now had an end. They observed everything around them live – then die. They both no doubt asked the question that every living soul since has pondered in their minds, and weighed on their hearts, when I die – what then?

True, that question evokes more questions, such as what comes after death? Where will I go? Who will I see? Will I remember and recoginze my loved ones? The Bibles' answers are cut and dry, and by faith, Farmer believed what it said. Those who trust in the Son of God, Jesus Christ as their Savior are taken to Heaven to live forever with God. Those who reject the Son and what He did on the cross for them are separated and alone for all eternity in a hellish place.

Amazingly, every generation since Adam and Eve has produced people who think, "God said that but He didn't really mean it". So they devise their own answers and beliefs to the questions about life after death.

"Everyone goes to a beautiful place," is a popular belief, "or we keep coming back until we get our life right, then we are transported to a wonderful existance." Many just hope it will work out for the best. Others believe they will come back as another person or in a different form. Those with a "do everything and get everything you can right now" attitude must believe there is no life at all after this one. But what if the Bible is true? What if God meant what He said? What if Heaven and Hell are real?

Chapter 1

NEWS

Farmer and Emile Trevor had faced near death experiences during the long and dangerous trip in a chuck wagon from their farm in Texas to claim their homestead land in Oregon. Even though they both were secure in knowing that Heaven was their home, they weren't homesick just yet. They had exciting living to do in a new land, and their thoughts were filled with raising their children, starting a herd of cattle and living each moment with vitality.

Christmas Day of 1925 was filled with meaning. They were warm and cozy in the log house neighbors had helped them erect. Leah was almost two months old. She was already displaying some of her Pa's restless spirit. Walter and Clifton had fallen in love with their new home. It was near impossible to keep them indoors, even on days that were freezing cold. Presents around their Christmas tree were sparse but special, and each opened with excitement.

"I reckon this to be our best Christmas!" Farmer declared as they feasted on wild turkey, potatoes and vegetables. The smell of fresh baked bread filled the room.

As 1925 drew to a close, Sections 8 and 12 of the homesteads remained unclaimed. The other ten homesteads had been settled on and homes built. The deadline was December 31st, but one day before the closing date, Olaf Anderson, a Swede, arrived from the northeast to claim Section 12.

Winter was raging, making any attempt to help Olaf build a house on his property impossible. He found a rental cabin in town owned by the Pacific Timberline Company and moved in there, taking a job at the mill.

The first months of 1926 were days of more snow and long nights of bitter cold. The Trevors fared well in their log home, but began to wonder if spring would ever come.

Farmer finally managed to get their stuck pickup back to the house – but driving into town was out of the question. Those days the wind howled, blowing drifting snow, Farmer had to cover the horses with blankets and keep them in the small shelter he had hastily thrown together. Farmer worried that if winter didn't end soon feed for the animals would run out.

By the time patches of green grass began to show amongst heaps of lingering snowdrifts, Farmer was restless to the point his patience was at an end.

He was eager to get going on all the activities he had worked out over and over in his mind during the course of the long winter months.

Emile was excited to at last go with Farmer into Douglas Landing for supplies – and news of what was happening in the world – hopefully news from home. It had been over two months since Farmer had ridden Dusty into town to check mail.

Emile went directly to O'Malley's Merchandise with baby Leah. Farmer went to the post office and the bank with Walter and Clifton right behind him. He wanted to make sure Rollin Graves would increase his loan so that a sizeable herd of cattle could be purchased. Rollin nodded his "go ahead when you are ready."

Emile took Leah to Dr. Put. This would be the first checkup since Leah's birth. The doctor assured Emile upon completion of their examinations that they were both in excellent health.

When Farmer came walking up to the truck, he waved letters for Emile to see. She excitedly ripped open a letter from her folks. They wrote of a possible trip to Oregon for a visit the summer of 1927. Emile squealed with delight when she read that her sister Susan was courting an attorney from Dallas, Texas named Andrew Neilson. The Holts wrote that the town was growing and now had a gasoline station. Hirum and Vivian had traveled to Dallas to see Susan and purchased a brand new Overland Six automobile while there.

Farmer's mother Allison also wrote. It was time for spring planting to get underway. Brother Jacob and Dorothy seemed happy in their marriage livin' in Farmer and Emile's old house. She suspected they might even be expecting! She told that Farmer's sister Stella was caught at school smoking a cigarette. Farmer was concerned when he read she didn't want to go to church anymore with the family and had tried to run away.

Farmer's heart broke when he opened a letter from his little brother William. William wrote how he longed to go off to school and Pa forbid it, 'cause he needed to stay an' help out on the farm. William told how he admired Farmer's fine courage to just up and leave. He hoped to be that brave!

A short letter from Margaret Hatchet brought tears to Emile's eyes. There was also a letter from Benjamin asking about the trip and did his maps help? He did promise to travel to Oregon to see them; however, most of his letter was full of talk of places he found easy liquor and women. This left Farmer greatly disturbed and again he breathed a prayer for his friend.

A letter telling news of the church members and how Farmer, Emile and the boys were missed came from Pastor

Beckner. He wrote they had heard of little Leah from Farmer's mother. Farmer was saddened that no one spoke of his Pa. Reverend Beckner went on to write that he hoped they had settled in their new home and church and were happy!

Emile took Farmer's hand, and without speaking a word both realized how much they missed their family, friends and church. There was no church in Douglas Landing, and Holt seemed so far away...

Chapter 2

BEST OF SUMMERS'

By the middle of spring, Farmer had bought a sizeable herd of Herefords. He was told that breed could withstand the long winters the best, so he made his buys at the cattle auctions in the Applegate Valley. He established his own brand and invited neighbors to help place a "Circle T" on the left flank of each heifer and steer.

Farmer increased the corrals and built a loading pen. He constructed a barn for hay storage, chicken coops and some hog pens. He cleared a patch of ground so Emile and the boys could grow a garden. He kept enough money from the cattle loan to buy a four-door automobile.

"Family's gettin' too big fer the pickup," he remarked to Emile one warm day. "Reckon we best go into the valley and get us a car." It didn't take them long to choose a Buick, and to go along with the new car; Farmer talked the local Forest Service into using their grader to clear a better road to the Trevors' log house.

The car was hardly broken in before Emile approached Farmer, "I want to learn to drive the car, dear."

"Don't know, Emile. The Buick is a powerful big one, and like herdin' six o' them horses at once!"

"I drove the chuck wagon."

"An' I reckon there were times it near got the best o' ya!"

"What if I need to go to town, and you can't go?"

"Jus' don't think it's a good idea. Women not as strong an' all an' air not made for drivin' cars like men air."

Farmer saw Emile's face get red and her jaw set, but she said no more.

By early summer the homesteaders gathered along with some of the loggers to make sure every ranch had adequate houses or outbuildings.

The first house-raising was for Olaf Anderson, then a barn for Beth Younger. Junior and Maybelle Springfield got a bigger home. Next, winter wood was gathered for the Millers when Lyman got down in his back. A road was in need of clearing' across the north property line of the McQuirk's to reach Clarence and Locust Tree Judd's house and on to Pendleton Green's place. Farmer had again enlisted the help of the Forest Service and was on the McQuirk ranch when Gardner Grubb emerged from a stand of pine trees.

"Howdy," Farmer acknowledged him. He had never met Gardner.

"Ye on my property?" Grubb growled.

"Don't reckon so," Farmer replied dryly. "Yer line be against those trees."

"Jus' make sure an' keep off my land!" Without further words Mr. Grubb disappeared into the trees. Farmer made up his mind to go visit the man one day. Gardner had never gathered with the rest to help – nor had he ever asked for help.

"Dang, he's a strange one," Joe replied when Farmer inquired about Grubb. "I keep invitin' him!"

Farmer and Emile were the happiest they had ever been. They felt a deep contentment and lacked nothing – except a church. They felt led to start a meeting in their home.

Joe and Sally were eager to come. With Rachel and the Trevor children they could have a Sunday school. Gordon, Ella May and little Gordie Brooks joined them by the second Sunday. The men decided to take turns giving a sermon. Junior and Maybelle came after Farmer and Emile paid them a visit. That very Sunday Maybelle announced they were expecting their first child, and the service turned into a celebration.

Beth told them when invited she was not a churchgoer.

It was not long after they started the home meetings that Farmer and Emile discovered an abandoned homestead. They had walked to the Baltmans for a Saturday lunch to talk over plans for the upcoming Fourth of July. After lunch Farmer and Emile decided to walk along the east bank of the Shanko River. The sun was warm with a gentle breeze echoing the sound of the river water as it brushed the treetops. It was a beautiful day for exploring! Walter and Clifton ran ahead and played – throwing rocks into the river. Farmer carried Leah, and Emile followed him through the trees. About halfway to Douglas Landing they happened upon a large, empty log house. The door hung on one hinge, windows were broken out, but it was in a beautiful setting on the bank of the Shanko.

They ventured inside. A wood rat's nest of sticks, pine needles and cones covered a corner. As they stood in the center of the log house, Farmer felt a chill run up his back.

"You thinking what I am?" Emile smiled.

"Yep! Reckon this be a good church in the woods. Need some cleanin' – ifen we can get this place, an' have ta build a bridge cross the river from the main road."

The next week Farmer drove Emile and the children into Applegate to the county seat to find out who owned the abandoned homestead. Emile disappeared with the children while he opened up the land records. She was waiting for him in the car with a strange, satisfied grin on her face.

"I reckon ya been up ta somethin', Emile," Farmer spoke curiously as he climbed in the car.

"Went to the library to borrow some books I can read to our children – and I also found this. It's a California paper from last year – last year!" Emile emphasized. She had her finger on an article. "I want you to read this!"

Farmer read the heading: "American Automobile Association Declares That Women Drivers Are As Competent as Men."

He looked at her for a moment with a blank stare – then burst out laughing. He shook his head as he slid out of the car and motioned for Emile to get behind the wheel.

"Now?" she gasped.

"Reckon it be as good a time as any. Long way home, so's ya should be learned or we be crashed," Farmer teased.

"Oh, no!" groaned Walter. He crawled down on the floorboard of the back seat.

"Will we be dead?" Clifton asked wide-eyed.

"Stop it! All of you! I'll drive this Buick if it kills me!" Emile shouted, grabbing hold of the steering wheel.

That night after supper and the children were in bed, Farmer and Emile sat on their porch. They listened to the tumbling creek below them and watched the moonlight shimmer over the fast moving water. They heard the lowing of their cattle in the distance.

"I've never been so happy!" Emile exclaimed.

"How so? 'Cause ya learned ta drive our Buick?"

"No, silly!" Emile hit him playfully.

"It's – just – all this!" she motioned widely, spreading her arms. "This has been the best of summers!"

Chapter 3

CHURCH IN THE WOODS

Records of deeds revealed that the same landowner who attempted to buy the unclaimed Section 8 owned the abandoned homestead. Section 8 was a prime piece of land with Cold Creek angling from the northeast to the southwest corner, cutting across the northwest tip of Beth Younger's place. When 1926 arrived and no one had presented themselves to settle Section 8, most of the homesteaders placed bids on it with the government; however, Cascade Lumber Company outbid them. The government had not yet made a decision to sell that section.

But Cascade did own the timberland where the abandoned log house was located. Farmer immediately made a trip into the mill at Douglas Landing to speak with the mill boss. Above the scream of the saws, Farmer could barely make out the boss's answer.

"Can't give permission to use the house for anything, but can tell you Cascade Lumber is interested only in the timber rights of the land it owns."

"Who ya reckon I needs talk ta?" Farmer shouted.

"Springdale!" was all Farmer heard and figured that was the head office.

Farmer and Emile planned a trip to Springdale with Joe and Sally for the following week. When the day arrived the two families piled their children into the Trevor's Buick and took off on the two-hour trip to Springdale. It took them some time to locate the headquarters for Cascade Lumber Company, as Springdale had grown into a sizeable city. Farmer and Joe went into the building and asked to see the owner Uriah Wallheim.

"It is not likely you can speak with Mr. Wallheim. He is an extremely busy man," they were told. "May I direct you to someone else?"

"Cascade Lumber owns some land in Douglas Landing that has an abandoned log house we could use for a church – if we get permission, of course," Joe explained.

They were directed to seats where they waited for nearly an hour before they were ushered into an office. The man behind the desk eyed them suspiciously as they made their request.

"And you expect Cascade to up and give you that house and land?" the man asked coldly.

"Not askin' fer givin'," Farmer replied, "Just usin'."

"I don't see the need for a church in Douglas Landing. What's to keep our mill hands from burning it down – just for the pure cussedness of it."

"The church is for us homesteaders, an' the townfolks – mostly," Joe tried to smooth the conversation out.

The man grew silent.

Finally Farmer spoke. "Our country is growin', an' I reckon thet churches is part o' thet growin'. Helpin' men replace their cussedness with better ways. Ya tell me which is the better worker – a man who's drunk an' beat up most the time – or one who is respectable with a family? We's jus' askin' fer a place ta let thet change happen."

"So, what do you want from this company?" the man questioned abruptly.

Joe started to speak, but Farmer interrupted. "Yer permission ta fix the house into a church on a acre o' land."

"Church going people I have known are always out to get something for nothing," the man snarled.

"Then we can pay for the use!" Joe retorted.

"How much?"

"What ya askin'?" Farmer felt angry.

The man eyed them thoughtfully for a moment. "You say you are homesteaders? You got land?"

"Yes, sir," they answered in unison.

"Then you give me permission to log the timber on your land."

Farmer felt he had been slapped in the face! Joe looked at him.

"Fer all my life," Farmer started slowly, "I hed me this dream o' comin' west ta raise cattle. Finally the Good Lord gave me my chance. I traveled months in a chuck wagon with my wife and babies ta get here. My place was more'n I could o' dreamt, and I met me some most givin' an' helpin' neighbors. We is growin' an' we want us a church buildin', I reckon, mighty powerful, but mister, ya is the taker – not us! Ya want ta come onto our land and strip off the timber which I reckon ta be worth a whole lot more than yer rundown empty house on a acre o' land."

The man's face turned scarlet as he began going through papers on his desk.

"Good day, gentlemen," he spoke with contempt.

Farmer and Joe were briskly escorted outside and found themselves standing on the boardwalk.

Little was said for sometime on the way home. The women chatted and the children played. Emile and Sally made futile attempts to cheer their men up. Farmer didn't know how Joe felt, but he felt like the air had been knocked out of him. He couldn't take it anymore – he had to say something about what had just transpired.

23

"I jus' don't understand this! I believed fer sure the Good Lord wanted thet log house ta be fixed into a church. I reckon we musta been the only ones hearin' it."

They spoke of other possibilities. Maybe some place in town.

"Maybe we could jus' borrow the money from Rollin at the bank and buy the land and house outright," Farmer suggested.

"Farmer, you know I'm against takin' out a loan," Joe objected angrily.

"Then how ya reckon we do it?" Farmer shot back.

Emile put her finger to Farmer's lips, but he brushed her hand aside. Joe and Farmer were becoming close and good friends, but they had disagreed on this one point from the start. Farmer took loans from the bank. He wanted to grow his ranch fast. Joe, on the other hand, started with what they had and was increasing his herd slowly. He and Sally wanted no debt. Farmer and Emile's Herefords were five times the number of Joe and Sally's. The Trevors drove a new Buick and the Baltmans drove an older Chevrolet they had come to Oregon in. At times Farmer saw Joe's wisdom – other times he saw Joe as afraid to take a chance. Farmer knew this much! Joe would never agree to a loan to buy the property for a church.

The next Sunday service at the Trevor house, Joe gave a report of the trip to Cascade Lumber Company in Springdale.

"We next to got booted out for askin'!" Joe laughed.

"Looks like the Lord didn't want us to have our church in the woods," Ella May spoke up.

Farmer put the matter out of his mind until the next week when he was in O'Malley's Merchandise, and Michael O'Malley told him, "The boss at the Cascade Mill has been lookin' for ye, man. Says he need be seeing ye."

Farmer wasn't sure he even wanted to talk with anyone from Cascade after the way he had been treated – but his curiosity overpowered any thought he harbored of ignoring him. He drove by the mill on the way home.

One of the workers directed Farmer to the office where the mill boss welcomed him.

"I have a letter from the owner of Cascade Lumber Company, Mr. Uriah Wallheim himself. He gives you his apology for the way you were treated. He overhead the conversation from his office, and assures you that employee you spoke with has been reprimanded. He goes on to say that he admires how you stood up for what you believe in, and he commends your pioneer spirit in making Douglas Landing a progressive and better community. Mr. Wallheim has begun the process to issue a title deed for the acre of land on which the log house sits for the purpose of building a church. And, Mr. Trevor, he has instructed me to assist with any materials you may have need of."

"I reckon – I don't – rightly – know – what I – should – be - a sayin'," Farmer stammered, "but – I know – this! We all is most powerful grateful ta Mr. Wallheim, an' ta ya too!"

Farmer couldn't wait to get home to tell Emile the exciting turn of events. They immediately got in the pickup and drove to the Baltmans to share the good news with Joe and Sally.

After Farmer relayed the conversation at the mill and let them read the letter from Uriah Wallheim, the four adults sat looking at one, then the other. Suddenly they burst out laughing and crying while they hugged.

"I'll never understand the Lord's ways as long as I live," Farmer shook his head. "'Bout the time I figure He ain't doin' nothin', is when He's a workin' it all out!"

"An' without the help of the bank!" Joe laughed.

"Let's start tonight," Sally clapped her hands gleefully.

"We're getting our church in the woods," Emile said softly.

Chapter 4

BETH

Widow Younger was attractive and immediately caught the men's eyes. In fact, it started with Pendleton Green at Beth Younger's house raising. Pendleton was from Chicago, and he seemed confident his big city polished charm would win Beth's heart. As the air turned warm in springtime, he hoped that Beth would also warm up to him. He called on her often.

When Farmer and Emile teased Beth about Pendleton and a wedding, she giggled and her cheeks flushed – then she grew sad as quickly as she had laughed.

"I miss Morgan so much," she spoke with a faraway look. "My thoughts for him have never dimmed, my love has not faded. I don't know if I could ever love any man as I did Morgan..." she turned her eyes away.

Olaf Anderson fell for Beth the first time he saw her. The day of his housewarming', Olaf asked her hand in marriage. She thanked him, but could not be his wife. Olaf was crushed and locked himself in his house for days. Farmer rode Sunset over to talk to him.

"Thet's the pain o' lovin' a woman," he told Olaf. "Yer love fer her can be so powerful ya think ya will die – but ya can't force her ta love ya back ifen her heart's with another. Beth still grieves fer her dead husband."

Beth Younger never attended a Sunday meeting at the Trevors, but she came to help clean and fix up the church in the woods. A wood floor was put down, doors and windows replaced, seats cut and nailed. Side rooms were fixed for the children, and, of course, Beth's presence guaranteed that Pendleton and Olaf would be there.

When the work was completed, Farmer was afraid Beth would not be back. He and Emile were delighted when she showed up for the first Sunday Service of the Church in the Woods – and the second – and third. It was Farmer's turn to give the sermon on that third Sunday which was the Fourth of July. They had planned a dinner on the grounds and an Independence Day celebration.

"This be our Independence Day." Farmer spoke. "From slavery an' death – from guilt thet makes ya sick - from tyrants!" He remembered the soldiers who had given their lives in the Great War to preserve our freedom, and Christ who gave His life on the cross to buy our freedom.

At the end of his talk, Farmer gave an invitation. "I ain't no preacher," he said, "an' I don't know ever'thing there be about God an' the Bible. But I know there be lots o' folks in the world with a great hunger ta be free an' ta know God. I met a woman in Utah, Ruth Riggs. She had a wantin' ta give her heart an' life to God – jus' didn't know how. I tol' her ta jus' ask. Jus' ask Jesus ta come inta her heart and make it well. She did an' I saw a transfermation in her face – right 'for my eyes! I'm sayin' ya can know Him in a real personal way today. Ifen I – or anybody else can help ya – come forward an' we can pray."

There was silence. Some began to squirm in embarrassment as no one said anything or did anything. Farmer prayed and waited. Beth slowly stood up. A gasp rippled across the room. She walked forward to take Farmer's hand.

"Farmer, I want to ask Jesus - " her voice broke, and she began to cry. She wept, asking Christ into her heart. In an instant Beth was a new person.

Chapter 5

UNLIKELY MATCH

October was truly an Indian summer. Caring for the cattle filled Farmer's days. He never tired of riding through trees and across sunny meadows – of spotting several steers with his and Emile's familiar brand – of herding his cattle off the other homesteaders' land back onto his own. Some evenings he would throw a line into Cold Creek near the house, and fish awhile with Walter and Clifton. It was near the same spot that Leah took her first step trying to reach her Pa.

Now Walter was attending school in Douglas Landing. Emile had completed her canning from the garden. In the summer, they had traveled several hours to a place called Huckleberry Mountain. The Baltmans, Brooks and Millers were also there. Tents were put up, and everyone picked and ate huckleberries by day, and talked and sang around the campfire at night. On the second day the women cooked preserves while the men continued picking berries.

Farmer was picking huckleberries in a thick patch when he felt a tug on his coat. He turned to look down at Walter who appeared upset.

"I caught Clifton and Rachel kissing!" he spoke as one sick to his stomach.

Farmer chuckled as Walter stormed off. The incident didn't cross his mind again until that mild October Sunday afternoon after church. He was sitting on the porch of their log house watching the boys and Leah play games.

"I love the sound of the water on the rocks," Emile remarked as she sat down beside Farmer. She watched the children for a while, and then said thoughtfully.

"I wonder who they will marry?"

"Well, I reckon Clifton will marry Rachel," Farmer responded in a definite tone.

"Yes, they play together well, don't they?"

"More'n thet, Emile. They's kissin'!"

"What!" Emile was shocked.

"Walter said he caught them in the huckleberry patch akissin'."

"They are just children, and their whole life ahead. They will meet others..."

"I was in third grade and ya in first when we fell in love, Emile."

Emile giggled.

"Anyway, I reckon Clifton and Rachel to be a likely match."

"Oh, look!" Emile pointed. "It's Beth."

Farmer caught a glimpse of Beth's old car she had bought that summer. She soon arrived and parked by the house. Farmer and Emile and their children met her as she stepped down.

"I just had to talk to somebody, and you all are my best friends!" She brushed her hair from a face that carried a look of perplexity on it.

"Come, sit and tell us," Emile invited.

"We missed seein' ya in church this morn," Farmer said – sensing a problem.

"That's just it! I feel I can't go nowhere!" Beth spoke in exasperation as she plunked down in a chair. She picked up Leah who was holding up her hands.

Walter and Clifton stood around a moment – then sensing this would be woman talk, wandered down to Cold Creek to resume their play.

"Being a single woman 'round here is likin' to being a honey pot in the barnyard. Attracts flies from ever'where. Pendleton drives me plumb nuts with his ways, an' Olaf is a good man, no doubt, but dull as a hammer. They came callin' at the same time the other day actin' like two little boys arguing an' near got into a fight. I have the feeling they just come to church to see me, and I want no part of that! I go into town and the loggers follow me – so I try to go when they are working. Then, even some men – I know they are married with families – try to get sweet on me!"

Beth shook her head in disgust. Leah got down.

"They can't understand that you are still grieving over Morgan and not thinking about courting or marriage now," Emile offered.

"But I am thinking about it! Yes, I miss Morgan – I love him with all my heart."

Tears filled Beth's eyes and spilled over and down her cheeks. She bared her heart.

"I get so lonely – especially at night. Sometimes I'm scared – sometimes I feel helpless and weak. My heart and soul aches for Morgan. I felt like part of me was ripped away the day he died. It seems so foreign – distant to me to think of loving another man like I did Morgan. I – wish he could have – seen this land – he had a dream too, Farmer. I – wish you could have - "

Beth covered her mouth; her face drew up in painful memory. After a moment of gaining her composure, she went on.

"Pendleton wants a wife and children – he wants me, but his ways are too cocky, and to be honest, I just don't love him – that way. And Olaf – I think he loves the possibility that our homesteads are next to each other, and we could have babies and a bigger ranch."

"I've talked to Olaf," Farmer wanted to defend the man's sincerity. "I reckon his love is real fer ya."

"Sure it is! He loves me about like a bull loves a heifer. I just can't love him – that way – to be his wife. In fact, I had decided that there would never be a second chance for me – until yesterday..." Beth's voice trailed off as she remembered.

"I was in town – not here but in Applegate. On the walk coming out of a store was Donald Parrigan – right in front of me. He removed his hat and stood in front of me. He asked to buy me some coffee and pie. Like a fool I accepted – and we talked – we talked through seven cups of coffee and two hours, and he – he stirred my heart."

"Oh, Beth! That's wonderful!" Emile exclaimed.

Beth buried her face in her hands.

"No, it's not!" she moaned. "He is rough and wild. He drinks all the time and fights. He ends up throwin' someone out Zeck's window every time he goes there. He's got a reputation he has to live up to. It's told that before we came – he and this woman got to drinking and they went off and got married. Next week when they finally sobered up, she got scared of him and ran away. He's nothing but a wild, crazy, drinking, fighting lumberjack. How could I feel anything for a man like that? Those feelings frighten and anger me both. I don't know what to do!"

"Oh, dear! Beth. Donald Parrigan? Oh, dear!" Emile put her arm around Beth.

Farmer rubbed his forehead. "Thet would plumb be a most unlikely match," he muttered.

Chapter 6

DONALD PARRIGAN

Little was known about Donald Parrigan's past. Story passed around that Donald's mother passed away giving birth. His father was a coarse, loud, cussing, drinking man who gave Donald to the grandmother to raise him. The rare moments of sweetness, gentleness and a manly kind of chivalry came from her influence.

But there was too much of his father in Donald. When the grandmother got too old and could no longer handle the boy, the father took him in. He taught Donald to fight and drink. Finally, the young lad ran away and took to the Northwest to find work in the lumber camps. He was strong and broad of shoulder. He displayed skill with an axe and saw, thus by his eighteenth birthday he proved himself as a capable timber faller. He had worked several years now for the smaller of the two Douglas Landing mills- Pacific Timberline.

Donald Parrigan fought and drank as hard on the weekends as he worked during the week. Despite his ways, Donald was well liked by the other men. He could always be counted on for a good joke as well as a hearty scrap.

When Donald put away some whiskey under his belt, he got mean. He could easily take on half a dozen strong guys.

He would deliver blow after crushing blow to the face. When he lost his temper he would always throw someone through the front window. When Zeck left the window boarded up and refused to replace the glass anymore, Donald threw his opponents out the door.

Women were afraid of him, and Donald found female company much lacking in his life. It was rumored that when he married the woman was drunk. When she sobered up and discovered to her horror that she was Mrs. Parrigan – she fled the town. Some weeks later Donald was served with an annulment.

Donald saw Beth for the first time at her house raisin'. He admired her beauty and watched her graceful movements. He began to feel a deep down inside longing for a wife. As he watched the families – especially the children, he realized how very much he had missed in his own upbringing.

Donald was at every house raising – working hard – secretly watching Beth. His heart grieved with hers when she spoke of Morgan. He tried to approach Beth at the house-warmings, but his legs turned to water, his heart raced and a lump formed in his throat. The one time he got close enough to Beth to speak – all that squawked out was a high pitched, nervous, "Howdy!"

He left that day frustrated and upset with himself. The tough lumberjack – fighter, was frightened by a little slip of a woman. Scared as a rabbit hoppin' up to a coyote! He gave up hope of ever having a woman like Beth. He couldn't compete with Pendleton's city charm – or Olaf's blundering boldness.

So when he walked into Beth in Applegate that day, he was so stunned before he could be frightened or nervous – out came,

"Would you have some coffee – maybe some pie with me, and we could – talk?"

He was flabbergasted when she accepted, and as they talked, she had a way of making him just be himself. All of the hard work he did – the cussing, drinking and fighting – he never felt as much a man as he did that day with Beth. He discovered how fulfilling, wonderful, exciting and fascinating the companionship of a woman could be. When Beth excused herself to leave that day, she took Donald's heart with her.

So it was no wonder when the next week's work was over that Donald drove out to Beth's place to call on her. She met him at the door, but didn't invite him inside. This surprised Donald and allowed his shyness to overtake him.

"I came – well – I thought – maybe we could talk some – more," he stumbled over his words.

"Donald, the only place I will see you or talk to you is in church," Beth spoke kindly.

"Miss Younger, I just came to - "

"Mr. Parrigan, I will only see and visit with you at church!"

Beth stepped inside and closed the door.

Donald was dumbfounded, but he didn't give up. Sunday afternoon he returned with flowers and a gift. He knocked and knocked, but Beth refused to answer the door.

He saw her in Douglas Landing and walked towards her. She held up her hand for him to stop!

"In church," is all she said.

His first thoughts were, "She's not worth gettin' duded up like some city slicker and church going like a weaklin'" But his heart refused to accept that – she was worth it!

Then he grew angry! "How dare she try an' force religion on me."

Then he reasoned, "Alright – I go to church an' see Beth. Once we get acquainted real close – I just don't go no more. Like a skunk sneakin' in the henhouse." Donald chuckled at his own joke.

When Donald finally mustered the courage to attend the Church in the Woods and walk through the doors – he wasn't sure if the congregation's reaction was one of surprise, or wonder why he had taken so long.

Joe Baltman gave the message that morning. When he finished he asked if anyone had anything to say. After a moment, Beth stood up.

"When I arrived in Oregon," she began slowly, "I had no one. My husband, Morgan, had died after a valiant battle against sickness, and my family was a thousand miles or more away. I was alone – lonely! You all became my family. The most wonderful thing you did for me was tell me about the Son of God, Jesus Christ – no, you showed me! With your lives and your - kind and loving deeds. I gave my heart to Him and believed. I am not the same person I was when I first came here."

Farmer watched Donald's face. He was intent, taking in every word which Beth spoke. After church everyone made Donald welcome, although Pendleton and Olaf acted threatened by Parrigan's presence.

Folks began leaving after awhile until only Farmer and Emile and their children were left with Beth and Donald. Donald spoke to Beth.

"I was hopin' we could get better acquainted and maybe like each other – a little?"

Farmer and Emile started to leave.

"Stay!" Beth implored.

Farmer could tell by the look on Beth's face she was struggling to be strong.

"Donald," Beth's voice was nervous. "We live in two different worlds. I'm headed to Heaven, and you're on a road to – to a burning hell!"

"What!" Donald sputtered, his face instantly growing red.

"Let me finish," she ordered. "Why would – how could I like you – or love you? You are nothing but a prideful, brawling, dirty talk drunk. You can't love a wife – you love your bottle too much, and you don't want a home. You already have one at Zeck's Tavern!"

Farmer felt the sting of Beth's verbal onslaught, and it wasn't even directed at him. Donald looked like he had been dealt a knockout blow!

"I'm changed, Donald Parrigan. I could never fall in love with a man who wasn't a Christian and who couldn't share my love for God, and the thought of a man coming to church just to see me, well – well it makes me..." Beth couldn't finish her thought. She was crying.

"Please, Donald, I don't – can't see you like you are – ever – again."

Farmer could only imagine what Donald felt as he climbed into his car to drive away. Would he be back, or was he lost forever? Only Donald Parrigan could make that decision.

Chapter 7

DECISIONS MADE

N
o one heard from Donald Parrigan. He neither called
on Beth nor returned to church. Word voiced around
town and out to the homesteaders was that Donald seemed
absorbed in his work.

Farmer thought about the Sunday Donald came to the
church service – and Beth's pointed and determined decision
about any kind of a friendship with him that hit Donald's
heart like a lightning bolt. Farmer prayed that God would
reach into the young man's life and hoped to see him in
Douglas Landing on one of his trips there.

But there was more wood to gather against a winter that
was soon to make its chilly presence felt. Some of the older
steers needed to be sold at the market and a bank payment
was due before the first of the year. With so much work to
be done, Parrigan faded into the background in Farmer's
thoughts – until the fourth Sunday after that one Donald was
in church.

"Please come see me!" Beth implored Emile after the
service was over. "Please come today, before the snows start!"

Farmer, Emile and their children drove to Beth's place
for a visit that afternoon.

Clifton would rather have gone to the Baltman's so he could play with Rachel. Walter didn't care to see Rachel, and the Brooks' son, Little Gordie, was closer to Clifton's age. He preferred to go into Douglas Landing where he had made friends with some boys his age.

But Leah adored Beth, and Beth felt the true aunt. She was present at Leah's birth. Leah got down out of the car and flew to Beth's door as fast as her little legs would run – falling down, getting up, running. The boys wandered towards the corral to pet Beth's horse.

Beth had coffee on and chattered about different things. Winter coming on – caring for her small cattle herd, her car not sounding so good.

Farmer listened to her and Emile make conversation and watched their faces. Beth seemed troubled and appeared nervous. Finally, at an opportune moment, he broke into their conversation.

"Beth, I ain't no expert on women, don't 'fess to be, but I reckon I know enough ta see ya be bothered 'bout somethin' an' are tryin' ta get a 'round to tellin' us."

"Farmer!" Emile scolded.

Beth dropped her eyes and stared at the floor.

"He's right, Beth," Emile took her hand. "He's no expert on women."

"No, he is right. I have been bothered. I have been harsh and hateful to the men who have come around, especially to Mr. Parrigan. I fear I have driven him completely away. I should have encouraged him more, but how can I love a man like him? There are nights I feel ashamed at how I treated him, then when the sun has come up, I think I did the right thing."

"Do Pendleton and Olaf continue to call on you?" Emile asked.

"Yes. They are friends. They are good men. But I do not love them. But I could have feelings for – Donald."

Farmer thought for awhile before he spoke. "I read in my Bible it ain't good ta hook a horse an' a ox ta the same plow. Ya know the Lord, Beth, an' Mr. Parrigan don't. Ifen ya was ta get hitched up an' he never got saved – thet would be a powerful big tragity! Why would ya want ta live with someone fer yer life – then be separated forever? I think ya did right. These matters need ta be settled first – ifen ya is ever to be Mr. and Mrs."

Nothing more was said concerning Donald Parrigan, and no one seemed to see or hear from him, until December 26, 1926, the Sunday after Christmas.

Snow had fallen on Christmas Eve; however, it was not uncommon to have a white Christmas in the mountains of Oregon. Families celebrated Christmas in their homes on Saturday, Christmas Day.

Farmer and Emile enjoyed their children around the Christmas tree and the warm crackling fire. They both were excited, and felt like children themselves, holding onto every expression of surprise and delight they saw in Walter, Clifton and Leah's faces when they opened their presents. The family laughed and sang – later Farmer told the Christmas story. They ate a bountiful dinner, which Emile had prepared.

Next morning the Trevor's drove to church. It was a beautiful day! The sky was clear and the sun glistened on the white snow.

"Remember Great Salt Flats?" Emile smiled.

"Yep – an' reckon it was a mite warmer – but just as bright!" Farmer laughed.

When they walked into the Church in the Woods, the fireplace was lit – the potbelly stove in the rear was toasty warm, but no one was there.

"Reckon Joe or Gordon musta come by early an' started the fires.

People began arriving. Sally led everyone in some hymns. It was Junior Springfield's turn to give the sermon. He told

43

how Jesus was in the lineage from David. Even his own family did not consider David a King, an' how Jesus, born, as a tiny baby in Bethlehem was not considered a King by most. Later some of His family an' neighbors rejected Him.

Suddenly, Junior stopped in the middle of a sentence, as if something had broken his thought. He was looking back at the door. Everyone turned to see Donald, his knit cap in his hands. His face turned red as he quietly came forward. Before Junior could resume his message, Donald spoke.

"I'm sorry to interrupt the meeting, but I got to get this out – before I bust wide open like a puffed up bullfrog, or I lose my backbone like a scared mouse runnin' from a mountain lion! Been here all night, pacin' back and forth, wishin' morning would hurry an' get here. Then when it did, I got as shaky as a drunk in a windstorm and walked to town – then walked back.

"I've had my share of fights in my life. Been hit hard by some big men, but Beth hit me hard 'tween the eyes with what she said."

Farmer heard Beth gasp and saw her drop her head.

"But, by golly, she was right. I'm a drunk and brawler who don't care about anybody or anything. Who could love a fella like me – or even want to!

"I did lots a thinkin'. I went way back an' remembered hearin' my grandmother pray. She told me many times, "If you get down or in trouble, find you a good preacher and ask for help. So that's what I did."

"Thank God for his grandmother," Emile whispered.

"I went to Applegate to find me a preacher, and I did. I didn't know nothing. I was ignorant as a Blue Jay in the schoolhouse. I had a hundred questions – an' the preacher took his Bible and taught me. Then when I understood, I fought God! Harder 'n I ever fought any man! It got so bad I couldn't sleep. Come Christmas, I knew! I knew I had to find my peace with – Him – or die! 'Twas just Him and me, not 'cause of anybody else – just Him and me.

"So Christmas I thought on ever'thing I remembered grandma tellin' me and what the preacher taught me – an', an', I just – just told Jesus how sorry I was – and believed!" By now many in the church were in tears. Emile dug in her purse for her hankie, and Farmer tried to wipe his eyes on his shirtsleeve.

"What I'm a tryin' to tell all of you is that yesterday something so strong and wonderful happened to me – I – I can't explain! I just know it was like a heavy mountain came off my back an' – an' – I felt clean inside and happy – an' – an' free! I couldn't wait to tell you, an'- I'm a Christmas, I mean, He saved me on Christmas an'-

The whole church was moved and surrounded this new child of the King to be the family he had lost so long ago.

Donald's life bore fruit. He was in church at every meeting. He was like a dry cloth soaking up water. The day came he took his place at the pulpit to speak.

His drinking buddies at Zeck's Tavern laughed and made a joke of Donald.

"He got religion," they said. He'll soon tire of that and miss the old times and his friends. He'll be back!"

The late spring of 1927 Donald and Beth were wed. Then his old drinking buddies laughed and joked some more.

"He got religion and a wife. He'll soon get tired of both, and he'll come back!"

But Donald never did.

Chapter 8

TWO WEDDINGS

The year 1927 brought winter days of cold and snow. The nights were long, and it seemed to Farmer they would never end. The first hint of spring touched the forest with an air of excitement that change was coming. Hope grew in the heart of good things to come. Something new, fresh!

A mild March settled on Douglas Landing and the homesteads. Farmer, Emile and their children drove into town as soon as the road cleared enough to be passable. It had been Christmas since they were able to come in for supplies and to check their mail.

The rest of the ranchers, undoubtedly, had the same idea, because every one of them was also in town, except for Gardner Grubb. Like a community of people waking up from a long winter's hibernation, they came out of their dens to feel the sun.

The Trevors went straight to the post office anxious to have letters from home. There was a letter from Susan for Emile. It was written and mailed before Christmas:

"Dear Emile,

I am writing to you to share the wonderful news. Andrew and I have decided to have a Valentine's Day wedding, February 14 at 3:00 p.m. We are Getting married in the church we attend in Dallas. Emile, I look at the map and see Oregon, you seem so very far away. I remember the things you told me about your trip – how long and difficult it was. At night, sometimes, I think of you – on your ranch with Farmer and your boys – who must be so grown by now. And Leah! I long to see her, but most of all, I wish with all my heart you could be here to stand by me as I wed Andrew and become Mrs. Neilson. Please write and tell me it would be possible to come home – please!

Love, Your sister, Susan."

Farmer heard Emile gasp as she put her hand to her heart! He saw a look of pain cloud her face and take away the warm smile she had bore all morning. She spoke not a word, but leaned against the post office wall as if to gain support. She held the letter out for Farmer to read.

When finished, Farmer started to speak, but nothing came out. Anything he could think of to say seemed to fall flat on the floor. Susan's wedding had been announced and taken place without Emile's knowledge.

In a moment, Emile gained her composure. She motioned to the other letter Farmer held in his hand – yet sealed – and gave a weak smile. "It's from Benjamin," Farmer mumbled and tore open the envelope. It read:

"Hey Pal, I'm for sure planning to drive to Oregon to see you all! That is as long as you got a place a

48

fella can get a drink. With prohibition – gets a mite risky sometimes.

I been doing real good. Got me a new car. A green colored Dodge roadster. Making me some good money, so with the car and money I am for sure planning to come your way. I hear tell that the road from Chicago to Los Angeles is being built mighty fine. They are calling it Route 66. Can't wait to drive it.

Now for my best news. I met this girl, Betty Jean. We love each other and plan to tie the knot – just as soon as I can get you all down here so you can be my best man. Or do we have to drive up there? Betty Jean and I talked about May or June hitchin'.

Can you come? Write me! Fast!

Your best pal, Benjamin"

Farmer and Emile stared at each other. He groaned inside. He knew full well that with what Emile had just found out, completely missing her sister's wedding, it was not possible to even consider trying to return to Texas for Benjamin's wedding.

Then as he recalled the trials and hardships of the trip west to Oregon, all that had taken place – the desert – the roughness of the terrain in much of the road – if there was even a road – the thought of a drive like that again – and back, made a trip to Texas very remote. Still he felt torn between wanting to help Emile, and the sense of being sensible of such a venture. He too, wanted to stand with Benjamin just as Emile longed to be with her sister. The drive home was in silence while they thought and listened to Walter, Clifton and Leah laugh and chatter. As they neared their log home, Emile began to share her feelings.

"Farmer, sometimes, I feel like we are as isolated here as we were in Holt. All we did was trade the wheat for pine trees, a plow for cattle. At least there we had our family near. Here we are so far away... I'm angry at this place, the distance, the hard winters that keep us from our mail. I'm – I'm angry at all this!" Emile's eyes flashed as she motioned around her with her hands, "for keeping me from my sister's wedding. Two weddings! One we knew nothing about until – too late. The other, we won't be at either."

When they pulled up to the house, Emile looked at Farmer.

"I don't know if I like living here anymore," she sobbed. She fled into the house to their bedroom.

Chapter 9

A VISIT FROM THE HOLTS

Well, there was one wedding Farmer and Emile got to be part of. Donald and Beth wed in the Church in the Woods, late spring of 1927. Farmer was best man, and Emile the matron of honor. It was a simple wedding, beautiful, well attended. Even Pendleton and Olaf were present, and carried the attitude, "The best man won Beth's heart."

A few days later a letter arrived from Jacob, announcing that Dorothy had given birth to a little boy, Sidney Dean Trevor, and he weighed 7 pounds, 2 ounces and was born April 19,1927. "Dorothy and the baby air doin' just fine," Jacob wrote.

"Pa hasn't been feeling so good, so more of the farmin' falls on William an' me. I think William is near as hankerin' to leave as you was. Ma is her same ol' gentle self. Stella has me worried 'cause she is so headstrong. Pray for us an' we pray for you. Sure do miss havin' you around here. Will ya ever come for a visit? We are still drivin' a wagon here. Pa won't never get a automobile. Jacob."

This was the first time since Farmer and Emile left Holt that his family had written anything about his Pa. Farmer wept alone later out by the corral for his Pa. He so wished that the rift between them could be repaired. He had written his Pa once from Oregon, but got no reply, and no one mentioned the letter.

A letter from Hirum and Vivian Holt was waiting for them the next trip Farmer took into Douglas Landing. He took the letter home to Emile and watched her face as she cut open the envelope. Her expression was serious, then she broke into a broad smile, then she began laughing and clapping her hands.

"Oh, Farmer!" she shouted with joy. "Mother and father are coming to see us in August. Susan and Andrew are coming with them!"

From that moment Emile became a whirlwind of activity. She went from being so excited she couldn't sleep, to fretting.

"Woman, I declare you aim ta drive me an' the children plumb crazy with yer cleanin' an' fixin'. We still have on ta two months 'fore they get here."

"But, Farmer, everything has to be just right," Emile laughed. "Don't you want them to be impressed with our home?"

"They be blind an' dumb if they ain't. I'm only mighty pleased fer ya ta see yer family, Emile."

Emile stopped what she was doing and turned to Farmer. Sadness filled her eyes. "Oh, Farmer, I wish you could see your family too," she said lovingly.

"Someday we will travel back, I reckon – soon's we be able."

Emile marked the days off on a calendar. They had only a few pictures of the Holts they were able to carry on their trip in the chuck wagon – Emile showed them to Walter,

Clifton and Leah. Walter remembered, but Clifton did not. Leah thought the pictures were to play with.

Farmer kept busy herding the cattle, guarding against predators, fixing what fence he had and repairing his out buildings. Emile, meanwhile, worked in the log house to stay busy – but still, for both of them it seemed that time stopped, and they realized the truth of the old saying, "A watched pot never boils." Farmer caught Emile looking down their road in the trees, or she would pick up a picture of her Ma and Pa, or look at the one of her and Susan.

"We gained a lot by our move," Farmer thought, "but we lost some too, I reckon. I uprooted her from her family and friends. An' my Pa and me ain't talkin', an' I sure miss my family a powerful bunch!"

August arrived at long last, but the Holts and Neilsons had not. Emile was concerned how they would know when her family arrived. Would they find Douglas Landing, or get lost in Applegate?

One warm evening in mid-August, Emile began to fret and worry while they ate supper. She had set the table on the porch where it was cooler, and they could watch the sun go down and listen to the creek a few yards beyond the house.

"Maybe they aren't coming!" Emile spoke.

"They woulda written ya a letter."

"What if there's one at the post office?"

"Just checked this mornin'."

"What if they get confused in Applegate and give up an' go home?" Emile almost cried.

"Would ya?"

"No!"

"Dallas is far bigger an' easier to get lost in then Applegate, Emile."

By now the children were finished eating and playing around the front of the house. Farmer and Emile ate quietly for a few minutes.

"How will we know when they arrive in Douglas Landing, Farmer?" she started in again.

"Reckon we could stay in town an' take us turns a sittin' in the car watchin' fer them, 'cause ifen they got to gazin' at the forest they might miss Douglas Landing fer sure, then where they be?" Farmer drawled dryly.

Emile looked at him over the brim of the jar she was drinking tea from, and then burst out laughing, spewing tea over herself.

"I'm being foolish, aren't I," Emile said after she had wiped herself off.

"Naw, just anxious fer yer people to get here! Wait! Listen! Emile, I hear a car on our road! Listen!"

"I hear it. You think it's them?"

The sound of the car's motor grew louder as it got closer. Soon it could be seen through the trees.

"It's Molly O'Malley – why do you think...?"

Then a second car they had never seen before came into view. Emile jumped up!

"Oh, it's them!" she shouted. "I knew it!"

Molly's car stopped in front of the house, and Emile went running to the second car – laughing – screaming – waving – arms open wide!

Chapter 10

OUTA PLACE

It felt good to Farmer to have Emile's family stay in his home. He had grown to love them as his own, and as he was out tending horses and doing chores at sunrise, he reflected on the night before.

The travelers were weary from long days of driving, but the excitement of arriving at Farmer and Emile's rejuvenated them all. There was getting acquainted with their new brother-in-law, Andrew. Both grandparents spent time holding and talking to Walter, Clifton and Leah. Walter ran to them, while Clifton held back and was shy. But it was obvious that Oregon-born Leah stole their hearts.

The scene at the car when the family opened the doors and scrambled out, was so vivid in Farmer's mind as to remain there forever. Emile flew into her mother's arms. Then she hugged her father. Farmer could see love in Vivian's looks and actions, and a kind gentleness in Hirum, the gruff old attorney. Emile and Susan held each other tight and wept for what seemed a timeless moment.

Vivian hugged Farmer talking all the while, "Farmer, we have been so eager to see you all, we wore poor Hirum and Andrew nearly to the bone driving our car day and night."

"And our Overland is a wonderful machine," Hirum spoke in his low growl. "It performed magnificently." Then they both turned to the grandchildren who were standing by Farmer. Walter ran to his grandpa, and while Vivian tried to talk to Clifton, Leah tugged at her grandma wanting to get her attention.

Farmer hugged Susan.

"Farmer, it has been so long. We are very happy to at last see you!" She was still sniffing. She turned to introduce her husband, Andrew.

Andrew was a tall, pale, skinny man. Not much to look upon in Farmer's view, and sort of sickly in appearance.

"He's very powerful in the court room and a tough criminal defense lawyer," Susan had written in one of her letters.

That night the Holts and Neilsons related all that happened on their trip and the sights they had seen.

"The road west is under major construction," old man Holt told. "They are calling it the Mother Road, and all the trails and road sections have been connected, with some parts now – what is termed – paved."

"Paved?" Farmer questioned.

"Made of oil and gravel and rolled hard. It surely made for a faster and smoother drive when we were on paved portions of the Mother Road."

"I heard it is called Route 66," Farmer added.

"'Tis so," Hirum went on.

"I liked Flagstaff, Arizona," Susan injected. "All of the tall trees remind me of your home here.

"Santa Fe was very interesting to me," Emile commented.

"A road is being cut straight across the state," Hirum explained. "Soon Route 66 will bypass Santa Fe."

"We never saw Flagstaff." Farmer spoke, remembering. "We turned north ta Utah. Did ya go thet way?"

"No,' Hirum answered, "from Flagstaff we went to Kingman."

"We stayed in a quaint hotel in a small town – Oakly, I think," Vivian interrupted.

"Oatman," Hirum corrected. "We crossed the Colorado at Toprock into California.

"Oh, Father," Emile, added to what he was saying. "We crossed the Colorado on a ferry boat at a place called Marble Canyon into Utah. We even swam in the river!"

"You swam in that muddy water?" Andrew was shocked.

"We had been days in the heat of the desert. There was more dirt on us than in the river!" Emile laughed.

"Darndest thing in the California desert. The road became boards laid down the width of a car. Drove on the boards to keep from sinking in the sand," Hirum went on.

"Oh, Los Angeles was so lovely a city. The Pacific was breathtaking – such blue water! That was my favorite," Vivian reflected.

"Talkin' 'bout blue water, Emile an' I air plannin' on takin' y'all to a place we heard 'bout. It's a lake in a volcano with the bluest water ya could ever see," Farmer told them. "The government made it into a park and named it Crater Lake."

"Oh, I can't wait to go!" Susan clapped her hands.

"Let's get some sleep first," groaned Andrew, and with that he and Hirum retired.

Farmer and Emile gave their bedroom to Hirum and Vivian, and Leah's bedroom was fixed up for Andrew and Susan. Farmer and Emile had made a bed for them and Leah with the boys in the loft. Farmer climbed up into bed and soon fell asleep. The women stayed up to talk, and it was the middle of the night when Farmer felt his wife slip into bed next to him.

As Farmer fed the chickens he caught sight of his father-in-law walking along the creek. It was the beginning of a beautiful day. The sky was clear and already the air was warming. Farmer walked to the house, and was met by Emile with a warm kiss and a cup of coffee. She had some breakfast prepared on the outside porch table. She went back inside to the kitchen. Hirum Holt came up from the creek and greeted Farmer with a grumbling, "Mornin'." Emile came out with a cup of coffee and kissed her father on the cheek. He took her hand and held it, his keen eyes looking into hers – searching deeper into his daughter to find what would be overlooked by just a surface glance. It seemed he wanted to know, is my daughter well, is she cared for, is she happy, is this place good for her? When he was satisfied with his answers, he smiled and let go of her hand. She returned inside.

"We is mighty pleased ta have y'all with us," Farmer attempted to start a conversation.

Hirum didn't respond. He looked at the creek, then the trees and beyond to mountaintops that were visible above the trees. He sipped his coffee and every once in awhile he would make a grunting sound. Farmer felt he was thinking and pacing the floor the way he did the day he and Emile announced they were moving to Oregon. So Farmer enjoyed his coffee and ate some breakfast and waited.

"Liquid gold..." Hirum spoke.

"Liquid gold – where?" Farmer asked.

"Do you realize what that water running on your property is worth; what Texas farmers would pay for it?"

"Yes, the good Lord has blessed us real good!" Farmer replied.

"Farmer, you did it. You followed your dream, you moved your family, and you claimed your land, got your cattle, found your place. I must admit, Farmer, I am surely taken aback by the beauty of this country." Hirum's voice broke, "I am proud of you, I envy you living in a place like this. I never imagined." Hirum shook his head, and took a drink of coffee. "Dang, you are carving out a life for you and Emile and your children – good for you, son!"

"Thank ya, sir; I jus' wished my Pa felt the same way."

Hirum studied Farmer a moment before he spoke. His voice was deep, full of emotion.

"I have spoken to your Pa, Farmer. He is a bitter, angry, unforgiving, stubborn, proud man who can't admit he is wrong."

No other words were spoken aloud, but volumes were said in the silence as the two men drank their coffee and ate breakfast.

After awhile the door opened, and Andrew stepped outside dressed in suit and tie. He carried a cup of coffee in his hand, and he joined Farmer and Hirum at the table.

Hirum nodded his head to the young attorney and grunted. Farmer spoke a friendly greeting, then laughing added, "Don't reckon ya needed ta dress up fer breakfast, Andrew!"

"I dress this way everyday, thank you. If I dressed up, I would be attired in coat and tails!" Andrew snapped coolly.

"Never had a coat with tails," Farmer joked.

"It is obvious you are uneducated – in social skills," Andrew snarled.

"Wasn't meanin' to rile ya, Mr. Neilson," Farmer could feel his neck and face heat up.

"I would dare say, you don't own a suit of clothes. This is what I wear for leisure. And might I add that you could do well, Mr. Trevor, to display a little class and taste in your wardrobe!"

Farmer studied Andrew Neilson for a moment and contemplated pokin' him in his snooty nose – but decided to be a better host than that.

"Well, Andrew," Farmer drawled slowly and deliberately, "I've been workin' this here mornin', but tell ya a promise. When I an' my family come to visit ya in yer place – I'll hunt me up one o' those coats with tails ya tol' me about."

Hirum verbally separated the two men with a reminder aimed at Andrew.

"Andrew, we are on vacation. Why don't you leave the courtroom in Dallas."

Later that morning, Farmer took Hirum and Andrew on horseback to check the cattle. Walter and Clifton begged to go, so Farmer let them ride bareback behind himself and Hirum. They weren't gone far when Walter tugged at Farmer's arm. Turning to look back at this son, he detected a scowl on Walter's face.

"He don't know spit 'bout ridin' a horse. If Wind wasn't followin' us, she would jus' stand still."

Walter's observations proved accurate. Andrew encountered difficulty giving any kind of commands that Wind would pay attention to. He couldn't get her to move, then she broke into a trot and Neilson shot out in front of the other two horses, losing the reins. He held tight to the horse's mane and neck until Wind came to a halt. Farmer retrieved the reins without a word.

The young tightlipped attorney made quite a spectacle riding a horse. Wind set a gait across a meadow that jolted Andrew up and down so hard his hat flew off. When he finally got Wind slowed down, attempts to turn around failed, so he dismounted and walked back to retrieve his hat. He left the reins upon the saddle allowing Wind to wander off, and Farmer had to catch her.

The final blow to Andrew Neilson's beat up ego hit its mark in a stand of White Pine. Wind ignored Andrew's efforts to follow a path, instead walking under a limb that swept Andrew right out of the saddle. He lit solidly on his rear – then fell backwards looking straight up through the trees.

Farmer came riding fast to him!

"Air ya hurt, Andrew?" he yelled as he dismounted.

"If I ever – ever – ride one of these animals again – I should have an examination to see if I have – a speck – of sanity!"

Farmer put Walter on Wind in front of Andrew, and they all made their way slowly back to the house.

"I must immediately bathe, and remove dust and filth from me," he told Susan. "I had a dreadful experience and wish to wash it away. Would you please draw my water."

Farmer could tell by the expression on his face Andrew was loaded for bear when he stormed into the living room a short time later. He was clean from his bath and had changed into another suit. He walked to Farmer in a confronting manner. Farmer looked up at him from his chair.

"I am aghast at how primitive you people live!"

Out of the corners of his eyes, Farmer could see the others sit up straight in surprise.

"In the city we have running water – plumbing. We can listen to a radio or buy a newspaper on the street corner. We have telephones to make calls. We have electricity for light!

"You carry your water in a bucket – no telephone – no electricity, you see with a kerosene lamp. The whole world could end, and you'll never know! You abuse your family making them live like this!"

Andrew was pacing back and forth like a caged animal.

"Tell me, Mr. Trevor, what gives you the right to force your family to live here – in this most primitive fashion?"

Hirum cleared his throat, and Farmer had a compelling urge to hit Andrew in the mouth with his fist. The women had drawn back in surprise at Andrew's assault of hot words.

"I reckon ya ta be a man who never lets a hair o' his head get outa place – an' ifen one does ya comb it down 'til it finally gives up outa plumb exhaustion," Farmer began.

"What does that have to do with my question? And can you please use proper English!"

"Reckon it has ever'thing ta do with yer question, 'cause it all ain't about where I live – or how I live – it's 'bout ya."

"Irrelevant!"

"It's 'bout ya gettin' a hair outa place. Ifen I was ta come to yer courtroom, I would be outa my place – 'cause I'd never been taught. I'd make a plumb fool outa myself tryin' to defend one o' yer criminals. It would be in yer power ta laugh and make a joke o' me – or -."

Andrew started to speak. Farmer held up his hand.

"Let me finish! Then ya can talk the night away if yer hankerin' ta.

"Yer outa yer place here. I love the open – the trees – the horses and cattle. The still nights with so many stars blazin' ya can't count 'em, the squawk of a Blue Jay to announce yer comin' to the deer, or seein' a herd o' doe an' their fawns in the spring, or helpin' a heifer deliver her first calf, or seein' Leah delivered right here in this house.

"Sure, I can't give Emile those pretties ya told 'bout, but Emile an' me agreed ta thet before Almighty God, when we tol' Him we would come and claim this land He had given us. An' I can't give ya water runnin' inta this house all warm an' such – but I know thet's changin'. I could see it as we traveled across this land. Our country is a changin'. I saw it – ya saw it! An' one day it will reach here. They has radio – an' newspapers – an' telephones – some – in Applegate. We saw even more progress in Springdale, an' there's talk o' electricity comin' to Applegate, an' when it does, it'll come to Douglas Landing fer the Forest Rangers. The government will see to thet. An' we'll get our plumbin' too. Jus' takes awhile.

"So ya see, Andrew, yer upset 'cause ya looked foolish out there today – 'cause ya was outa yer place, jus' like I'd look powerful foolish ifen I was in yer courtroom. I'd be outa my place. But we can't make Douglas Landing inta Dallas. Least not completely."

Andrew had not taken his eyes off Farmer the whole time. He began biting on his lip, nodded his head in a contemplative "yes" several times. This attorney bowed to

Farmer, admitting defeat to a wisdom he recognized coming – from a source far beyond the education and knowledge of his opponent.

"Brilliant," he declared as he turned and strode off to his bedroom.

Chapter 11

CRATER LAKE

Andrew Neilson did not attempt to join Farmer on horseback anymore. He did seem to enjoy and be content with taking a book and chair down by Cold Creek and sit in the early morning sun and read.

Hirum, on the other hand, seemed to find new life and energy riding with Farmer and the boys across the Circle T property. He relished in herding cattle from one place to another. Sometimes they crossed onto another homestead to drive Farmer's cattle back home.

"You make a powerful argument to come here often, besides to visit my daughter and grandchildren, and of course, you... son," Hirum spoke low as they rode through the trees. Farmer's heart swelled! Then sadness swept over him as he longed to hear his own Pa speak tender words, and call him son.

"We have spent the day inviting friends and neighbors to join us for a camping trip to Crater Lake!" Emile announced happily when the men returned to the house.

"We met such lovely people!" Vivian exclaimed.

"I absolutely loved Sally and Molly. They had me laughing the whole time!" Susan's voice reflected her excitement and pleasure of the day's visits.

"Air the Baltmans a goin' campin' with us?" Farmer asked.

"No," Emile answered, "but Clifton talked them into – no, begged them to let Rachel go with us. Sally finally said yes."

"Reckon it's settled then," Farmer declared in a commanding voice. "Tomorrow we pack tents an' food an' such, then next day early mornin' we leave fer Crater Lake."

Word spread when the party was leaving for their camping trip to Crater Lake. Most folks would have been most pleased to go, for a change of routine, and to go to a cooler place. Douglas Landing was in the hot, dry days of August, so the high elevation along the rim of the crater would be more comfortable. However, they could not leave their ranches or work at such a short notice.

There were others who did not think camping to be their idea of an enjoyable experience. The McQuirks and Millers fit into that category. So Farmer and Emile figured there would be no one joining their caravan.

In the grey of dawn everyone talked and laughed; except for Andrew who was sullen, but attempting to help load the cars. Tents, blankets, pillows, changes of clothes and lanterns were all carefully packed in the trunks of the Buick and Overland.

They were ready to begin the journey when headlights appeared on the Trevor's road, bobbing through the trees. Soon, Donald and Beth Parrigan drove up and parked. Farmer and Emile were pleasantly surprised and pleased to see them.

"This where we sign up to go campin'?" Donald shouted above the noise of his car's engine.

"Sure is!" everyone yelled back in unison.

Donald and Beth were introduced to the family, and the campers were off on a trip that would require most of the day to reach the rim of the ancient volcano. The road was well graded, and gravel in some places. Since the lake became a National Park, the government maintained and improved the growing roadway.

When the sun stood overhead, they stopped along a fast running stream that tumbled under a bridge made from logs.

From the base of Mount Mazama up to the top the road grew steeper. That posed no obstacle to the Overland or Buick, but Beth's old car kept overheating. They would go a mile or two and have to stop to let it cool.

Exasperated, Donald removed his hat to scratch his head as he eyed the steaming radiator. "We're slowin' you down like a peg leg on a roadrunner. Go on! We'll catch up to you."

"No," Farmer snapped.

"Go on, we'll be along directly."

"No!" Farmer was emphatic. "Won't leave ya. There was folks on our trip left us on the side o' the road. Won't do it ta ya'."

So the travelers made their way slowly up the side of the mountain. Wildlife was free and uninhibited as they drove. Multitudes of squirrels and chipmunks darted across the road. Walter spied a skunk below them running amongst the ferns. Several times they came upon deer whose heads snapped up, ears erect. On one sharp turn in the road, a momma bear and two cubs came into view and ambled slowly down the roadside. Farmer slowed the car down to see them better. As they came alongside the black bears, Farmer realized how large an animal they were. The older bear raised its head and sniffed the air in loud snorts.

"Oh, Farmer, please hurry!" Emile cried weakly as she grabbed his arm.

In his rearview mirror, Farmer saw that Hirum sped past the bears, but Donald and Beth stopped by them.

Emile was looking back, "That Donald is such a fool-hardy boy!" she blurted out.

Farmer smiled as he had almost done the same thing a moment ago.

Somewhere around 4:00 in the afternoon, the three cars reached the rim campground. Other campers were already there and numerous campsites were set up. Emile and Susan selected a spot in a patch of fir trees.

"What a beautiful place!" Beth declared, trying to take it all in.

But nothing could have prepared them for their first sight of Crater Lake. The jagged rocky rim stood above the bluest water they had ever seen. The size was massive. Mount Mazama had blown its top, and the volcano somehow collapsed inside itself. Slowly, the huge crater filled with water until it became the deepest lake in the country. To the left they could see a small island out in the water.

"That's called Wizard Island," Vivian said, reading from a pamphlet a ranger had given them when they entered the park.

They stood in reverent silence before a Holy God who had created a spot upon this planet Earth, of such magnitude and beauty that words and thoughts to describe it could not be found. No photograph would ever do it justice. No painter could ever represent it. In its awesome beauty, Crater Lake gave glory and honor to the God who had made it! A thing of great beauty formed out of fire and ash.

Chapter 12

CAMPFIRE

The four couples went about setting up their tents and making their campsite comfortable before night overtook them.

They had passed a marker – 5,000 ft. Elev. on the road as they neared the rim, so Farmer knew that the early morning would be brisk. Emile had planned for such coldness and had made sure of ample bedding and jackets.

Farmer deducted from watching him struggle with the tent that Andrew had never been camping before. But he also observed that Andrew had a clear and concise mind and caught on quickly when instructed in a matter.

Donald Parrigan, as always, brought life to the party with his wit and humor. The women hardly knew when he was serious or joking. Even Beth was unsure at times, although she had begun to detect a little upward curl in each corner of Donald's mouth. Though he tried to keep a straight face, those little curls gave him away to Beth.

Andrew seemed amused by Donald and more or less tolerated him being present. Hirum, however, liked having Donald on the excursion, and enjoyed the young man's homespun rough lumberjack demeanor. The children, on the other hand, saw Donald as a big kid, fun to have around to laugh and joke with.

The campsite secure, Farmer collected rocks and formed a sizeable circle with them. He gathered twigs and leaves for a campfire. While he was trying to start a fire, he heard Emile telling Vivian and Susan, "I miss our chuck wagon we traveled in... My kitchen was handy at the rear of the wagon."

Farmer smiled as he recalled campfires spread along the road and trails from Texas to Oregon. He was thankful for this place at Crater Lake where firewood was abundant. He remembered some areas they camped that wood was so sparse a fire could not be maintained.

"Men and children gather firewood while the womenfolk fix supper! We needs us a powerful fire to light our camp 'til we's done with it – an' I reckon some wood left over fer mornin' coffee an' breakfast," Farmer shouted out the instructions.

After eating and finishing chores, everyone gathered around the warmth and light of the campfire. The dancing flame created a dreamy mood for the campers.

Leah had crawled up in her grandmother's lap, her eyes watching the fire. Scout lay quietly beside Walter; Rachel sat next to Clifton who was poking a stick in the fire. Susan sat by her mother and Andrew was near her. Hirum sat on a log slightly behind his youngest daughter who was by Farmer. Donald and Beth were on his other side.

Farmer saw Scout raise his head and perk his ears. The sharp, rapid barks of a pack of coyotes split the quiet night air. The barks were loud and close – then a mournful howl answered from a distance.

"Reckon they could be yonder in thet stand o' fir trees," Farmer drawled. He had seen some of their guests start with the second unexpected yapping of the coyotes.

"Jus' some ol' coyotes," Walter remarked.

"They are hunting;" Beth added, "the one far away seemed such a sad and lonely sound!"

"Oh, they frighten me!" Susan spoke in a fearful tone. "Do you think they will bother us?"

Donald spoke before anyone could answer.

"I was duly scared by coyotes one time. It was on a night jus' like this'n, and by a campfire like – well – maybe a smig smaller – but I sure got me a fright!"

Farmer eyed the faces glowing in the firelight. The children were immediately intent on Donald's story. The women were hooked and hung on his words – except for Beth who kept trying to look around at her husband's face – which was lit up in a broad grin.

Andrew seemed skeptical and Farmer could only dimly see ol' man Holt, making it difficult to tell what he was thinking.

"Now, it went like this as I recollect," Donald continued. "We were up in high country an' I was so all fired intent on fallen trees that the crew jus' left me there. I have to admit, I was a bit nervous, bein' so far away an' all, but I had my axe, and I built me a big fire like this'n."

Donald paused to look at each face – then off into the darkness as if to picture it all over again.

"Now, I had calmed down all content like, feeling secure as a Canary bird in a wire cage. That's when it happened!"

Donald paused again. Susan had caught her breath!

"This squirrel ran by my campfire – eyes wide with unnatural fear. But 'fore I could think to be scared, this bobtailed cat came right behind the squirrel. I got me to thinkin' the bobcat is a chasin' the squirrel, but danged ifen a pack o' mean coyotes came breakneck speed right through my campfire!"

"Oh, dear!" Susan exclaimed.

Farmer heard Emile softly snicker.

71

"Hev to tell you, by now I grabbed my axe, 'cause it's a dawnin' on me that something's a chasin' the lot o' them. Donald jumped up, imaginary axe in one hand.

"Jus' then the meanest mountain lion I'd ever laid eyes on, 'course I'd only seen one twice before, landed on all fours right before my very eyes – then leaped over my campfire and disappeared into the darkness after the coyotes!"

Farmer felt Emile shiver as she slid her hand inside his arm.

"Ya get the ol' cougar with yer axe?" Clifton asked.

"Didn't have me a chance, 'cause right behind that mountain lion came the biggest, meanest black bear I ever did see with my own eyes. He was growlin' and runnin' fast like a runaway train rollin' down a steep grade. I raised my axe!"

Donald paused again. Susan had her hand on her heart – her mouth aghast. Vivian was frowning.

"I raised my axe!" Donald continued, "this bear was runnin' straight towards me, and I figured this to be the last time to use my axe and figured never to see another day.

"But danged ifen that bear didn't jus' bust right on by me – fear in its eyes – I coulda swore it had turned white as a polar bear.'

No one moved nor made a sound. All eyes were fixed on Donald Parrigan.

"Now, folks, that's when I seen what was scarin' all these critters. Plumb raised the hair on my neck. Comin' into the firelight was – a skunk."

With that, Donald sat down in triumph.

"You are awful!" Beth exclaimed as she playfully hit him.

"And what did you do next, Mr. Parrigan?" Andrew used his lawyer voice.

"What did I do?" Donald laughed. "Now, I'll tell you, wasn't but a minute an' I was passin' up the squirrel."

"Oh, for goodness sake!" Susan threw up her hands.

From out of the shadows a low growling sound began to build.

"Haargh – haargh!"

"Haargh – haargh – haargh!" It was Hirum. Soon the old man was bellowing out in a laughter that came from deep down inside. The kind that leaves you spent and feeling good – and everyone around you laughs too – because of you. Farmer had never heard Hirum laugh like that, but Farmer saw his father-in-law in a different way that night. Farmer realized that the gruff attorney had built something into his daughters that was very special, a spontaneity that was always surprising and refreshing.

The laughing finally subsided, leaving everyone in a thoughtful frame of mind.

Susan broke the silence.

"I must confess – this is my first campfire ever," she said.

"Closest I ever came to one, was the fire in the heater in our home. City folks don't have much chance for campfires," Andrew added. Farmer thought he detected a twinge of regret.

"Vivian and I had us a real true campfire scare," Hirum's gravelly voice boomed from the shadows where he sat on the log.

Farmer could tell by the look on Vivian's face that she knew exactly of what her husband spoke.

"We were young – not married long – I had just finished law school. We drove a carriage up into the Wichita Mountains of Oklahoma. That was still a wild territory then.

"Night fell with no town and accommodations near. We built us a fire in a grove of trees – a place to stay the night."

"Oh, Hirum, must you tell this!" Vivian protested.

The puzzled glance told Farmer that the Holt's two daughters did not know of this incident.

73

"It happened, Vivian!" Mr. Holt was determined to get through this.

"In the night as the campfire was burning down, two highwaymen appeared. Demanded money and food. They had hard looks towards Vivian, and I feared for her. They spoke of – taking her and the horses.

"They held guns on us, but never figured for me to have a hidden pistol. I learned when confronted in the manner we were – to act quickly. I fired – wounding one in the leg – the other I shot in the stomach. They screamed as they fled into the dark."

"Oh, father – mother!" Emile and Susan cried out at the same time. "You both must have been so scared!"

"Yes, we were very shaken," Vivian, reflected.

"Now, I'd a been as shaky as a man standin' on a nail keg in a windstorm. Ifen I ever need me a strong attorney, I'm lookin' for you," Donald spoke seriously.

Everyone laughed!

"I remember a campfire," Beth spoke quietly. "It was when I was a young girl. My Pa was still alive, and we were on the edge of a mining camp in the Rockies. It was a happy time," she said sadly – then she cheered up. "Tonight is happy too – for me..."

"We had so many campfires traveling to Oregon," Emile spoke softly, "but one we had in Arizona was very frightening to me and the boys. A fierce mountain lion tried to attack the horses and us. Farmer built up the fire and set out lanterns, and he shot his rifle at it – like you did the robbers, father."

Farmer added wood to the fire. Everyone sat in silence, remembering, thinking, and looking into the flames.

"I reckon ever'one else has told a campfire story, so's I'm gonna tell one. Don't rightly know ifen I was plumb powerful scared – or just plain not knowin' enough to be scared.

"We was talkin' an' laughin' by the campfire, almost ready to eat our supper. This was in the desert an' wood was hard to find, so's our campfire was a tad small. All's a sudden like, this Indian walks right inta our camp. There I was with my heart jumpin' an' my rifle in the wagon! Reckon we felt like ya did, Hirum; ya an' Vivian when the robbers came at ya.

"Hev ta tell ya all, thet since Indians stole from the wagon and lied to us – there in Gallop, New Mexico, I hed me some right bad ideas 'bout Indians – an' I was powerful suspicious o' this'n standin' by our campfire.

"Well, I reckon he was 'bout as scared and suspicious o' us as we finds out thet he had his wife an' two children hid in the bushes."

"Poor dears!" Susan exclaimed compassionately.

"We shared our food an' water with 'em, but they weren't fer takin' a hand-out. They went out an' gathered wood, fer the meal they had eaten. Their names was Henry an' Hettie Wild Eagle, an' – an' – their boy an' girl – ah – was - "

"Curtis and Omney," Emile helped him out.

"Struck me as odd – them runnin' from a reservation in Montana an' us from a farm in Texas, meetin' like that in the desert. Our campfire talk changed my notion 'bout the Indians."

"Pa gave Injun Wild Eagle his Bible," Walter spoke of something that had touched his heart.

"An' we gave them our airplane," Clifton added.

"Then I got all suspicious an' 'fraid and sat in the dark to keep lookout with my rifle – 'cept my eyes got heavy an' I reckon I plumb fell asleep," Farmer went on.

"Then what happened, Mr. Trevor?" asked a skeptical Andrew.

"They tied us up an' left us ta the buzzards fer not trustin' them," Farmer joked.

"Oh, Farmer, they did not!" Emile hit his shoulder.

Hirum's hearty growling laugh started up again, and everyone joined him.

"This conversation has gone to the dogs," declared Andrew.

"Scout's the only dog here," Rachel spoke timidly.

"An' he don't want it," Clifton yawned and stretched.

Chapter 13

1929

When a visit with loved ones nears an end, sadness settles in, and an ache creeps into the heart. Nothing is said, but the silent awareness is in thought, that the time of parting is near.

When the day arrives, tenderhearted women grow weepy, and the men are quiet and reserved. Children will act up, and a temper flares now and then.

"I think the most difficult thing for men and women to deal with is separation," Farmer pondered as he watched the family struggle with parting goodbyes. "Separation by distance, death or a relationship turned sour," he thought of his own Pa.

There were tears when time for the Holts and Neilsons to climb back into their Overland and start their six-day journey back to Texas all too soon arrived. They promised to again come for a visit two years later in 1929 – and they did.

Appearances pointed to another prosperous and happy year. The year 1929 marked the last year of the "Roaring Twenties;" however, all projections pointed to the fact that the thirties would roar as loud and as well.

This would be the year that the government deeded the land to him. The herd of cattle was much larger now. Of course, so was his debt, but no one seemed concerned. He was able to market enough cattle each year to pay on his note, and he and Emile had a comfortable life.

Walter was nine; Clifton seven and Leah would be four in November. Donald and Beth had a baby girl that spring they named Beverly Ann Parrigan.

The Holts and Neilsons arrived August 13th in much the same fashion as they had in 1927. The Holts sported a new Cadillac, and Andrew actually showed some excitement upon arrival. He had finally admitted to Susan that he did have some degree of enjoyment from his brief stay at the Trevor's Oregon ranch. He was desirous to return and ride horses with Farmer and Hirum, although Hirum was experiencing more difficulty getting around. Some days he relinquished his saddle to Walter, Clifton or even Leah, who was quite the rider.

Farmer proudly displayed the water system he designed upstream on Cold Creek and piped down to the house. He built a bathroom with toilet, sink and tub. He also piped water to the kitchen sink and through a coil in the wood stove that gave them hot water.

He made sure to inform Andrew that electricity and telephones were promised Douglas Landing for the next year. That meant the homesteads would have power and telephone lines put up as well.

Late one evening the three men were engaged in a long and lively discussion. They had remained on the porch long after dark. Farmer brought a lantern from the house and placed it on the table where they were seated. The women and children were playing games inside.

"I predict more good times ahead," Hirum spoke gruffly with conviction. "We have a new President who will lead our country into even greater prosperity."

"Yes, yet there is such unrest," Andrew commented. "Clashes and fighting in Europe, and gangsters in America."

"I read that Al Capone was sentenced to a year in prison," Hirum spoke in a tone of unbelief, "it should have been ten!"

"Yes, I heard that on the radio. They found nothing to charge him with except having a concealed weapon. In a year he will be free and more powerful. You watch and see!" Andrew grew angry.

"We see stronger gangster activities in Dallas. Prohibition has spawned corruption, and in my estimation is a miserable failure," he went on.

"Think the Yankees will make the World Series?" Hirum changed the subject.

"Philadelphia will be the team to beat," Andrew answered with his opinion.

Farmer felt lost in the conversation.

"I listened to the Indianapolis 500 on the radio in May. Cars neared 100 miles per hour. Will your Buick do that?" Andrew kidded.

"Do fifty on a good road," Farmer answered.

"Reached sixty in my Cadillac one time on a California road – this trip," Hirum growled.

"I read about a box they are testing. It receives sound like a radio, and has a picture," Andrew continued.

"Do tell?" Hirum revealed interest.

"Said the picture is in color or black and white. Like a movie, but it comes on air waves."

"Humm," Hirum grumbled thoughtfully.

"I heard on the radio that a banquet was held in Hollywood, California to give awards to movies. Have you ever seen a moving picture, Farmer?" Andrew asked, and seemed to enjoy prodding his host.

"Reckon I can't say I hev," Farmer replied dryly.

"Oh, Farmer, it is such entertainment," Susan exclaimed as she stepped through the door onto the porch. "I hear one of the songs on the radio all the time – 'Happy Days Are Here Again.'"

Farmer had vowed to never let himself get so out of touch with changes happening around the world. Yet tonight he was hit in the face with the ugly reality – he had allowed himself to hide in the forest of his ranch while the world of change passed him by. He made up his mind to correct the problem!

The visiting guests begged to go back to Crater Lake. Donald and Beth's baby was too little to make the trip, and Donald couldn't get off work. The Baltmans and Brooks followed the caravan up to the rim, which gave the campout a new life and different dimension. Everyone agreed, however, that they still missed Donald's tall tales.

"It's been a perfect year," Farmer thought to himself as he looked out at a starlit sky through an opening in his tent. He could hear Emile and their children breathing in contented sleep next to him. Yet he sensed an uneasiness that he could not explain. This heaviness on his heart had persisted for months, unfounded, with no reason.

One time he thought he heard the Lord whisper to him, "Sell your cattle, and pay your debt." He felt shocked – confused. Why would God instruct in such a manner? That would put him back to a very small herd like Joe and Sally. To do that made no logical sense. He finally dismissed the thought as one of his own fears and not of the Lord. Still the uneasy feeling hung on him.

The time to say, "Goodbye," seemed to come even sooner in 1929.

"Farmer, I truly have had a good time. I must admit, I envy you living in this place and slow pace," Andrew spoke with genuine feeling as he shook Farmer's hand. By the way, you are friends with Benjamin Harrison?"

"Yes, we grew up together."

"He has been keeping dark company. You would do well to warn him of danger."

"Oh, Farmer, you all please come see us in Texas next year," Susan pleaded. "Promise!"

"Yes, yes," he agreed. "I think it is time."

"And we shall be back in 1931," Hirum's deep voice broke as he hugged each of his grandchildren. Vivian was sobbing.

How could they all have known of the black and difficult days and years that lay ahead?

October 29, 1929, the Stock Market crashed!

Chapter 14

A WITNESS TO TWO MEN

Farmer knew the Lord wanted him to talk to two men about their salvation. He felt positive that this must be done and before the snows arrived and 1929 slipped out into the history books.

Benjamin Harrison, Farmer's lifelong friend had remained heavy on his heart for years. Andrew's warning only reinforced the urgency of again talking to Benjamin concerning his relationship with Christ.

Accomplishing a witness to Benjamin would not be easy. Two thousand miles of mountain and desert separated them. Telephones were not a part of everyday life in Douglas Landing, at least not until next year.

Farmer decided he could write Benjamin a letter, but it would take the Spirit of God to write the words on his friend's heart. Farmer set about composing a letter one evening. He tore up several attempts before he completed a letter he could mail:

"Dear Benjamin,

We all send a howdy to ya an' Betty Jean. Hope ya both air well an' the Good Lord has been good to ya.

Emile's Ma an' Pa came ta visit us a spell in August. Susan an' her husband Andrew rode along. He tol' me thet ya seemed ta be courtin' some trouble. This news weighed heavy like a big boulder on me, so's I reckon I hed ta write ya 'bout it. Ya've been a powerful good friend ta me. It was y'ar maps an' all thet helped us make the long an' dangerous trip to Oregon. I felt ya was with us all the way.

My heart longs ta see ya, Benjamin. An' Betty Jean too. But even more'n ta see ya, I hev me a powerful yernin' ta see ya know my friend, Jesus Christ. Ta know Him in yer hearts like me an' Emile has known Him all these years.

Benjamin, ifen I could hev me one wish it would be fer thet. When ya read this would ya jus' have a quiet talk with God. Ask Him ta fergive yer sins. Believe thet the Son o' God, Jesus, died fer ya on the cross. Then, jus' invite Him inta yer heart – like askin' a friend ta come in yer house ta stay. I'm a beggin' ya both to do this now!

Love, Farmer."

The letter was mailed the next day sealed with the prayers of Farmer and Emile.

Farmer was apprehensive about the second man, Gardner Grubb.

"Why send me, Lord?" Farmer found himself praying. "Ya need to bring in a preacher fer this'n!"

No one in Douglas Landing, or even Applegate knew anything about the man. He was the first of the homesteaders to arrive, and he had section one. He was alone, no one knew where he came from, nothing of his past, he entertained no visitors. The few who ventured on or near his property – like Joe Baltman, Junior Springfield, Scott McQuirk, Clarence Judd or Farmer had been met with a shotgun, cruel words and been run off. Gardner had not participated in any of the house raisin's or warmin's. He never attended church, only went into Douglas Landing once or twice a month, and no farther as far as folks knew.

Gardner lived in a small but sturdy log cabin by himself. He added some out buildings Joe reported. He and Clarence were the only living souls who had actually been to Gardner's cabin. No one had seen inside.

Gardner had a handful of cattle, some pigs and chickens, just enough to satisfy government requirements to prove his homestead.

One strange thing about Gardner, he owned a nice car. The automobile was much too fancy to be parked by a small cabin in the woods. It was out of place in a lumber town like Douglas Landing – even a car, which went beyond Applegate or Springdale. The whole mystery had left folks scratching their heads.

Farmer put off making a call on Mr. Grubb as long as he could, until he knew, "I must go today!"

He decided to take his pick-up. The motor would alert Gardner as to a visitor, and Farmer could drive in fast – maybe all the way to the Grubb cabin.

Farmer grabbed a Bible, and with his heart in his throat he took off to see Gardner. Farmer was surprised to see fence on the Grubb property that ran along the northern part of section one. His heart sank when he came to a locked gate. He sat there for a minute before he shut the engine off. He slowly got out of his pick-up and climbed through the fence.

He followed the little worn road that was nothing more than a trail that led to Gardner Grubb's cabin. He walked quickly, Bible in hand, unsure of what he would encounter or say.

He walked about twenty minutes. Gardner had no doubt built his cabin far into his section of land, and Farmer had not come upon it yet. As he passed by a thicket he felt the cold barrel of a gun touch his neck, and the click of the hammer being cocked.

Farmer froze!

"You better have a good reason for trespassing or I'll plant you right here," a chilling voice from an unseen person spoke.

"Gardner?" Farmer choked. "I'm yer neighbor, Farmer Trevor – come ta visit."

"I'm not in the mood for a visit," the man snapped as he stepped from the shadows of the thicket. He moved around in front of Farmer, his shotgun leveled at his chest. Gardner was a thin man, well dressed, his hat pulled down where his eyes could not be seen. He was clean-shaven, and Farmer detected the faint odor of cologne.

"Gardner, I'm yer neighbor for gosh sakes. I ain't got me no gun, so's ifen yer not fixin' to hold me up, ya can please aim thet shotgun somewhere else," Farmer spoke nervously.

"I told you! I'm not in the visiting mood, and I'm not in a joking mood with a smart mouth," Gardner's words bit, but he did lower his shotgun.

"So state your business – and quick!"

"Well, I reckon I'll start with invitin' ya to our Church in the Woods, an' tell ya 'bout my friend Jesus Christ." Farmer raised his Bible to open it.

The man began to laugh. He laughed long and hard in Farmer's face. It was not a happy or hearty laugh, but carried a mocking tone.

Then Gardner stopped as abruptly as he had started.

"I have no use for church!" Gardner exploded. "How dare you come on my property to preach to me! You think you can convert me? I've killed men for less than that!"

Farmer felt his heart stop when Gardner raised his shotgun again, and this time he saw the piercing eyes from under the hat. Farmer wished he had never come, and he prayed that God would spare him. He tried frantically to collect his thoughts.

"Didn't mean ya no offense," Farmer gulped to clear his throat. "We just want ta be yer friend. Know it must get powerful lonesome, bein' here by yerself and all..."

"I don't want friends! How I live is no concern of yours, Mr. Trevor."

"When I believed on Jesus Christ and thet he died in my place on the cross – I asked Him ta come into my heart. He did, an' He changed me. His love is most powerful!"

"I don't want you or your Christ for my friend. I'm not buying what you're selling. I don't need either of you!" Gardner thundered.

"Get out! Get out! Before I open your chest with this shotgun!" He yelled.

The fire in Gardner's eyes and the rage in his face convinced Farmer it was time to leave. He ran all the way back to his truck.

He spoke little of the details concerning the encounter with Gardner to Emile. Farmer chose not to frighten and upset her.

Two weeks after the visit to the Grubb homestead, a letter arrived from Benjamin. It read:

"Hi Pal,

I just wanted to tell you that I'm doing fine and for you not to worry about me and Betty Jean. You know me, Farmer, I never was much about church going, and what has God done for me? Maybe when I'm old and grey haired, I'll have time to get to know Him like you do. But for now, there's money to make, people to meet, places to go. You go to church, we party at the speak-easys. But don't tell anyone. Ha! You wrote the letter before your last one that you planned on a trip next year. I too long to see you my good friend. We've had some good times – you and me. When you come next year, I want you and Emile to meet Betty Jean. She's a real beauty. Then maybe we can come to Oregon in 1931.

Walter and Clifton must be almost grown, and haven't even seen Leah yet.

Write soon,
Benjamin."

After reading Benjamin's letter, Farmer wept. He remembered summer days he and his friend walked wooded paths, hunted game, rode horses together. He wished he could live some of those precious moments again. Not to change anything – just to savor them a little more fully.

He recalled the day he trusted Christ as his Savior, and his life changed forever – never to be as it was before. Benjamin didn't understand what had happened to his close friend, nor did he ever quite accept it. He certainly didn't embrace a loving God who had brought about the change, or to even acknowledge that He had anything to do with it.

Yet their friendship had remained strong over the years. But no matter how strong, it was not enough to bring Benjamin to Christ.

Farmer felt he had failed to reach either of these men. Farmer had a great love for Benjamin, and even felt love for the cold, cruel Gardner. But to no avail...

The Lord seemed to slip His arm around Farmer's shoulder as He gently whispered, "Not all is lost. Not all is lost."

Chapter 15

DEATH COMES IN THREES

In 1930, the United States plunged into the Great Depression. The bottom dropped out from under the cattle market, not only making the Texas trip impossible, but also forcing Farmer to sell a much larger portion of his herd in order to make the bank note. When New Year's Eve finally arrived, Farmer, Emile, Walter, Clifton and Leah joined hands in a prayer thanking God for His blessings and a hope that 1931 would be better.

This was the first New Year's since they had begun their lives in Oregon that friends and neighbors did not grace their living room and warm themselves around the Trevor's fireplace.

There was no air of celebration! Everyone was simply glad to get through the year, and wished for better times again.

That hope was not to be fulfilled yet. The country did not climb out of the Depression. Instead, it sank deeper into the financial, jobless, homeless mire. News came from the east of fortunes lost, suicides, soup lines and rampant crime. That uneasiness that Farmer felt in 1929 relentlessly hung on him. He thought about it during the day, it stared him in the eyes when he awoke in the night – this uncertainty of the future – this refusal of money to flow. It mounted an assault against Farmer's faith and trust in his Heavenly Father.

It was a warm spring day in 1931. The snow had melted, grass grown green, and the heifers mostly finished calving. It was some time in mid-morning, and Farmer was riding Sunset checking cattle – especially looking for the baby calves.

He thought he heard Emile calling him faintly from afar. He called Scout back from his hunting of some small animal, and turned Sunset towards the sound of Emile's voice. It took probably an hour to locate her because she too was moving.

Farmer was surprised to see Emile on Wind, and Leah on Dusty searching for him. She was holding something in her hand. When Farmer rode up close he could tell that Emile's face was tear stained.

"A messenger – drove – out from Applegate – this morning with – this – telegram," Emile choked out the words.

"Did ya read it?" Farmer asked.

"Yes," Emile said, and then burst into tears.

Leah began to cry too, as she pulled on Dusty's reins to settle him down.

Farmer took the telegram from Emile and read:

"Farmer – stop. Your Pa died suddenly yesterday in the field planting crops – stop. Doctor said his heart gave out – stop. Funeral in two days unless you all can come –stop. Ma."

"No! Oh, no!" Farmer cried aloud in shock and anguish. "Oh – please – no, God, please!"

"Oh, Farmer, I'm so sorry!" Emile tried to comfort him.

"What is it, Pa?" Leah asked half crying, trying to understand.

"Your grandfather has died, Leah," Emile explained. She had not revealed the telegram's content until Farmer saw it.

On the ride to the house, Farmer grieved. He pictured times growing up, the times they went fishing. He remembered working the fields with his Pa. He wished he could take back every harsh word he had spoken; every mean thought that had entered his mind about his Pa. He wept bitter tears of remorse that they never settled their differences. He just wanted to tell his Pa he loved him.

Reaching the house, Farmer unsaddled the horses, got Emile and Leah into the Buick and drove to Applegate. He wanted to be at his Pa's funeral more than anything, but felt caged in by the hard times.

He felt himself grow angry over the condition the country was in. Was the United States reaping the whirlwind of ten years of loose living? Wasn't that what the Roaring Twenties stood for: drinking, smoking, murder, robbery, broken homes, broken lives and reckless abandonment?

But why should decent folks pay for the sins of many? Why should he be denied going to his Pa's funeral because thousands desired to booze their lives away? Farmer's anger flashed hot – then he shook his head. He was blaming thousands upon thousands for his grief, which they knew nothing about. They had grief of their own, the likes of which Farmer had no idea. He just had to face the reality that a trip to Texas for any reason was impossible.

He thought of hitchin' rides – that could take weeks. It could be dangerous – these were desperate times. Farmer felt his hands were tied while he was being beaten. The worse part, which hurt and confused Farmer, was that God let it happen and remained silent.

Farmer sent a telegram to his Ma. That night they told the boys. Sadness filled both Trevor homes, separated by so many miles.

A few days later Farmer was surprised to find a letter from Clem Harrison at the post office. He had perhaps written once since the Trevors came to Oregon. Farmer's heart sank as he read:

"Dear Farmer,

I hope this letter finds you and your family well. I regret to send you bad news, but was sure you would want to know.

Benjamin and two other men were murdered in what the police described as a gangster execution. We just returned yesterday from Fort Worth where the funeral was held. His wife Betty insisted that he be buried there near their home. Benjamin had a small but nice funeral. I wanted to write because you and Benjamin were such close friends. You two seemed inseparable. Also, I don't know if you heard that Margaret Hatchet closed up her Mercantile when the Depression started. She passed on in her sleep a month ago.

Clem."

Farmer stood outside the post office and wept again from an aching heart. There had never been any indication of Benjamin embracing and loving the Lord, Jesus Christ. The thought of turning to Christ when he got old would never happen for Benjamin Harrison. All of his living for pleasure only robbed him of life, perhaps forever. Yet Farmer held on to hope that maybe – just maybe Benjamin had opened his heart to the Lord – at the last minute! No one could know for sure.

On the ride home, Farmer remembered special memories of his good friend and the times they laughed, played, fought and grew from boys into men. Pictures came to his mind of the last time Benjamin came to their house in Holt, big grin on his face, talking miles a minute, his arms loaded up with maps for Farmer and Emile's long trip.

"Thank you for my friend," Farmer prayed in sobs, and then had to stop the car to wipe his eyes.

It struck him as odd that Clem Harrison had not mentioned his Pa's death in his letter. He picked up the envelope from the car seat and saw that it was postmarked two days before Franklin Trevor's sudden passing.

When he resumed driving, his thoughts turned towards Margaret Hatchet. It saddened him that her warm laughter and smile could be heard and seen only in the memories of those who knew and loved her. Her old Mercantile no longer filled a place in Holt, Texas.

Scenes from the past touching his Pa, Benjamin and Mrs. Hatchet flooded into his thoughts. Farmer concluded that what folks fear most is separation, separation by time, by distance, by anger or hate, by death. The ultimate is separation from God, but some don't pay that much mind – 'til they are dying.

Within a short time, three people he knew and loved had passed into eternity. The saying, "Death comes in threes," has been told for generations. Farmer considered it a superstitious notion. He did not believe it – until now...

Chapter 16

POACHERS

A letter of condolences arrived from the Holts. Hirum and Vivian voiced all of their sympathy to Farmer for the loss of his Pa. They told that the family was holding up, but crops were not good this year. Farmer's Ma, brothers and sister were struggling to hang onto the farm.

Vivian wrote the letter. She went on to say that Hirum and she had lost much in the stock market crash and were barely getting by. The number of clients for both Hirum and Andrew had dropped drastically. The ones they did have could not pay. The planned trip for 1931 would have to be postponed until times got better.

When the Great Depression began, most Americans believed it would be over soon. They kept thinking – we'll pull out of this next month. Then it became – we'll surely climb back up next year.

But with each passing month, conditions grew even more desperate. Hopes faded, even the most stouthearted fell, and the Depression that had crept across the land now laid its black icy hand on the neck of a nation.

That nation was again on the move, but this time not out of joy and sheer excitement of travel to see new places.

Now men rode the rails or hitchhiked. Families piled meager belongings on their cars, all-making their way to places rumored to provide some work.

Farmer had also applied for a job at the two mills in Douglas Landing, and some companies in Applegate. He discovered that for every position two hundred men were in line ahead of him, clamoring for the job.

To add to their woes, January and February 1932 was the most extreme winter anyone could remember. As the bitter cold days wore on, Farmer faced the realization that if winter didn't break soon, he would not have enough feed for his cattle.

It was on a grey February morning when Farmer heard it. A rifle shot – just one – not far from where he was riding Dusty. He had left the house early to check cattle and make sure they had some feed.

He was near the eastern line of his section, which bordered the Miller ranch. He was riding along Cold Creek, because most of the cattle gathered on the east side, where, if it were possible, was warmer and they could water. Farmer knew he would usually find much of his herd here.

The rifle shot puzzled him; maybe Lyman was hunting. Farmer decided to see, and rode Dusty quietly through the trees.

Soon he came upon a man's footprints, visible in the crusted snow. He saw where someone had crossed Cold Creek and walked north.

"This be on my side o' the property line," he thought. "Would be a bit odd fer Lyman ta be a huntin' over here."

He turned Dusty to follow the tracks. He had not gone far when he heard a noise. Then a man on his knees came into view through the brush and trees. The man was intent on what he was doing, his back towards Farmer. He was unaware of the rider's approach.

As Farmer came closer he saw the man was cutting one of his steers with a knife. A rifle was propped up against a near tree stump.

Farmer exploded inside with anger upon discovering this poacher. He drew his 30-30 out of its saddle sheath, and dismounted from Dusty.

He stealthily stepped through the trees to a position behind the man who was feverishly butchering the steer. Farmer leveled his rifle and took a bead on the man.

The sound of Farmer cocking the hammer on his rifle startled the man. He jumped up and spun around. Terror was written all over his face at the sight of looking down the barrel of Farmer's rifle. He collapsed to his knees and began to beg.

"Oh, God! Please don't kill me, mister. I got a family – I have pictures – here," he frantically dug some pictures out of his billfold. His hands shook so much everything he was holding fell to the ground.

Farmer was incensed. "Yo're a no good cattle rustler. Ya killed one o' my Herefords. Where I come from, we buried rustlers where we shot 'em," Farmer growled, his eyes blazing.

"I could finish ya right here – right now, an' leave ya fer the coyotes."

The man turned ashen. "Awwh, no," he choked. "Have mercy. I'll pay you. I'll work, anything – just don't kill me!"

With that the man wrapped his arms around Farmer's legs pleading for his life. Farmer freed himself and kicked the man away. Farmer aimed the rifle between the man's eyes; he was ready to pull the trigger, when the Lord stopped him.

Farmer had never seen such fear in any man, and in that instant he realized that he was the cause of it. It was in his power to take another's life – and God stopped him. He didn't quite know how he knew that; he just knew He did. He lowered his rifle and slowly released the hammer.

The man scrambled to pick up his pictures, holding them up to Farmer. He began pleading again.

"Please, mister, don't kill me. I ain't never done anything like this before. I was raised by God-fearin' parents, been outa work so long, my wife and family are cold and hungry, couldn't stand to see that – awwh, please, let me go! I'll work – anything to pay you back -!"

"Shut up!" Farmer ordered.

Farmer took the pictures. One was of the man, a modest looking woman and two small children. The other picture was of two small girls.

"How'd ya get here?" Farmer demanded.

"I drove my car from Applegate. I parked on the road and walked – to here."

"Thet yer rifle?" Farmer motioned towards the gun.

"No, I borrowed it. Only had two shells."

"Yo're family in Applegate?"

"Yes, sir."

"Y'all take me to 'em."

"What!" the man gasped.

"Y'all take me to 'em, an' they better be what ya say, or y'all be goin' ta the sheriff."

Farmer finished gutting the steer and threw it on Dusty's back. Farmer carried the man's rifle, and they trudged to Farmer's house. Emile was curious; Farmer told her he was taking this fellow into town.

Farmer hung the meat up in a shed. The cold would keep it. He instructed the fellow to get into the pick-up, and they drove to Applegate mostly in silence. The man appeared fidgety and nervous.

When the pair arrived in Applegate, the man gave directions into a part of the city that had streets lined with plain but comfortable looking homes. The man pointed out one of them, and Farmer stopped at the gate.

Farmer entered the door right behind the man. Two young girls came scrambling out of the shadow of a dark corner, yelling, "Daddy!" Hands held out. They leaped into his arms; he wrapped them close to him and buried his face against their heads. He looked up to see his wife who appeared right behind their daughters. She spoke not a word, but her glance towards Farmer holding the man's rifle, and the questioning look to her husband revealed she knew something must be wrong. Farmer sensed in an instant neither she nor the children had any knowledge of what had been intended or happened.

"Did you bring us something to eat – like you said," one of the little girls asked her daddy. From the side Farmer could see the man's lip quiver and his face squint up in pain. He looked at his wife.

"Awwh, Grace, I've done a terrible thing!" he began to confess. Farmer grabbed the man's shoulder to stop him from saying anymore.

"Actually, misses," Farmer interrupted, "Yer man got a steer from me – fer work. It's a curin' at my ranch right now. We jus' needs ta be gettin' it. Y'all will have meat on yer table."

Relief came over the woman's face.

"Oh, thank you," she spoke softly, as she took the girls from her husband. They stood beside their mother and peeked around her to see Farmer.

As Farmer looked around, he realized that the electricity, which had come to Applegate the year before, was turned off. Studying the family's faces and actions, he deducted they were all weak from hunger.

"My name is Farmer Trevor," he handed the rifle to the man.

"I forgot my manners. I am Mitchell, my wife Grace, and our twins Jane and Shirley."

"When can we eat?" Jane timidly asked.

"I sure am hungry, Daddy," Shirley was anxious. Both parents turned their faces from Farmer and their children.

Farmer drove Mitchell back to the ranch as quickly as he could. He was thankful no new snow had fallen from the grey overcast. He dropped Mitchell off at his car and instructed him to follow to the house. Farmer arrived a little ahead, and told Emile about Mitchell, Grace and their twins. Tears filled her eyes with an, "Oh, dear!" as she gathered some of her canning from the pantry.

Farmer showed Mitchell how to skin and cut up the meat. He told him how to preserve the meat and placed it in the trunk of the car.

"Ifen there be other families thet truly be in need an' nothin' ta eat, ya hev them ta come see us," Farmer told Mitchell. "I sware ta ya thet as long as we hev somethin' ta give, none shall go hungry."

Mitchell stood looking at Farmer for a long time.

"I don't know – what to say," he finally spoke. "How can we ever thank you!"

"Ya said ya would do anythin'," Farmer reminded Mitchell.

"Yes."

"Promise me thet ya will find a good church in Applegate an' get yerself, Grace an' yer little girls in it!"

Chapter 17

BLACK CLOUDS – DARK DAYS

B ecause of the U.S. Forest Service Ranger Station located in Douglas Landing, electric poles were installed along the main road, and power was brought in from Applegate. Telephones soon followed. Everyone in town had electric and telephone lines to their house or business, but few could afford those new luxuries.

Business suffered. Both mills cut back and laid off many of their workers. Donald Parrigan was fortunate to hang onto his job, but they did cut his hours. There were rumors that Michael and Molly O'Malley might be forced to close O'Malley's Merchandise, and Dr. Put was considering moving back east.

Prohibition agents acting on a complaint arrested Zeck and closed his tavern. Zeck spent ninety days behind bars. When he got out he reopened his establishment selling soft drinks and sandwiches in the front, but he had a hidden back room where he sold bootleg whiskey.

The summer of 1932 brought extreme hardship for the homesteaders. Junior and Maybelle Springfield sold their section to Cascade Mountains Timber Company, and took their child and went back to Alabama. Pendleton Green gave up and sold out. He hoped to find work in Chicago. Soon after that, Scott and Catherine McQuirk sold their property and left for California. The homesteaders felt a tight bond. They had helped build each others homes and out buildings, watched over their cattle, ate together, formed a church together, saw babies born, shared dreams of the future. Now those dreams were vanishing – like sand through their fingers.

"I feel like we are losing part of our family," Emile related sadly one summer evening as the couple sat on their porch.

"Junior and Maybelle air mighty fine folks," Farmer knew what Emile was referring to. "I am proud to hev known them fer friends an' neighbors."

"Their family is precious," Emile seemed lost in thought. "Pendleton – the McQuirks gone. Farmer, what is to become of us? When will this dreadful..." she stopped.

Farmer could see the worry in her face.

"Will it ever get better – again?" Emile asked.

"It has ta I reckon," Farmer mumbled halfheartedly.

But it didn't get better. The end of 1932 came on with a vengeance. More people were out of work when the snow fell. One by one families came to the Trevors – desperate folks who were hungry. Farmer and Emile gave each person both physical and spiritual food. With each steer Farmer butchered, the sinking, hopeless feeling that he was depleting his herd continually forced its presence upon him.

When 1933 arrived, Farmer did not have the money to make the bank note. He trusted God to provide – hadn't the Lord always taken care of them in the past? He remembered and found comfort in recalling ways God's provision came to them on the long trip from Texas to Oregon. And their needs had always been met on the ranch. Farmer didn't know quite how God would take care of it – only that He would.

The Trevors were snowed in for weeks in January and February. The children could not attend school, and Farmer could not get to the bank, but he was plagued with the nagging need to see Rollin Graves. The small bank had been struck hard when the '29 crash hit. It closed for several days, and even though it was a part of a larger chain, the bank nearly went under. It would have were it not for the simple trust of the townsfolk, loggers and homesteaders who refused to give in to panic.

Farmer would have to face Rollin and tell him he couldn't make the note payment. He was responsible, and as soon as the weather broke and roads cleared, Farmer drove to Douglas Landing.

Rollin Graves greeted him warmly and motioned him into his small office.

"How are you, Farmer? How is your family?" Rollin asked.

"Fine – all fine, Rollin. I'll get right ta the reason fer my visit I reckon. I can't sell any cattle, an' I don't hev the money ta make the note, but I'm a hopin' that the market will get better this spring an' I can catch up."

Rollin Graves grew serious.

"I know it's a down market, Farmer. Let's hold off until spring and see what happens then."

Farmer was relieved and drove home happy, thanking God. He shared the good news with Emile who hugged him tightly for a long time. He felt that a weight was taken off her as well. Emile had not voiced her fears, but Farmer knew she did worry about the finances, and her faith was being tested as much as his. He held her close and stroked her hair.

"See, Emile, God *is* taking care of us," he spoke gently.

Farmer went about daily routines and chores. He didn't think too much about it anymore, except that soon he would have to go to market.

Farmer was surprised to see Rollin Graves' car coming through the trees one warm spring morning. Snow was melting and roads drying. Farmer met Rollin at his car when it stopped by the house.

"Well, mornin', Rollin," Farmer drawled with a cheerful, cautious manner. "Reckon I'm a mite surprised ta see ya, but powerful glad."

"Good morning, Farmer. How are you?"

"As Donald Parrigan says – 'bout as happy as a fly in a bucket of hog slop," Farmer laughed.

"Yes, Donald would say that," Rollin chuckled with him. The two men shook hands.

"Come have coffee!" Emile called from the porch.

"You certainly have fixed up your place," Rollin commented, looking around.

"Yes, sir, we hev. God has been mighty kind ta us" Farmer agreed.

"Put a lot of work into it, you have?" Rollin asked.

"Yes, sir – reckon seven year's worth. Can't rightly count this year, 'cause I ain't done me no buildin' yet."

Rollin greeted Emile who had two coffee cups waiting on the table. She retreated into the bedroom. Farmer's mind was racing – wondering why the unannounced visit from his banker. Rollin sipped his coffee intent on the inside of the log house where he sat. He appeared sad and nervous.

"Farmer, I've been told you've been feeding the whole of Oregon with your cattle."

Farmer felt his face get hot.

"Well, thet's partial true, Rollin, only I ain't got a big enough herd to feed ever'body, so's it's only been the families most needin.' "

"You have been slaughtering your cattle to feed people you don't know?"

"I reckon I know 'em by the time I feed 'em."

"How big is your herd now?"

"Haven't killed any heifers – only steers. Probably hev a hundred heifers, most hev calves to be born soon."

"How many steers?"

"I reckon I hev twenty or so left."

"So you have none to sell this spring, Farmer?"

"No, sir, I don't."

"Don't call me sir, Farmer! Don't make this harder than it is!"

Farmer was stunned and speechless. He had never seen Rollin like this. The banker looked around quickly to make sure Emile was not in the room. He lowered his voice.

"Cattle market is down, Farmer, and you've been giving your cattle away to strangers." Rollin shook his head. "Business-minded men would call that crazy as a fool!"

"Rollin, me an' Emile couldn't see hungry men, women an' children goin' without ifen we had somethin' ta give."

"Farmer, you don't seem to understand the severity of your situation. A larger banking organization bought out the company who owned us. The new management wants to know how you will pay your note. Your loan far exceeds the value of your cattle, your automobiles and your property – even considering timber rights."

"Ifen ya can hold off 'til fall an' I can sell - "

"Farmer, they won't wait until fall. They have instructed me to inform you that your note payment is due in full thirty days from now, or they will foreclose on you. I'm sorry, Farmer, but I have no say in this matter anymore."

Rollin could have hit Farmer in the face with a full swing of a rafter beam and not dealt the blow he had just given! Farmer reeled from the shock of Rollin's pronouncement. He tried to stand to see Rollin out, but his legs gave way beneath him. His mind refused to think – he steadied himself with the table – sitting – dazed.

The sky was a clear sunny blue, but in Farmer's world black clouds covered the blue and the day grew dark.

Chapter 18

WILL GOD TAKE CARE OF US?

Farmer tried to shield Emile and the children from worry.

"Rollin jus' wanted us ta get the note payment in," Farmer told Emile when she asked why banker Graves came to their house.

"Do we have enough to pay it?" she asked.

"Not yet, but I'm workin' on it," Farmer replied, but didn't look her in the eye.

And work on it, he did. He drove into Applegate the next day to wire Hirum and Vivian Holt to see if they could help. He even thought about rancher Thomas Redkin, but couldn't bring himself to wire him. He next made the rounds of the remaining homesteaders to see how deeply the Depression had taken its toll. The vice grip that held the nation also had its jaws locked on Oregon. Jobs were scarce, money tight – most folks just tried to hold on and prayed to survive.

"I tried to tell you not to borrow from the bank!" Joe Baltman scolded when Farmer told him about Rollin Graves' visit. "I wished I could help you, Farmer. My spread is free an' clear, but me an' Sally an' Rachel are just livin' off our land. You practically give your cattle away at the sales. We'll make it, but we got no money. The Brooks borrowed against their place like you did. Ella May told my misses that they was gonna lose their place if they can't gather the note payment."

"God's not gonna let us lose our ranch, Joe!" Farmer exclaimed. "I jus' know He won't. He didn't bring us here ta take it all away!"

Joe held a steady gaze with Farmer for some time. It seemed he wanted to say something, but didn't or couldn't. He finally spoke.

"I sure hope you don't lose your spread, I surely do. I pray God will spare you."

Farmer saw Joe's face soften.

"You know you all have a place here to – stay – if..." Joe's voice trailed off.

Clarence and Locust Tree Judd had not borrowed as much as Farmer and had managed to pay off their note before the Depression reached its depth. It was much the same with the German couple, Lyman and Helen Miller.

"Thirty dollars we have saven. You habben it to help you, Herr Farmer, mine friend," Lyman shoved some wadded bills into Farmer's hand.

"I can't take yer savin's – money," Farmer tried to give it back.

"Nicht! You givin' it to Herr Graves, you helpin' us, we helpin' you. Besser times comin', you will see them, mine Herr."

Farmer left with a sense of shame taking the Miller's savings.

Donald and Beth Parrigan and Olaf Anderson were making it barely, and that was only because Donald and Olaf had jobs at the mills. And they, like the fortunate ones to have work, lived just month-to-month, hand to mouth.

A few days later a return telegram from the Holts informed Farmer that they regretfully could not help, and prayed that the ranch would not be lost.

Farmer spent restless days and sleepless night. There were times in the dead of night that the weight of the problems crushed him right through his bed. He had flashes of panic if he allowed himself to mull over their situation. It seemed hopeless! Even if he could sell everything they had, besides the land, it would not be enough to pay the bank note.

But God had always brought them through – even desperate times, and Farmer knew and took comfort now by faith that His God would do it again.

In Sunday Service, Donald gave the message. "God's ways are higher'n our ways and we can't always understand 'em," Donald said. "'Bout the time we think we have Him figured out, He does a turn to surprise us. Who woulda dreamed thet God would use a woman to get this lumberjack's attention? God has a broader way a workin' out what we be facin' – but it will be His way, like a lovin' Father who can see the whole picture. Like God told Paul to go to Jerusalem, an' that wasn't a pleasant trip. He had all kinds a troubles. His enemies finally jailed him. Seemed a cruel thing – I mean, God sendin' Paul just so he would encounter all manner a trouble. But ya see, the Lord had a bigger tree spotted for Paul to cut down, and had to get him to Rome to talk to Caesar."

The church prayed for the Trevors and the Brooks at the end of the service, but Farmer left with uneasiness in his heart over the message Donald had given.

Farmer decided to sell as many cattle as he could market and take what money he had into Rollin. Although it fell short of the figure required to pay the note, Farmer prayed that it would buy him some time. If only the black clouds of the terrible Depression would break apart and the sun shine once again, they would all make it.

The dreaded day arrived when Farmer drug himself into Douglas Landing to the bank. Rollin saw him enter the bank and motioned him into his office. He greeted Farmer warmly as a longtime friend, then went to a cabinet to dig among files until he pulled one out which Farmer reckoned was his. Farmer laid out the cash he had accumulated on Rollin's desk.

"I sold most all my cattle, Rollin, an' had me some money besides. This be all I got. I knows it don't match what ya was a askin' fer, but I reckoned maybe y'all could – well, maybe it would buy me a little more time."

Rollin Graves silently counted the money, and then gave a sigh.

"I knows it ain't enough, Rollin, but ifen ya could jus'..." Farmer was pleading, but couldn't go on.

Graves slowly stood as if heavy weights would pull him to the floor. "I will make a phone call to see what I can do," he spoke quietly as he left out the office door to another room in the bank. Farmer could see him talking into a phone. At times he appeared angry.

After what seemed an hour, banker Graves returned to his desk. He handed Farmer back his money.

"I have been instructed not to accept a partial payment, Farmer."

Farmer felt pain in the pit of his stomach. "What does – thet – mean?" he stuttered.

Rollin shuffled through papers in Farmer's file. "Your loan lists for collateral, your ranch and cattle you have left, your pick-up, your Buick and certain furniture items. The bank will take possession of all I named immediately."

"An' ifen I refuse to leave?"

"The banking firm which has your note will obtain a court order against you, and a sheriff will come out and remove you and your family from the property."

Farmer's heart sunk, he felt sick; he was confused! Why hadn't God helped? He felt his faith crumple in a heap on the floor of the bank office.

"I trusted God ta take care o' us – to provide – I never reckoned on this..." Farmer spoke half to Rollin – half to himself.

"Well, unless God adds a sizeable amount to what you just showed me – Farmer, I have no choice. Please don't make this any harder, I don't want to do this either. If I don't, the main office will send someone in who will. I can't afford to lose my position here. I hope you won't force us into court."

Farmer's whole life caved in as he realized he was losing everything he had – all he had worked so hard for. Gone in a day! His mind swam in racing – painful – thoughts. He buried his head in his hands to hide tears he could not stop. How could he face Emile – his children? Where would they go!

"Oh, God! Where will we go?" he cried out. "We have nowhere!" What have I done? Oh, God! Help us! What will become of my family?"

Farmer sobbed violently, his body shaking in convulsions as his heart broke, and his life came apart.

Rollin got up and closed the door so other bank personnel and customers could not hear Farmer's grieving. Graves was sitting quietly, watching sadly when Farmer finally looked up.

"Sorry," Farmer coughed, trying to clear his throat. "I reckon I made a mighty dumb fool a myself. Ya been a good an' generous friend, Rollin. Won't make ya no trouble. We'll gather up some belongin's."

Farmer saw the banker's eyes get watery, then his face lit up like he had an idea. He went out into the bank to another cabinet and soon returned with two files.

"I just remembered that the bank repossessed two houses in town almost three years ago. No one has the interest or money to buy them. I have felt sick to the point I can't sleep over taking everything from you, Farmer, which I can't do anything about, but danged if I can't deed one of those houses to you and the other to the Brooks. Yes! That's exactly what I'll do, so you and Emile and your children have a – place to stay – a home!"

Rollin seemed relieved – even a bit excited to have found some sort of solution to help the Trevors and Brooks.

"The house I give you is on the corner of Peppertree and Breach Road. It is a small house, but has several acres going back into the trees; there is room for your horses. You can keep all the furniture items not listed in the note. I'll let you use your truck 'til you move, and you keep the money you have. You'll need it to get by."

That night, Farmer told Emile, "I feel such a failure and so ashamed!" The sense of loss overwhelmed them both, and they cried in each other's arms well into the night.

"I thought God would take care of us. I believed He would, an' He didn't!" Farmer was hurt and confused. "He let us lose éver'thing! I don't reckon I understand – Him atall!"

"I think – He *did* - take care of us," Emile murmured softly between sniffs, "just not – the way – we expected."

Chapter 19

HOUSE ON PEPPERTREE
AND BREACH ROAD

W alter, Clifton and Leah did not take it well the next morning when they were told the family would have to move into town. Walter and Clifton sort of pulled themselves together and went out to the road to catch the ride to school; however, Leah was too upset to go and locked herself in the bedroom.

With heavy hearts Farmer and Emile set about the task of packing up their belongings. Emile knocked on Leah's bedroom door to inform her the pick-up was loaded up, and it was time to take their first trip into town. Directly, Leah stormed out of her room, face puffed up and refusing to look at either her mother or father. She spoke no words on the drive to Douglas Landing.

Farmer stopped first at the bank to get the key to the house. Rollin had some papers for him to sign.

When Farmer turned the pick-up off the main highway onto Peppertree, Leah spoke.

"Can see that ol' house from the school. Ever'body says ghosts stay in it. Says people were murdered there!"

"Ridiculous!" Emile retorted.

"Banker Graves tol' me a few minutes ago thet a soldier from the Great War built the house an' named the street," Farmer explained. "When the town started they graded three roads off the main one due west startin' at the Ranger Station. Named 'em fer trees – Peppertree, Aspen thet the school's on – an' Myrtlewood. The soldier said thet there be no connected road on the other end – needed a breach. The name stuck, an' he built his house on it."

"An' he got murdered!"

"No, Leah, he got laid off'n his work an' – an' he lost his house an' moved – on."

"Bet we find a body!"

"Oh, for goodness sake, stop, Leah," Emile ordered. "There's no dead bodies – 'cept yours if you keep on talking like this!"

The three were shocked when they walked into the house. It seemed tight and well constructed, but three years of lying empty had left its fill of cobwebs, dirt, and mouse and rat droppings.

Several faded pictures hung crooked on random walls. Strips of ripped, water-stained cloth hung from a wire over two of the windows. Papers were scattered on the floor.

The house consisted of a living room, which was the largest room in the house. There was a kitchen with room for a table. Water was piped into the house, so the kitchen had a sink and wood cook stove. Emile tried the faucet, but the water was turned off.

Next they looked in the bathroom. It displayed a small sink, a tub for bathing and a commode.

"Where is my room?" Leah demanded. "There's only one bedroom, an' it has dirty ol' springs on the floor!"

Farmer and Emile looked and for sure there was only one bedroom. It had metal box springs in a corner of the room.

116

"You and the boys won't have a room. You will have to sleep in the living room."

Farmer's mind refused to work at this juncture.

"This is a bad dream! What's happening to us? I don't understand!" Leah howled.

"We will have to make the best of it," Emile tried to console their daughter.

"I don't want to make the best of it! I won't make the best of it. I want our own house back. I want to go home!"

Anger flashed hot in Farmer. "This is yer home!" he raised his voice. "Be thankful ya have someplace. We could be standin' on a road somewhere -."

Leah ran out to the pick-up and sat on the running board crying.

"This is a difficult change for her, Farmer," Emile spoke softly. "We'll make do."

"Emile, what is wrong with ya? Look at this place – it's dirty! Mice an' rats livin' in it – no place fer our children, an' yer talkin' like it's jus' fine. What's wrong with ya? I done lost our ranch an' home an' ever'thing. Get mad! Cuss me out! Tell me thet I'm a lowdown dirty skunk o' man – not fit fer ya or -!"

Emile came close and put her hand on his mouth to quiet his ranting. He couldn't cry, there were no tears left!

"You must understand, Farmer, to be with you and our children – that's all that matters. Yes, it hurts to lose what we've worked so hard for. I hurt for you – but Farmer, it's not the end of the world. Think on this: the children won't miss so much school in the winter, and we don't have to trudge in the cold to the road when the snow is deep – and – and – look we can have electric!"

Farmer threw up his hands and walked out onto a small back porch and into the grass behind the house. He paced back and forth making his way to the pine and fir trees. A grove of glimmering aspen lined a small creek on the back-side of his property. He had to settle down.

"This is terrible hard on Emile – she never accuses or complains. She be a mighty fine woman, Lord. I sure can't understand yer way o' thinkin', but I hev ta accept it. I want ta accept it; Ya know I'm a grievin' loss, Lord. I'm a thinkin' right along I was a doin' it all Yer way...but maybe I wasn't. I sure got my family in a bad spot.

"An' this be a hard time fer my children. The boys loved the open range an' trees an' herdin' the cattle. An' Leah is growin' into a woman soon – pretty as her Ma. She already speaks her mind too. She don't understan' bein' booted outa her home – ta come – ta this. What's ta happen ta us, Lord?"

When Farmer returned to the house, Emile and Leah were busy converting a dirty neglected house into a livable home. They had already placed a woman's touch on it. Leah approached Farmer.

"I'm sorry, Daddy. I know you are doing the best you can to take care of us. I didn't mean those – what I said."

"Yes, ya did," Farmer responded. "We all air a hurtin' 'bout this turn. But we can trust God ta make it good." Farmer folded her into his arms and held her tight.

"Like yer Ma said, "we'll make do.'"

By the time school was out, four trips had been made to the log house. The boys walked down the dirt road to their new home. Rachel Baltman came with them.

"Been thinkin', Pa," Walter announced the second he walked through the door. "Seein' as this be one bedroom – thet's fer you an' Ma – an' Leah needs her privacy. Well, me an' Clifton could set up our tent behind the house. We could camp out there fer the summer."

Farmer eyed them suspiciously. Rachel was already exploring the house.

"How ya boys know this be one bedroom?" Farmer asked, puzzled.

"'Fore school we came lookin' in the windows. What ya think, Pa? 'Bout campin' in the tent out back?"

Farmer saw his sons differently for the first time. Walter had shot up and was getting tall for his thirteen years. Clifton was shorter, but growing and seemed to display maturity beyond his age of eleven.

"I reckon it to be a fine idea, an' I'm a mite proud o' ya," Farmer put his arms around both boys.

Rachel slipped next to Clifton, and looking up at Farmer, giggled in her girlish way. "I like your little house that sits on Peppertree and Breach Road."

Chapter 20

GREEN CHAIN

It was an emotional farewell on the last trip from the ranch house.

"Are ya gonna take our wagon?" Clifton asked.

"No, son. Thet chuck wagon brung us ta the ranch, not Douglas Landing. We ain't a movin' it from its place by the barn."

The Model T pick-up sat by the ranch house where Farmer parked it. They were to drive their Buick to the bank and leave it with Rollin.

"What's gonna happen to our home, Daddy?" Leah questioned sadly.

"I reckon the bank will sell off all they can – the pick-up, Buick, livestock, what's left o' the cattle. Not much ta sell in the house."

"I'm thankful Mr. Graves told us to take most of our furnishings. He wasn't supposed to do that," Emile added.

"Nor give us the house in town," Farmer said.

"Pa, who's gonna get our ranch?" Walter asked.

"I reckon Cascade Mountains Lumber Company's Uriah Wallheim will grab it up likin' he did the other sections. His outfit will come in and cut down the best trees fer lumber. Now y'all climb in the car – time fer us to – leave."

Walter and Clifton got in the front seat with Farmer. Emile and Leah sat in the back.

"This has been a good home to us for eight years," Emile spoke, looking back, as the car pulled away.

"Remember how we looked back one last time at our farm house when we left Holt," she went on.

"Yes," Farmer replied, but he refused to look back as the rest of his family did. He vowed to himself never to return until he could buy the ranch back. He could see Emile and Leah holding each other when he did glance in his rearview mirror.

Everyone was submerged in their own thoughts on the drive into town. Except for the rumble of the Buick's engine and the bumps and jars there were no sounds.

Giving the keys to Rollin Graves seemed to symbolize the end of Farmer's ranching days. He didn't know what to do with himself. Emile stayed busy fixing the house, but Farmer just had no interest. He felt lost on an ocean of "what ifs". He had no direction, no purpose. Failure seemed written across his forehead – he even began to think that was what others were saying behind his back. He wanted to crawl in a hole and never come out.

On the third night in their tiny house, Farmer cried himself to sleep like a little boy. He was dying inside and knew it, but helpless to stop it.

In the darkest hour of that night, the Lord gently spoke to him.

"Farmer, you will see the wisdom of what I am doing, and My complete purpose will be revealed in due time."

Farmer lay awake until dawn pondering the Lord's Words. He didn't understand God's ways, but knew he must surrender to His Will and trust Him – for everything.

When Friday rolled around, Farmer was surprised to see Donald Parrigan stop in front of the house. It was going on sundown, and Donald must have just come in from the woods.

"Howdy, Donald, come on in," Farmer greeted the lumberjack at the front door.

"Glad to see you, Farmer. Me an' Beth is deeply sorrowin' to lose ya as neighbors, but we be thankful you are stayin' in Douglas Landing."

Donald had to look over the house, poke his head in each room, and make kidding remarks to Emile and Leah. He then went out back to holler at Walter and Clifton.

"Why you boys look as snug as a couple of beavers sittin' in their beaver house," he laughed when he looked in on them in their tent.

Farmer and Donald walked in the field behind the house. Sunset, Wind and Dusty came trotting up to them – hoping to be ridden somewhere.

"I'm as proud as a gambler findin' a silver dollar to see you kept your horses," Donald beamed. Then he grew more serious.

"Just got in from the woods an' the crew stopped by the mill. It's payday. The mill boss told me that one of their green chainmen is too old to keep up. He quit today. Going somewhere else to live. I told the boss 'bout you. He said if you want the job to be there Monday morning at 6:30."

"Of course, I want it!" Farmer answered, before he could think. "I reckon to do anything! What is the green chain?"

"That's where fresh cut lumber comes off the chain. You grab the pieces, and stack 'em. Be sure and wear good gloves 'cause the wood will splinter and cut your hands. An' those boards will come at you fast an' nasty as a nest of Yellowjackets that got riled up! The first few days you will think you died and went to a bad place – but stick to it and you'll toughen up to the job. That's what happened to me when I first started fallin' timber."

"I'm mighty grateful fer the job," Farmer's tone confirmed his gratitude. "An' fer ya tellin' 'bout me, Donald."

"The boss said this is the first hiring by Pacific Timberline in over a year!" Donald exclaimed.

"The Good Lord has done given me a right dandy job!" Farmer slapped Donald on the back.

"He's given you the green chain," Donald laughed heartily. "After you've done it awhile, then judge how dandy it be!"

Chapter 21

GOD'S WISDOM

Donald Parrigan's description of working on the green chain was most accurate. Farmer nearly crawled home from his first day of work. He had never worked that hard in his life, and was too tired to eat. He flopped into bed.

"Merciful Lord, I don't reckon I can do this 'cept ya give me a big fillin' o' yer strength," Farmer breathed as he closed his eyes.

The next day was not quite as difficult, and as Donald had predicted, Farmer adapted to the work, and it got better.

The Depression, however, was not getting better. Economic forecasts predicted that 1932 was the darkest it would get. Farmer and Emile had gone to the school in November of that year to vote. It seemed most of Douglas Landing rallied together to help vote in Franklin D. Roosevelt and remove Hoover from office.

With the promise of a new President to be sworn in March of 1933, folks felt encouraged. Yet from the election, into the New Year the nation's conditions hit bottom. Bank closings continued, one locked its doors in Applegate. President Roosevelt on his first day in office called for a four-day bank holiday across the country. Rollin Graves joined in on the closure.

That night the President spoke to Americans by radio in what he called the first of his "Fireside Chats." Much of Douglas Landing and some of the homesteaders gathered at one of the four homes that had radios. Farmer and Emile with their children were present at the O'Malleys to hear that talk.

Newspapers coming from San Francisco and Portland displayed articles about Roosevelt's "New Deal" and the "Hundred Days of Congress." They seemed optimistic that measures were being taken that would guarantee the end of the Depression. If there was any relief from this black grip that had held the United States in a hammerlock for three long years, it was not loosening in the slightest on Douglas Landing.

By late fall the Baltmans depleted their small herd of cattle. They now had no income. The Judds and Millers were in similar straits. Farmer returned the thirty dollars that Lyman and Helen Miller had generously given Farmer to try and save his ranch. The story was different for the Brooks and the Trevors.

The Brooks also lost their ranch, but banker Graves deeded the house on the other end of Breach Road to them. Gordon was given some work repairing cars and pumping gasoline at old man Francis Haywood's service station.

Farmer enjoyed receiving his monthly paycheck from Pacific Timberline. Their house was free and clear. They had no car, so the family expense was low. They had water, electricity and plans for a phone the next year. Farmer approached his boss soon after he started his job about buying the miscuts.

"We jus' throw the miscuts and scraps into the burner. Some of the mill hands take the scraps for firewood. Help yourself to whatever you can use," the boss told him.

Farmer got Donald to carry atop his car, defective and miscut lumber that he collected after work to the house. By the time winter was setting in, Farmer had expanded the house nicely with the addition of a large bedroom for Emile and him, another bedroom for Walter and Clifton to share, a sun porch on the front of the house to catch the morning sun, and a large porch on the rear with chairs to watch the sun set. Farmer enclosed one side of the back porch and made that into a washroom for Emile.

Farmer was constantly amazed and fascinated to watch what Emile did to the house. "I make the rough framework – she puts on all the finishin' touches," he thought.

First night in their new bedroom, Farmer sat on the edge of the bed taking off his boots. Emile came over with a sweet smile on her face and sat in his lap. She held his face between her hands and looked him steady in the eyes.

"Farmer, I am so proud of you, and what you have done to our home. Thank you for that, and for being my husband, and the father of our children. I am very happy and so glad you are my man," she purred as she kissed him softly – then deeply.

That night Farmer felt man enough to take on the whole world.

Winter was predicted to be a cold one with heavy snow-packs. Farmer wasn't sure he would get his turn to speak again at the Church in the Woods before the weather turned bad. It was cold on the Sunday morning he was to give the message, the sky clear and sunny, the ground dry.

Gordon Brooks had traded work for a car, so for a month now they would stop by to pick up the Trevors on Sunday morning and take them to church. Little Gordie Brooks was between the ages of Walter and Clifton. They had become even closer friends – forming a common bond around the loss of the ranches and moving into town.

"Clifton loves Rachel!" Gordie blurted out from the front seat.

"Yer jus' jealous, Gordie!" Clifton smirked.

"Enough!" all four adults ordered in unison.

Farmer's heart was full when the singing of hymns concluded, and he stood to speak. The Lord had given him a message.

"I want ta bring y'all to rememberin' what Donald tol' us in the spring," Farmer began.

"I was most disturbed by what he said 'cause mainly I didn't want to hear it or believe it atall. Donald was sayin' thet the Lord don't always do things the way we think He should, 'cause He sees what we don't.

"The Good Lord gave us a chance at a new life. He made it so the Government gave us some of the finest land to be found. He guided and protected us on the long journey here in a chuck wagon – thet bein' a whole chapter o' our life right ther'.

"God, with y'all's help, gave us a most beautiful log house. This spring it was all taken away - jus' as was the Brooks."

Farmer saw hankies come up to the faces of Emile, Ella May and Beth.

"I jus' couldn't understan' why God would give us land and bring us this far jus' ta take it all away. So's when Donald said thet maybe God had different plans – I couldn't accept it. Jus' couldn't make no sense o' it – fer God ta – ta – let us lose – all." Farmer had to stop to regain his composure. After a moment he went on.

"I was angry at God an' was sayin' some mighty ugly words ta Him. I was reckonin' thet I was doin' ever'thin' the ways He wanted it done. Then I got ta thinkin' – maybe the Lord didn't tell me to go borrow thet money, an' I jus' done thet on my own. Then my anger turned towards me. I reckoned I was a failure – I let my family down – let y'all down – I was most shamed.

"The Good Book says thet God will turn even bad things out good. Donald was right! His ways air so much higher then our thinkin' an' He always has Him a plan. "On the blackest night o' my life the Lord whispered in the dark. He said, 'Farmer, ya will see the wisdom o' what I be a doin'. My full purpose will be seen in time.' "I'm a beginnin' to understan' the first part, but the second is muddy water to see into. Y'all know I grieved 'bout losin' the ranch. I miss it powerful, an' the life me an' Emile an' our children lived there. But God has given us a house thet's comfortable ta be in, with land fer our horses. We own it with no money borrowed. An' the Lord done give me a job – workin' harder then I ever be in my whole life!"

Farmer attempted a weak smile at Donald.

"So I reckon I can see God's wisdom in what He's a doin' – an' I can thank Him."

After church a solemn Joe Baltman caught Farmer alone. His face was pained.

"Farmer, you know it's difficult for me to ask for prayer in church."

"What is it, Joe?"

"I don't know what to do. Sold all our cattle and that money is all gone. Farmer, we are out of food – this will be our last trip 'til I can buy gasoline."

Farmer was shocked. He had no idea Joe and Sally were in such want. Without a second thought he thrust his hand into his pocket and produced the few bills he had on him.

"Joe, here's some money fer a little food an' gasoline. I had no idee o' yer... How air the Judds an' Millers?"

"Hurtin' bad," Joe's face was pale. He dropped his eyes.

"Joe, as long as I'm a workin' an' money comin' in, I sware, we will be bringin' y'all food – 'til better times come!"

Chapter 22

PROGRESS!

Another country in the world was also in desperate depression and they too brought a new leader into office. This occurred a few days before Roosevelt's inauguration; however, none in Douglas Landing paid him any mind. His name was Adolf Hitler, and he seemed a world away.

Conditions did begin to improve in Douglas Landing with the spring thaw of 1934. A sizeable force of young men, the government Civilian Conservation Corps, or Roosevelt's CCC's as they were called, arrived at the Ranger Station. They were assigned to plant seedlings in areas stripped of timber by loggers or fire. These men purchased gasoline for their rigs, ate in the café and kept the O'Malley's scrambling to keep their shelves stocked.

With the removal of prohibition, Zeck moved his back-room trade to the front, and restored his tavern. The CCC boys of age were Zeck's good-paying customers. This greatly concerned Farmer and Emile, but they could only pray.

Orders for lumber to be shipped east were on the rise. Pacific Timberline increased the working hours and gave their people small raises. Farmer decided to have a telephone installed in their house, feeling they could afford the monthly fee.

"Who should we call? How do we use it?" Emile was talking excited and fast as the whole family stood looking at the contraption hanging on their wall, almost afraid to touch it. They jumped with a start when it came to life with its first ring. The boys snickered and Leah giggled. They counted the long – short – two longs.

"Not ours, but a neighbor," Farmer looked over the paper the phone company had given them. The phone rang again. "Rinnnnnnng – ring – rinnnnnnng – rinnnnnnng!"

Farmer scanned over the names of the eighteen neighbors on their party line.

"Thet was Rollin Graves."

"Oh, let's listen!" Emile reached for the phone.

"Mom!" Leah objected and pushed at her.

"How are we going to know if it's clear for us to use?" Emile teased.

"Ya wait a spell," Farmer answered.

"Alright... We've waited," and Emile picked up the listening handle off its cradle hook and put it to her ear. Her eyes got big; then she hung it up.

"Hummph," she grumbled, "talking business."

"Emile, I reckon we didn't get this here phone fer ya ta spy on folks," Farmer admonished.

"Don't be silly! I'm not going to spy."

"I am!" and Leah grabbed the handle off the hook to listen before Farmer or Emile could stop her.

"Hey!" she was surprised. "It's just buzzing."

"Thet means it's clear. Emile, call yer folks in Texas," Farmer told her.

"Yeh, Ma," Clifton encouraged.

"I don't know how – what to do!" Emile protested. "You call them, Farmer."

"Somebody call them!" Leah howled.

"Fer Pete's sakes, I'll do it!" Walter took the handle and gave one short ring. Farmer and Emile looked at each other as if to say – "How did he learn this?" They both stared at Walter. Walter looking back from his position at the phone, "What? I listen to folks on the phone at Haywood's Station all the time."

"Why are ya at Haywood's?" Farmer asked.

"I go after school. Mr. Haywood let's me do a little work on the cars. Mr. Brooks been showin' me too."

"Ya knowed 'bout this?" Farmer asked Emile.

She shook her head, no.

"Hello! Hello! Yes, ma'am. I'd like to call Grandpa an' Grandma Holt in Texas, please. They live in Holt."

Walter was pleased with himself and proud of his confidence, but it came crashing down when his face got red, and he turned to ask, "What is Grandpa an' Grandma's first names?"

Emile tried to suppress bursting out laughing. Farmer managed to remain calm, but knew he and Emile would enjoy a good hee-haa later in their bedroom.

"Ahem – Hirum an' Vivian... son."

"Hirum an' Vivian Holt," Walter repeated.

It took some time as numerous connections had to be made. Suddenly Walter straightened up.

"Grandpa! Is that you? It's Walter," he started laughing. "It's Grandpa!" he shouted, his face beaming.

Walter talked. Leah had to be next, then Clifton. Emile was so happy she was laughing, crying, asking questions. Farmer feared he'd never get her off that phone an' it'd be glued to her. Finally, she handed the receiver to him.

After he caught up on some of the news from back home, and telling how they were faring in Oregon, he made a request.

"Hirum, would ya reckon ya could arrange fer my family ta come ta yer place at a time we set, so's I can talk ta my

Ma? Ain't been able ta do thet since we left there. An' my brothers an' sister?"

"I will do my best, Farmer." Hirum's voice crackled over the line. "I'm afraid yer sister got into trouble an' ran off an' got married. Your two brothers are trying to survive and hold onto the ranch. Conditions are very bad here; we have not had rain for months. I am sure your people would do well to hear from you – and the children."

The very next Saturday, Farmer walked down to Haywood's. Gordon Brooks was running the station.

"My son, Walter, been comin' here an' gettin' in yer way?" Farmer asked as he approached Gordon, who came up from under the hood of a car.

"Howdy, Farmer. He surely ain't a bother. For sure he's a good hand an' he's learnin' the mechanic business fast."

"Jus' makin' sure he ain't a wearin' out his welcome."

"No, please let him come. Clifton too. He and Gordie can help out. Ol' man Haywood's health ain't so good, so more of the work falls on me."

"I'll tell Clifton. Thank ya kindly fer givin' my boys work, Gordon."

"Come take a look," Gordon motioned for Farmer to follow. He led him to a car parked beside the garage.

"What you think of it?" he asked Farmer.

"Mighty fine automobile ta be sure. What is it?" Farmer walked around the car looking it over.

"It is a 1929 four-door Chrysler sedan. Has the six cylinder engine."

"Mighty fine!" Farmer exclaimed again.

"You want to buy it?"

"Well, I ain't a goin' ta Rollin Graves askin' fer no loan ifen thet's what yer thinkin'!"

The two men laughed together.

"A fella owed Francis Haywood an' tol' him to take the car. Then we found out the motor needs work. I can fix it for – uh – probably hundred fifty. You can have it for two hundred..."

"Sold!" Farmer shook Gordon's hand to firm the deal.

The Trevors had a car again, and their first family trip was to Easter Service at Church in the Woods.

The next week Farmer and his family had a tearful phone reunion with Farmer's Ma, his brother Jacob and wife Dorothy. Even got to say hello to their little boy Sidney Dean who was seven years old. Farmer's heart filled with compassion for all of them as he heard the hardship and struggle in their voices, especially his Ma and little brother William.

"Ma, soon's this cripplin' Depression is over an' we be able, we is comin' ta see ya. I promise!" were Farmer's closing words.

Chapter 23

THE MYSTERY OF
GARDNER GRUB

That peaceful summer morning in early June of 1935 gave not even the slightest hint of what had taken place the night before. The talk of what happened came upon the town of Douglas Landing like the roar of a passing airplane; faint and distant at first – then louder and louder – until it swept by you.

Farmer noticed different workers in the mill talking to one another in a much more animated manner than usual, but as he pulled the green chain he had little time to consider it. Not until morning break did he hear what most of the others already knew.

"Some homesteader's place burned to the ground last night," the mill foreman informed Farmer. "Townsfolk's sayin' somebody burned up in the house."

"What?!" Farmer gasped, standing up from the break room table where he had sat down to drink coffee. "Who?"

"I think it was that strange fella that stays to his self mostly," the foreman spoke in a low voice. "That's all I know."

The rest of the day, Farmer could not get the tragic news out of his mind. He reviewed over and over in his thoughts the few times he had encountered Gardner Grubb, especially the time he ventured onto Grubb's homestead with his Bible to witness to him. If Gardner never accepted Christ as his Savior, then he is lost forever now. A feeling, dark and cold, swept over Farmer.

He had seen Gardner in town after that visit a few times, but Farmer was afraid to approach this mean, strange and mysterious man. Once, Farmer pulled into Haywood's Station on a Friday evening just this spring. It was near dark, and Francis Haywood was pumping gas into Gardner Grubb's big, long hooded car. Farmer wanted to speak, but his courage turned to gelatin. All he could think about was looking down the barrel of Grubb's loaded and cocked shotgun. The big car drove off that evening from the station, and that was the last time Farmer saw the man.

Then the sting of guilt pressed heavy on his chest. What if God was giving Farmer one last chance to speak to Gardner about his eternal destiny? One last time before he – burned...

Farmer's leg got hit by a board coming off the green chain, and he was immediately jolted back to the mill and his work. He spent the rest of the day with a clouded and troubled mind.

When the mill whistle shrieked its announcement of another workday at Pacific Timberline finished, Farmer decided to stop by O'Malley's Merchandise before going home. "Michael and Molly will know what happened by now. They are good at hearing gossip and wringing out the truth," Farmer thought.

Suddenly a shocking posibility hit him as he approached the O'Malley's – one that hadn't even crossed his mind. What if it was one of the other homesteaders? What if it was Joe or Sally – or Rachel – or Beth or Donald – or little Beverly Ann?

"Dear God!" he breathed aloud.

"What happened?" he questioned Molly as soon as he entered the door.

Molly's face was flushed – she grew intense with the telling of the story.

"Clarence Judd told me first hand by golly. He saw the bright red glow in the sky and figured a fire to be on the Grubb place – by the direction, you know. He's wonderin' what to do, whether to go over there. Seems that fire got bigger, so's Clarence drives to the Grubb gate. He told me he was surprised the chain had been cut plumb off – that was odd, you know ' cause Grubb always keeps that bloomen gate o' his locked tight, he does.

"Clarence told me that when he found the house – the flames was so high and hot, he couldn't even get near. Said all he could do was keep it from spreadin' into the trees."

"Is Gardner -?" Farmer started to ask.

"Now, this is the part I ain't told many folks, Farmer, but by golly, yesterday I had these strangers come in the store. Two of them, an' were they pokin' around for a wee bit o' information – askin' 'bout the homesteaders, and who lived where. Well, I didn't tell 'em much, but they surely talked around."

Molly stopped to catch her breath – then she drew closer to Farmer, speaking softly and looking him steady in the eyes.

"An' this beats all!" she went on. "Today FBI Agents showed up and went out to the Grubb place. I heard rumor that they found remains of a body in the – well, what's left of Grubb's house."

Farmer shook his head in disbelief.

"Some of us are driving out there as soon as I close the store. Want to come?"

"Yep! I will get Emile an' the kids," Farmer was out the door.

Emile, Walter, Clifton and Leah were in the house waiting for him.

"Have you heard?" they asked at the same time when Farmer walked onto the porch.

"Yah – terrible news," Farmer declared as he hugged and kissed each of his family.

"That's all the whole town has been talking about. Oh, Farmer, it's so dreadful – oh, poor Gardner!" Emile's voice expressed her grief.

"Pa, can we go out there?" Clifton asked.

"We can't do that!" gasped Emile.

"Sure we can. Some's already been," Walter sided with his brother.

"I want to see!" Leah voiced her curiosity.

"We'd be trespassing," Emile countered.

"I don't reckon Gardner would mind," Farmer remarked grimly.

Emile studied Farmer for a moment, acted like she started to laugh, but caught herself.

"Farmer, you are an awful man," she concluded.

"I know – so let's go!" Farmer felt excited and ashamed for being so.

Walter, Clifton and Leah scrambled for the car. Emile and Farmer followed.

Gardner Grubb had settled on section one of the homesteads. He was the first settler to arrive in Douglas Landing, and his section, which bordered the Shanko River, was the closest to the town. The bridge, which the government built across the Shanko, allowing the homesteaders to drive into Douglas Landing was closest to the Grubb section. The Church in the Woods was a short distance from the northern edge of the Grubb homestead, and the town a short distance beyond the church.

It took considerable time to drive to where Gardner's home once stood. It appeared he had gone to great lengths to make the house hidden and inaccessible. When the remaining out buildings came into view, Farmer could see several cars parked and numerous people walking about. As they drove closer, a man Farmer had never seen before stopped them and informed them they could not go any closer. When Farmer parked the car, he glanced in the rear view mirror. Leah's eyes were big as silver dollars.

"Hey, there's Rachel," Clifton shouted – pointing.

"Yes, there's Joe and Sally by that cedar tree," Emile touched Farmer's arm to get his attention.

The Baltmans started towards the Trevor's car; Rachel ran ahead.

Farmer greeted Joe with a question. "What ya reckon this all ta be?"

"It's a mystery, for sure," Joe grabbed Farmer in a bear hug.

"FBI has been here all afternoon an' won't let no one close. I got to talkin' to one agent who was some friendly, an' he told me that they found casings from handguns. Appeared someone cut the lock on Gardner's gate an' drove a car in here!" Joe's excited words shot from his mouth in rapid succession – like bullets from a tommy gun.

The children wandered over to where the government cars were parked, for a closer look.

Joe pointed everyone's gaze to the blackened remains of Gardner Grubb's house.

"The agent told me there was lots o' shootin' here last night. They don't think the fire was no accident. The agent said there's one body – dead in the house – burned up – no one else - . Jus' Gardner's car in the shed an' the body – what's left of it..." Joe's voice trailed off.

Farmer, Emile, Joe and Sally stood – staring at the charred rubble that seemed to represent Gardner's remains. Finally, Emile broke the silence.

"The mystery of Gardner Grubb. We may never find out in this life what took place here..."

Chapter 24

REACHING OUT TO
THE WORLD

Farmer had vowed years before to never be so out of touch with the world around him as he had been in Holt, Texas. The radio became one link towards keeping that vow.

Right after the tragedy at Gardner Grubb's place, Farmer decided to purchase a radio. Walter found the idea in a book to string a wire for an antenna. This greatly improved the reception, making it possible to pick up Portland and San Francisco stations. Late one night, Clifton woke Farmer and Emile up to tell them he was getting a station in Oklahoma City loud and clear. Soon the whole family was huddled around the talking box, feeling the voices brought them a little closer to their long ago home in Texas. Farmer didn't realize how a simple late night broadcast could affect them all so much – except for Leah, who promptly told them she couldn't see anything so special about hearing someone in Oklahoma, and she was going back to bed.

Farmer gave that radio to Walter, and bought the family a new model. Next year he gave that one to Clifton. For

Christmas of 1937, he got a radio for Leah and an electric toaster for Emile.

"I've been saving my present for you until last," Emile announced with excitement as she produced a beautifully wrapped gift from its secret hiding place.

Farmer was surprised and felt that same sense of opening a gift he had experienced as a young lad. He tore at the wrapping to open a box.

"My very own radio!" Farmer proclaimed with a shout, holding it up for all to see.

"Thank the Lord, you won't have to keep listening on ours," Walter laughed.

That Christmas night as Farmer listened to his Christmas gift, he grew uneasy and keenly aware that war in Europe could be a possibility.

The movies also provided a connection to the vast world outside of Douglas Landing. Applegate had its first movie theatre built in the summer of 1938.

"Don't reckon thet be somethin' we be attendin'," Farmer remarked matter of factly at the dinner table one evening after the theatre was open. "Heard me a preacher on radio say it was a devil's tool ta drag us inta sin."

"Aw, Pa," Clifton protested. "Rachel and her folks have been already. She said it was like a movin' storybook before yer eyes."

"An' the Brooks saw a cowboy movie an' didn't see no harm in it," Walter added.

"There was fightin' an' killin', Walter! What's the good in thet?" Farmer raised his voice. "Seems there's too much o' thet in the world already!"

Leah in a soft calm voice that reminded Farmer of her mother spoke next. "Daddy, how can you decide for all of us about something you haven't seen?"

"'Cause I say so! It's bad an' – an' evil – an' we won't be a takin' part – an' I don't want ta hear no more 'bout it,"

Farmer sputtered out the words, red-faced, and making wild hand motions.

Emile tried to change the subject, but the family fell into sullen silence. One by one they left the table.

That night Farmer wrestled with himself. Leah's piercing question haunted him. He was judging something he hadn't seen. What was so different from a movie and radio? Both told stories.

"But I hear news on the radio," Farmer argued. Then he remembered a mill worker telling him that a cartoon like the Sunday funnies, and a newsreel preceded the movie.

Newsreel! The word stuck in Farmer's thoughts and refused to leave. It seemed the Lord was reminding Farmer of his vow to stay in touch with the world.

"You're sure a hard one ta disagree with, Lord," Farmer sighed. Shame filled his heart as he thought how he had treated his wife and children at the dinner table. He wished he could undo his words and actions. He prayed that the Lord would erase them from the minds of his family. Hot tears burned his face as he repented before God over something he thought he had been so right about. Farmer couldn't wait for the sun to come up to make amends with those he loved so dearly.

"I was sorely wrong," Farmer confessed at breakfast. "I was wrong ta make a judgment on one man's say-so – even ifen he be a preacher. So's, I reckon we will go ta Applegate ta see us a movie an' decide fer ourselves ifen it be good or evil."

Everyone at the table cheered – even Emile, and to the movie theatre the Trevors did go just as Farmer had said.

The movie took place during World War I. The airplanes fascinated Walter and Clifton. Leah thought the young soldier was handsome. Emile was touched by the wives and mothers being left behind and went to digging in her purse for a hankie.

Farmer, on the other hand, for the first time, saw another part of the world - a world he had only heard about on the radio. A world so far away, yet the newsreel brought it to where Farmer lived. He had no idea that night how important the newsreels would become, or how the world he wanted to reach out to would invade and disrupt his quiet and peaceful life in Douglas Landing.

Chapter 25

WHAT IN THE WORLD IS URIAH WALLHEIM BUILDING?

The country was climbing out of the Depression. Change and construction was happening everywhere, so it was no big surprise when trucks and large equipment arrived at the Cascade Mountains Company mill one October Saturday in 1939. Most of Douglas Landing just figured that the mill was expanding.

Donald and Beth Parrigan, along with their daughter Beverly Ann, stopped by the Trevor's for a visit later that afternoon.

"We don't see you enough being just on Sundays goin' to church – so we're seeing you twice this week," Donald shouted into the house from the porch.

"Oh, do come in," Emile called to them from the kitchen.

Farmer was always glad to see these dear friends and met Donald with a smile, steady gaze and firm handshake. He placed his free hand on Donald's shoulder.

"Reckon I could do ta see more of you myself," Farmer's voice projected his love for this brother. "An' who air these lovely ladies with you?" Farmer teased.

Beth hit at him and gave Emile a hug.

"My father says I'm old enough to ride one of your horses, Mr. Trevor, all by myself – if you'll let me," Beverly Ann spoke with an eager politeness.

Farmer studied her a moment, making a face that made her giggle.

"Oh, Daddy, stop being silly!" ordered Leah, who had just walked into the living room.

"Well, Beverly, ya has always ridden with Leah or the boys, but the horses air gettin' old. I reckon they would be hard pressed ta get up much steam, so's I reckon it be fine ifen it's agreeable ta yer Ma an' Pa."

"Can I, Father," Beverly tugged at Donald's arm. He nodded.

"Leah, ask the boys ta saddle the horses so's this young lady can ride," Farmer spoke with a jolly tone.

"Walter's gone, but Clifton's here," Leah informed them.

"Where's Walter?" Farmer asked.

"Said he was going to snoop around Cascade Mountains to see what's going on."

"Hmmm," Farmer said thoughtfully.

"I'll saddle the horses, Pa," Clifton called from the back porch. Leah and Beverly Ann ran out the kitchen door to join Clifton.

"You must stay for supper," Emile implored. "Beth, come help me."

As the women went to prepare the evening meal, Farmer and Donald went out on the back porch. Sitting at the old wooden table and watching the children call in the horses, Farmer's mind went back to the ranch. This table and chairs had sat on the porch there. At times it seemed like only a few days ago Farmer was riding one of the horses on his own spread, checking on his cattle. But today it seemed like the years were many and long.

Donald broke his thoughts. "You've had those horses a long while. I'd a wagered you to sell them when times were so bad."

Farmer reflected awhile, and Donald was quiet. All three horses emerged from the trees.

"They air on in years, Donald. Sunset will likely be the first ta go. Dusty is the youngest an' will live longest, but no matter how old, they have never lost their love fer my family an' ta be ridden. They'll be happy tonight."

The two men sat quietly, the setting sun giving their faces and the tops of the pines a golden glow.

Farmer continued. "In 1925 my horses made as long an' dangerous a journey as any animals ever made. They never gave up or gave out an' pulled us in thet chuck wagon all the way from Texas. The night Leah was borned; I made the horses a promise. I was so overcome with joy an' happy feelin's an' full o' thanksgivin' an' gratitude ta God. I reckoned these horses had been faithful ta the task an' – an' I promised 'em thet I would never sell 'em!"

Donald gave Farmer a strange look, and then his expression softened as if to convey a kind understanding.

The men again sat in silence, Farmer deep in thought.

"I made me a request ta God thet same night," Farmer went on.

"What was that?" Donald turned to look in Farmer's face.

"Seems a mite foolish as I think on it."

"Then why'd you say it – gettin' my curiosity all aroused? I'll be squawkin' like a spooked Blue Jay if you don't tell."

Farmer never looked at Donald or cracked a smile. He spoke in a reverent and serious tone.

"I got ta lookin' at the trees an' listenin' ta the wind blowin' through 'em a soundin' like a mountain stream. The moon was glistenin' on the snow an' reflectin' so beautiful like offen the water in Cold Creek. Then there was a hush an' the whole world was at peace. Thet's when I made my request. 'Lord,' I said. 'I don't reckon ta know much 'bout Heaven, but ifen the place ya fin' fer me could look like this, I'd be mighty pleased.' Thet's what I told the Lord."

"I always thought of Heaven as pearly gates and golden streets and houses of crystal and glass," Donald gave his own impression.

The two men watched the three youngsters ride – both looking without seeing, lost in their individual thoughts until the harsh brackish noise of trucks on the highway brought them back to Douglas Landing.

"What ya reckon is happening at Cascade Mountains?" Farmer questioned Donald.

"You know Uriah Wallheim is like a bulldog, bitin' off ever bit of business he can chew. I hear tell he landed some big state and federal contracts. His crews are out cuttin' timber like grasshoppers in a pea patch. You been out to your old place? They cut the biggest and best of your trees."

Farmer's heart sank, but he didn't say anything. He had made a promise to himself to never step foot on his ranch until he could own it for himself again. He had kept his vow.

"Anyway, I'm guessin' that Wallheim is expanding the operation here to keep up with business. Maybe more saws – or extra dryin' kilns."

Farmer was conscious of Walter's voice in the kitchen. Soon the young man was out on the porch – an air of excitement had ahold of him, and he was hopping around like a dancing man on a hot stove.

"I reckon ya discovered what Uriah Wallheim is a gonna build, an' yer 'bout ta tell us," Farmer smiled at Walter.

"Yer dang tootin'," the words burst from Walter's mouth, "but gotta tell ya first how I found out!"

"Ya was snoopin'," Farmer tried to keep a straight face.

"Sure was! I asked some of the truck drivers, but none seemed ta know what ol' man Wallheim is a fixin' ta build, or they weren't tellin'. So's I just kept on askin' 'til finally this logger at Zeck's - "

"Ya were in Zeck's?" Farmer and Donald asked in unison.

"I was outside. Anyway, he told me thet whatever Cascade Mountains was buildin', Wallheim sent a fella to oversee it – ta run it – an' thet he came in one of the trucks an' had gottin' settled in one of the Cascade cabins."

Walter paused to take a breath.

"So I made up my mind to be neighborly an' welcome this fella to Douglas Landing an' give him a invite to church.

"Glory be!" Donald exclaimed. "You're as hard to hold back as my bull when it gets loose."

"Did ya see this fella?" Farmer asked.

"Sure did. He's not much older'n me. Name's Harold is all he tol' me. Said he would maybe come ta church."

"Plumb glad ya got thet settled," Farmer replied sarcastically – but he realized the importance of what Walter had done. Both men sat staring at Walter, waiting for more. Finally Donald spoke.

"I'm guessin' that Cascade is growin' their mill."

"Not so!" Walter answered with a grin as wide as his face.

"They are buildin' an airfield for ol' man Wallheim's plane – an' others who will be flyin' in here. There will be – a – place for the planes, and Harold will do the mechanic work, an' he said I could help an' – an' – it's gonna be a airfield!"

Chapter 26

HAROLD MOONWOLF STEMPER

The building went up quickly at the same time the landing strip was being graded and leveled. Two rows of lights would illuminate the runway, and Mr. Wallheim made arrangements for a county road crew to bring in their equipment and lay down hard surface, both on the runway and around the front of the buildings.

Wallheim was looking ahead to not only accommodate smaller airplanes, but larger ones that could fly in visitors for Crater Lake. The buildings were constructed to be oversized; the airstrip longer, and the hard surface assured all weather use for even the larger aircraft.

The windsock was mounted, and the whole town turned out to watch Uriah Wallheim be the first to land his plane on the newly finished airfield.

Walter and Clifton were up at dawn and down at the airfield hours before Wallheim's arrival. When Farmer, Emile and Leah pulled up in their car, a crowd was already formed, lining along the side of the airstrip near the buildings. Walter and Clifton shouted and waved when they saw them walking towards the assembled onlookers. A dark tanned young man was with the boys who Farmer recognized as Harold. Farmer had seen the lad at a distance but never met him.

"Ol' man Wallheim's airplane should be comin' in soon," Walter informed Farmer, Emile and Leah.

"Don't be disrespectful!" Emile scolded.

"Everbody calls him that," Walter laughed. "Even ol' Harold here!"

Farmer looked into pale blue eyes that held his gaze for an instant, then broke away. A red tinge could be detected on his cheeks and neck.

"Walter, don't tease your friend," Emile said with a smile.

"Ma – Pa, this is Harold," Clifton spoke up. "An' my little sister."

"Ma'am," Harold uttered and tipped a worn brown cap. He nodded to Leah and extended a nervous hand to Farmer.

Harold was a lean young man, tall with reddish brown skin and blackish hair. His clothes hung on his thin frame and had worn, faded patches on the shirtsleeves and the knees of his pants.

His eyes were striking, and Farmer looked deep into them when their hands locked in a handshake. He hoped to see into Harold's soul for a glimpse of what was there. Harold's eye contact was only a glance, and then averted.

"See all those trees that had to be cut down on the south end of the airfield," Walter pointed out. "The strip runs close to the highway there."

"Yes," Farmer answered.

"Why?" asked Leah.

"So thet - "

"Why doesn't Harold tell me?" Leah cut Walter off, and looked at Harold impishly.

Harold dropped his eyes and grinned.

"Is Harold shy?" Leah taunted.

"Stop acting like a baby, Leah!" Walter said irritably. "They cut the trees so as ta give the planes more room ta take off an' not hit the treetops. 'Specially, the bigger airplanes – ol' – er – Mr. Wallheim says will be landin' here!"

"Ho!" Clifton shouted and waved to the Baltmans who he saw coming through the crowd. Rachel came running to him.

"I swear – those two!" Farmer heard Emile exclaim under her breath.

Soon the Baltmans joined them.

"This be most excitin' as a picture show!" Joe Baltman spoke loudly above the noise of the crowd.

"Whole towns in a tizzy!" Sally Baltman added.

"An' you must be Wallheim's engine mechanic," Joe directed his attention to Harold and extended his hand.

"Who said I was a Injun!" Harold bristled up.

"Oh, Harold, use yer ears," Walter interjected. "Mr. Baltman said engine – motor."

"Oh!" Harold dropped his eyes that had flashed so angrily a moment before. He realized his mistake, and shuffled around on his feet.

"Harold," Joe wouldn't let go. "I'm Joe Baltman. Welcome to Douglas Landing. Right proud to have you... an' I couldn't give a hoot if you was a Injun or not."

Harold's face grew red again, and he looked away.

Farmer started to speak, but a roar from the crowd took everyone's attention. Next the sound of an airplane engine could be heard, and then suddenly a plane made its appearance above the trees. Engine speed was cut, and the plane drifted down onto the end of the runway. It touched the hardtop with a bounce and rolled to the other end of the runway where it slowly turned and made its way towards the buildings.

The crowd went wild when the plane stopped, and the engine shut off. Amid screams, whistles and clapping, Uriah

155

Wallheim and his wife made their grand entrance. Harold had disappeared when the plane topped the trees, and now he took his place by the plane. Uriah shook his hand and spoke something to him. Mrs. Wallheim patted his face.

The Wallheims faced the crowd of townsfolk who pressed closer to see them and their airplane. Uriah was in a nice suit, and Mrs. Wallheim's dress was very elegant. The owner of Cascade Mountains Lumber Company gave a speech about the airfield, and progress in Douglas Landing, but Farmer couldn't get Harold out of his mind. Why did this young man have such favor with this powerful couple? He was puzzled.

Now, it's strange about the spreading of news in a small town. Words can flare like a fanned fire, and the tellers relish in the telling of it. The problem, though, is to figure which is truth and which is exaggerated, because the story can change its shape and size many times. Farmer heard numerous versions about Harold over the next few days. Rumors flew of Harold being Wallheim's bastard son, to a runaway renegade Indian in trouble with the law, to a cheap worker.

Farmer wasn't one to take a story at face value that had been hashed around, chewed up and spit out by fifty or more people – so he decided to go ask Harold himself. He needed to know more about this young man who was beginning to also have a powerful influence over his two boys.

For years now, Walter and Clifton had helped Gordon Brooks and Little Gordie around Haywood's Service Station. All three boys were accomplished auto mechanics, however, since the arrival of Harold, Farmer's boys had been spending more of their time at the airfield. Farmer questioned what they were doing there since there were no airplanes yet.

"Harold is teaching us about airplane engines and how a airplane works," they were quick to reply.

"Where did he learn?"

"Ol' man Wallheim sent him to a school in Portland."

Farmer realized his boys were not children any longer. War had erupted in Europe, and there was talk of joining the Army, which Emile didn't want to hear of. Moments of fleeting fear for his family would pass over him. Events were becoming too big for him to do anything about.

He was concerned that the world might present a strong pull down the wrong path for his boys. They told Farmer one night how Harold frequented Zeck's and got drunk. In addition to tales of drunkenness, Harold had not joined the family in church as he had promised Walter. These were concerns along with his curiosity that prompted Farmer to pay a visit on Harold.

He waited for a Saturday when the boys were off with friends, to approach Harold in the main hangar. He was fueling Wallheim's plane parked there, as Uriah was back at Douglas Landing.

"Hello there, Harold," Farmer greeted warmly as he walked up to the young man.

Harold glanced his way.

"Hello yourself."

"I came ta get better acquainted with ya," Farmer went on. "Like ta know 'bout yer family."

"Not much to tell," Harold spoke in a low voice, not looking up from his work.

"I reckon there's a lot. Everbody has a life story. I don't know yer name."

"Harold Stemper."

"Where ya hail from? How 'bout yer Ma an' yer Pa? Ya have brothers and sisters?"

Harold shut off the fuel valve and turned squarely to face Farmer.

"My life isn't any of your concern!"

"If my boys are gonna be a comin' here, I think it is!" Farmer retorted.

"You can't stop them, an' you can't stop me! Not even if I wanted to court your daughter."

Farmer felt his body stiffen, and the hair rise on the back of his neck.

"How old air ya, Harold?"

"Born in 1913 – I'm 26," Harold shot the answer at Farmer never taking his eyes off him.

"Leah is 14!" Farmer roared in anger.

"So what! My mother married when she was 15."

"Well, it won't happen with Leah!" Farmer retorted. Then he leveled a barrage at this man who had suddenly chosen to attack him with his words.

"Ya boastn' about drinkin' an' gettin' drunk to my boys?"

"An' I'll get them to join me – only a matter of time 'til your hold is over," Harold's eyes flashed.

Farmer fought back the urge to punch Harold in the face.

"An' ya promised Walter ta come ta church with us an' thet ain't happened either."

"I have a strong dislike for church. I told Walter, 'Maybe,' and maybe is a long way off – maybe never!"

Farmer was amazed and dazed by this quiet young man's defiance and aggression. He stepped closer to Harold. Harold put up clenched fists – ready to fight. Farmer got ready to dive into him and throw punches.

"Come on," Harold taunted, "hit me! Hit me here!" He thumbed his chin. "You coward. Big church phony! Hit me! You think you are such a wonderful father – you are a joke! Come on! Hit me! Coward!"

Farmer dropped his arms. The anger subsided, and Farmer felt pity for this sad, lanky, brown-skinned young man who stood before him, fists raised, face distorted in anger, burning eyes.

"Why air ya so angry, son? Ya don't even know me, an' ya air ready ta fight?"

"You came in here all high and mighty, asking questions about me; I'll throw you out!"

"I wasn't diggin' inta yer personal life, but ta get ta know ya better. I'm tryin' ta be yer friend, but I will have my answers, son. I have had conversation with Uriah Wallheim, so's I reckon I'll talk ta him 'bout ya an' how ya acted here today."

Harold's expression turned to one of horror! He dropped his arms and sat down on a wood crate. He buried his face in his hands, and Farmer saw dark dots where Harold's tears fell on his jeans.

"I'm sorry..." Harold's voice was so low Farmer could barely hear him.

"My father's dead," Harold looked up at Farmer as he continued. As he spoke he looked out the hangar door across the runway and the Shanko River. He was dredging up a painful past.

"He came from Denmark and finally ended up in Oregon working for Cascade Mountains Lumber. He met my mother. She was half Indian and half – something else. She never seemed to fit in – anywhere – except with my father. They loved each other, Mr. Trevor, and I loved them, and we had a happy family.

"When I was born, my mother named me Harold Moonwolf Stemper. She said when I was born the moon was full, and she remembered hearing the cry of a wolf in the distant forest. She wanted me to remember I was part Indian, but I grew to hate it...after..."

It was a long time before Harold went on. He never looked at Farmer, but kept his gaze fixed outside the hangar. Farmer could see the tracks of tears on the side of Harold's face made noticeable by the sun that now shafted light into the hangar and onto Harold.

"My father worked in the woods for Mr. Wallheim. One day Mr. Wallheim came to our house. He told us that his own son had gone out to check on the crew. As he was walking with the landing foreman where they were pulling cut trees, a widow maker, dead snag, toppled over."

Harold was saying the words now as if in a dream. Farmer felt that the boy had recited this part so many times – it was as if all emotion was drained out of him.

"My father saw the dead tree falling towards Wallheim's son and the landing foreman. He ran to push them, but was too late. All three died. My father died for nothing. He ran to his death, Wallheim's son died anyway. My father died for nothing."

"Thet ain't so, Harold!" Farmer's words jolted the young man back from his grief and sad memories.

"Thet ain't so; as I see it, yer Pa was a hero. He tried to save two lives. Do ya reckon he coulda lived with his self-jus' standin' by watchin' it happen? He did do somethin' thet counted, an' ya should be proud!"

"Mr. Wallheim told my mother and me that day he would take care of her as long as she lived."

"Where is she now?"

"She lives in a company house in Springdale. Mr. Wallheim promised to fly me to see her often and maybe bring her here – some."

"An' Uriah Wallheim sent ya ta school ta work on these here airplanes?" Farmer was fitting the pieces together now.

Farmer walked over to Harold and placed a hand on his shoulder. Harold looked up at him.

"Thank ya fer tellin' thet, son. There be enough folk around tellin' tales on ya. I wanted the true one so's I came ta ya. They all got enough ta jaw on 'bout, so's they won't be hearin' anything from me. I reckon y'all have ta tell 'em yerself."

As Farmer walked towards the hangar door to leave, he heard a soft voice from behind him, "Harold Moonwolf Stemper is serious about what he said about your daughter."

Farmer turned slowly, without cracking a smile, speaking in a very stern tone.

"So was I, Harold. So was I!"

Chapter 27

TRAIN UP A CHILD

Farmer received a late evening phone call from Holt, Texas, in April of 1941. He heard his brother William on the other end of the line telling him he had just been given his draft notice into the Army. By the time Farmer finished talking, Emile, Walter, Clifton and Leah were huddled around him.

"William has been drafted into the Army," Farmer announced, hanging up the phone.

"Oh, dear God, no!" Emile exclaimed, covering her mouth.

"What about Uncle Jacob?" Walter asked.

"The Selective Service age is 21 to 35. Jacob is past thet. William said the government wants him to stay on the farm where he is needed," Farmer answered.

Farmer could see Emile's lip quiver, and tears filled her eyes.

"What will – this – mean – for Walter?" she had trouble getting the words out.

"It means I gotta register on my birthday in September, Ma. I'm thinkin' I should just enlist an' be done," Walter spoke with a newfound resolve.

"Me too!" Clifton agreed.

"Oh, boys! You don't know what you are saying!" Emile appeared almost frantic.

"Ma, we ain't little boys no more! We be men thet need to do their duty!"

"Oh, no! God help us! No!" Emile placed a trembling hand on the table to steady herself.

By now, most all of Europe was under the control of Germany and Italy. Only Great Britain and Russia remained. Great Britain hung on by a thread and desperately needed America's help. The Nazis had already struck into Russian territory, and it appeared a major offensive would come soon.

Americans were joining the Canadian Royal Air Force, and a few others were helping the Chinese against Japan. Most folks hoped that the United States could remain neutral on our side of the world, and not get involved in the war. Charles Lindbergh, along with others, spoke openly against U.S. Involvement. He even travelled to Germany to speak with leaders there.

Walter and Clifton discussed the possibility of going to Canada to join the war effort there; until Harold threw cold water on their eagerness with, "This ain't our war! Why should we get killed over people we don't know – or even like?"

Farmer had enough difficulties on the home front to keep up with all that was going on in Europe and Asia. His children were grown up and wanting their freedom to try their wings.

Walter was a tall, gangly young man, almost 21. He could rebuild a car or airplane engine in his sleep. He had saved his money working for Gordon Brooks at the gasoline station and purchased a '40 Ford coupe with a flathead V8. Walter worked hard and was gone from home more frequently now. Gordie Brooks was his closest friend and Walter didn't pay much attention to the girls.

Clifton, on the other hand, was shorter and stouter than Walter and good looking. Most of his time was spent with

Rachel. The two had been inseparable since the Trevors and the Baltmans arrived in Oregon. They reminded Farmer of he and Emile. It was like they were in love from the time they met as children.

Clifton hadn't spent much time at the Brook's service station over the past year. His love was airplanes, so he was always at the airfield.

Harold had instructed both Walter and Clifton thoroughly on the workings of several different kinds of airplanes. Farmer was sure it was Harold's attitude about the war that prevented the boys from leaving for Canada. But he was disturbed over the hold that Harold exercised on both his boys. They seemed to admire Harold's rebellious nature and his drinking. He was openly critical of Christians and the church, and to Farmer's frustration and annoyance, he could tell the boys something, and they would pay little attention to it – even disbelieving what Farmer said. Harold, though, could tell them the same thing a week later, and it became law. Yet he knew that to insist they stay away from Harold at this juncture was futile.

Leah, on the other hand, was headstrong, testing every limit. She seemed to have her Grandpa Trevor's stubbornness, Grandfather Holt's biting words and her Pa's quick temper.

"Poor girl don't stand a chance this side o' Heaven!" Farmer told Emile in exasperation one day.

Leah had shown an interest in Harold that neither Farmer nor Emile felt comfortable with, and Harold had already made himself clear about his intentions towards Leah Trevor. At that point, both parents forbid Leah to be around Harold, except at church if he should come. To Emile and Farmer's surprise, she didn't seem upset over this and concentrated on spending time with her friends she knew at school. Leah would turn 16, November of that year, and Farmer knew the older she got the more difficult to exert that kind of control over her would be.

So it was a hot afternoon in late August that Farmer knew the instant he got out of the car and looked up to see Emile stumbling on the porch that something was wrong – dreadfully wrong.

Farmer had felt good all day and was cheerful. He enjoyed a closeness with the Lord in prayer early this same morning. It seemed for the first time in months that things were settling down and made some sense. He had heard that boys weren't being drafted for 6 to 8 months after they registered. That would go well into 1942 – and maybe peace would come again to Europe and Asia, and the boys might not have to go into the military after all. Leah was active in school and had settled down, and Emile seemed happy and content.

Was it too good to be true? Had the Lord blessed them, and the enemy snatched it away? Perhaps he was mis-reading what he saw in his wife's face. Not so!

When he approached the porch, Emile had her mouth covered with her hand. That meant she was trying to keep from crying. Her eyes were red and her face splochy. Farmer started to ask what was wrong as he stepped onto the porch, but before he could speak, she flew to him and buried her face against his chest. Her whole body convulsed in labored sobs. Farmer held her tight until the crying stopped.

"What is it, Emile? What's wrong?" Farmer stroked her hair.

Emile finally pulled back so she could look at him.

"Oh, Farmer! It's Leah!" Emile covered her quivering lips again.

"What's wrong with Leah? Is she hurt?"

Emile shook her head and cried again.

"Emile, what is it?"

"Oh, Farmer! She's pregnant!"

For a moment Farmer felt like his body went numb and his mind blank. Next he saw Emile looking, searching into his eyes.

"Wha?" he choked. "When – who?"

"It's Harold! She's been with him! When she told us she was with her friends, she was with Harold!"

Rage filled Farmer.

"I'll kill him! Let me get my rifle!"

Emile blocked his way.

"You'll do no such thing! You can't go around shooting someone who angered you!"

"A snake like him don't deserve ta live – doin' this ta our little girl." He moved towards the front door.

"Farmer! Stop! Think! She's not a little girl anymore! She loves him – she gave herself to him."

Suddenly emotion washed over both of them, and they crumpled to the porch, feeling a pain they had never known before. They could only cling to each other and cry out to God, their Father.

It says in His Word: "Train up a child in the way he should go and when he gets older he will not depart from it." Right now this promise didn't seem to be working very well for Farmer and Emile. Maybe it only applied to the boys, maybe at some future time.

Chapter 28

LEAH

Farmer helped Emile into the house, and he staggered into the kitchen.

"Where is she?" he asked in a low voice.

"In her bedroom, and – she is frightened out of her wits to face you," Emile whispered.

"How long have you known?"

"I've suspected for several days. When she got sick this morning – I asked her. She broke down and confessed."

Farmer fell into a chair at the table. His head was spinning. He felt weak, and his hands shook.

"I need ta think," he mumbled and buried his face in his hands.

"Leah with child," he thought. "What will she do? What will we do? She's so young!"

Farmer remembered that cold, clear, starry night in 1925. The first sounds his daughter made. It was as if he could still hear her cry. Now she would have a baby of her own.

He pictured Leah nursing at her mother's breast, warm and safe in Emile's arms. The times he carried her around the ranch house, so tiny and wiggly. The times he heard her cries in the night – her laughter in the day.

He could see her running through the trees – and riding swiftly on one of the horses – her long hair flying in the wind. Oh how had the time slipped by? She was not that little girl he told stories to anymore – she had somewhere become a young woman.

"Farmer," Emile's voice broke into his thoughts. "She really needs her Pa right now."

Farmer looked into the face of his wife and saw a mother whose child was hurting, and she felt helpless to protect or shield her from that hurt. The look on Emile's face told him that she looked to him for his strength and help, and that how he dealt with their daughter would be most crucial. She touched his arm as he walked by her to Leah's door.

As he reached the door he paused. A flash of anger spread over him. She had lied to both of them. She had snuck around behind their backs. She disobeyed! She fooled around with a man much too old for her. Farmer was angry over the foolish decisions his daughter had made.

He wanted to scold her! She should be punished! He knocked soundly on Leah's door. He heard a faint, "Come in," from inside. He pushed open the door – then halted. Instead of the woman she was supposed to be, Farmer saw only a tearful, frightened little girl sitting on the edge of her bed – his little girl!

The anger quickly faded away, and a father's love for his daughter filled his heart. He sat down by her and put his arms around her and held her like he did years ago. Nothing was said as he let her cry awhile. Finally he spoke in as calm and gentle a voice as he could muster up.

"Leah, I reckon I won't always agree with what ya do or how ya do it, but ya can know thet yer Pa will always love ya an' believe in ya, an' so will yer Ma."

Leah's body shook in his arms as she cried even harder.

"How can you ever forgive me, Daddy?" Leah spoke between sobs. "I've done a terrible thing and hurt you an' Mom so deeply. I know I have!"

"We've already forgiven ya, Leah, but ya hev ta settle with the Lord."

"I've never done so much prayin' in my whole life – the last two weeks, Daddy. I am so scared!"

Farmer sat back to look in her face. "Does Harold know 'bout this?"

"Yes, I told him two days ago," Leah dropped her eyes. "I told him we were going to have a baby. He seemed nervous – or upset. He didn't mention getting married like we'd talked before."

Then Farmer saw Leah's face scrunched up in pain, and she put her hand over her mouth. "When I – stopped – by – yesterday – yesterday – he – he – an' his things – were all gone," Leah sobbed out.

"Daddy, he's gone – an' – I don't – know – what – to do!"

Farmer heard the back door slam. Next Emile appeared in the bedroom doorway.

"That was Clifton! He came in the back door. I tried to get him to go back out, but he wanted to know what was going on."

"Did he hear?" Farmer stood up.

"Enough. He's gone to find Harold. Farmer, you must stop him!"

Farmer headed toward the front door.

"Y'all stay put. I'll be back!" he ordered.

"No, Pa, I'm going with you!" Leah was right behind him.

He spun around, "I said stay, Leah!" but now he looked in the face of a young woman who would fight for her man. Her eyes blazed with determination and fire.

"Alright, Emile ya come too, an' y'all can stay in the car."

Farmer sped to the airstrip and pulled up next to the building where Harold stayed. Walter and Clifton were standing by the door; Walter had his hat in his hand and was scratching his head. Clifton was talking to him.

"Stay put!" Farmer ordered the two women.

He got out of the car and approached his sons. Clifton's face was red; Walter was somber.

"I heard it all," Clifton blurted out. "I'll whoop Harold good ifen I find him."

"He ain't here, Pa," Walter motioned towards the building. "Yesterday, I came over ta work a spell – all his clothes – gone. I ain't seen hide nor hair of him. I been doin' work I knowed needs doin'."

"He's been a fox creepin' in our house!" Clifton smashed a fist against the door. "We just gotta hunt him down like the animal he is, Pa. He's gotta pay!"

"Don't talk foolishness, Clifton. I wanted ta kill him – I did, an' I know how ya feel, but thet's not the answer."

"I'm powerful hurt fer Leah," Walter spoke and sadness filled his eyes. "Can't believe Harold ta do such a disgraceful thing."

"Well, he did!" Clifton snapped.

"Did Wallheim fly him out?" Farmer asked.

"Don't think so. We'd a heard the plane," Walter spoke as he rubbed his chin.

"Then how could he go? He has no car."

"Beats me."

"Maybe he's holed up 'round here," Clifton suggested.

The family spread out and searched around town. No one had seen or heard from Harold for two days.

That night a tired and spent Trevor family gathered around the dinner table. As they held hands to pray, Farmer spoke.

"This has been a tryin' day. I don't know how or when, but I reckon the Good Lord ta take care of all this hurt an' confusion, an' make some sense o' it fer us. An' He'll take care o' us, an' Leah an' her baby, an' Harold wherever he be, 'cause he needs more prayer then us!"

Chapter 29

THANKSGIVING

Farmer contacted Uriah Wallheim by telephone to inquire as to the whereabouts of Harold Stemper. The old man was unaware Harold was gone. He was shocked and vowed to make the young man "do what was right by Leah and her family." At the same time, he hired both Walter and Clifton to fill in Harold's place.

As the weeks passed, nothing about Harold surfaced, and Leah fought bouts with feelings of sadness, then anger. She loved and missed him, and then she would think, "How could he leave me like this?"

Long before she even began to show, the whole community knew of Leah's condition. Shameful news travels rapidly, and Farmer and Emile were concerned about how their daughter would be treated. People can be so cruel!

Emile told Farmer one evening when he came home from work that Dr. Put had stopped by. "He said since Leah hadn't come to see him, he was coming to see her," Emile laughed.

"He was so funny, Daddy," Leah sounded happy. "He said - " she tried to make her voice sound like Dr. Put. "Missy, I spanked your bottom when you were born, now I shall spank your baby's tiny bottom next year."

The members of the Church in the Woods gathered around Leah and loved and accepted her. Farmer and Emile knew that if other Christians condemned their daughter, they could not continue attending there.

Donald Parrigan expressed it the best in a message he gave on a Sunday morning.

He spoke about when Jesus asked the question, "How can you see a speck in yer brother's – or sister's eye when you have a log in your own big enough to fill a log truck?" Donald stopped and gave everyone time to catch his joke.

"Ain't a one of us that don't have things in our lives we ain't proud of. Don't mean that what we do is always right, 'cause we all sin. But if I understand the Bible right, Jesus died for all our sins. Our part is to ask Him to forgive us 'cause He loves us, and the price has been paid. Then we are to forgive each other and love each other as He does for us."

After the service, Joe teased Donald. "Preacher, I was tryin' to find in my Bible where Jesus was talkin' 'bout a loggin' truck."

"Well, Joe, wouldn't I a sounded most profound if I'd a said, 'fill up a donkey cart?' I'd had to gone another hour to explain, and you woulda dozed off for sure."

Both men laughed heartily, and Joe came to where Farmer was standing.

"Sure sorry for Leah, dear friend, but Sally an' I are here for you all – any way we can help – you know that," Joe spoke with sincerity.

"I know," Farmer answered. "You hev been good friends since we arrived. We have watched our children grow up."

"That we have, an' I sometimes worry over our two young'ns. They been close since they were babies – seems more so now."

Farmer drew back in shock, but instantly realized the truth Joe spoke.

"Ya be right, an' I caution Clifton ta treat Rachel with respect."

"I think Leah's troubles have been a warnin' for Rachel," Joe spoke thoughtfully.

"For all the young people – 'cept Clifton wouldn't leave Rachel thet way like Harold did Leah." Joe slapped Farmer on the shoulder, "You won't be hearin' any cruel words from us – or any other of your friends here at church."

But cruel words did come. Words like whore – loose – devil girl – wicked. Accusations like that came, not from church members or townsfolk, but from Leah's schoolmates. It exploded one morning during recess into a hairpulling fight. Leah stormed out of the school and marched home.

"I refuse to go to school anymore," she fumed to her mother. "They are such immature brats."

That night Emile told Farmer about it and explained that as Leah got bigger, the taunts from her friends would also. They decided that next morning Emile would go to the school and see if Leah could do her work at home.

Weeks rolled by, and Thanksgiving arrived. Farmer and Emile sensed this would be a special day. They had invited the Baltmans, the Brooks, the Parrigans, Dr. Put and the O'Malleys. It would be potluck.

"Where will we put them all?" Emile threw up her hands in despair.

"Everywhere, I reckon!" Farmer laughed.

Excitement grew as Farmer and the boys prepared the house with extra tables and chairs.

"We can have tables on the front and back porches, Lord willin' the weather stay warm a few days," Farmer directed. Emile and Leah busied themselves preparing a turkey and mashed potatoes with turkey giblet gravy. The Brooks would bring corn and a fruit salad, Sally would be sure to bake fresh bread and make tea. Molly cooked a most delicious Irish ham

– a recipe given her by her grandmother. What Beth would bring would never be known until the Parrigans arrived.

The night before Thanksgiving Day Emile stayed up late finishing preparations.

"I reckon she will be worn out come mornin'," Farmer thought.

But she was up early, bubbly, full of life and eager for their guests to arrive. Farmer shook his head in amazement.

"I think we are ready," Emile announced. She kept looking out the front window.

"You want me to sit on the porch an' tell you when anybody arrives so you won't have to stand by the window," Clifton teased.

"You just want to watch for Rachel," Leah threw it back at him.

"Surprised he don't wanta sit where the food's at," Walter remarked trying to keep a straight face.

"Shoo – out! All of you!" Emile shooed them out the door with her hands. A minute later Clifton stuck his head back in with a silly grin.

"Dr. Put is here." He tried to announce with an appropriate accent.

Farmer watched Sirikin Put walk to the house. His dark hair turning grey, his face showed age, as did his hands. How many times had the doctor decided to leave for another city, but couldn't leave the people he had grown to love. He hadn't married, just been a doctor in the lumber town of Douglas Landing.

"Welcome, Sirikin. We are glad for you to share this day and eat with us," Farmer and Emile greeted him.

Soon the rest arrived - the Brooks, the Baltmans next – then Molly alone.

"Can't be long, my Michael's a bit under the weather today, but I brung ye all a ham to make yer mouths water for sure."

The Parrigans arrived last. Donald and Beth had cooked sweet potatoes, squash from their garden and venison steaks.

Everyone gathered in the kitchen to thank God for the bountiful meal that lay before them. Before prayer, Farmer told the brief story of the Pilgrims.

"We don't have any Indians," Gordie piped up.

"What?" Walter asked him.

"Indians – the Pilgrims invited the Indians."

Out of the corner of his eye, Farmer saw Leah stiffen.

"I'm an Indian," Dr. Put said with a mischievous smile, "and a British one."

"Not that kind of Indian, Dr. Put," Rachel spoke sweetly, "but we are very glad you are here."

After prayer, everyone filled their plates. The young people went out on the front porch.

Farmer and Emile spent time with different guests. Farmer went over to Sirikin who was seated alone, and pulled up a chair.

"Doctor, how many times have I invited ya ta our church?" Farmer asked.

"Same number of times I have not attended," Dr. Put smiled.

"So's I'm invitin' again."

"Farmer, I am not of your faith."

"Reckon I'm not askin' ya ta be. Jus' come be with us. Ya have doctored us and seen our babies born – come worship with us. Perhaps God will speak ta ya there."

Sirikin started to raise an objection when a commotion erupted outside. Farmer jumped up. He could make out two men on the ground fighting. He bolted out the door and to the men wrestling in the grass. He separated them pulling Clifton off of – Harold?

Leah was instantly there, crying, holding Harold in her arms.

"Let me whip 'im, Pa. Let me beat him to a inch of his life for what he done!" Clifton was spitting words out.

Farmer held him back. "We don't meet those who come ta our house with our fists, Clifton."

Leah's concern suddenly turned to rage. She began beating Harold's chest and arms and face.

"Where have you been? Why did you run away? Why didn't you write – call? I hate you!"

Emile pulled her away from Harold. Farmer stood above Harold who lay on the ground. The men were beside Farmer and towered above Harold.

"You're not welcome here," Farmer growled.

Harold raised his hand to shield his face. He spoke in a soft voice.

"Please, I know you hate me. I've been disgraceful – a wolf, but please, I've got to talk to Leah – alone – then to the rest of you."

Harold's eyes were pleading. His gaze went from Farmer to Emile to Leah.

"Please," he implored again.

A long tense silence followed. Farmer was unsure of what to do. He wanted to protect his daughter – his family. Why had Harold picked such an awkward time to reappear? Had he come to claim his property? Farmer could feel his blood boil. How dare this young man come boldly to his home – to insult his family – Leah – to add hurt to the insult? Everyone seemed to be waiting for someone to say something.

"I'll talk to you," Leah spoke with a tone of disgust, "you have a lot of explaining to do."

Against Farmer and Emile's better judgment they and everyone else left Harold and Leah alone on the front porch steps, but Farmer kept a nervous eye on the two.

"I don't trust him, Emile," Farmer whispered.

"I know," she replied wistfully.

Time passed, the meal finished and the visiting began to wane. Molly was the first to say goodbye. After awhile longer, Joe, Gordon and Donald gathered around Farmer. Joe nodded towards the pair still seated outside on the porch steps.

"Think we need to hang around?" he asked.

"Don't see no need. I reckon me an' the boys can take care o' Harold ifen he gives us any trouble," Farmer replied.

One by one their guests expressed their appreciation for a good Thanksgiving and their hopes that all would be well for the Trevors and especially for Leah.

Farmer made up his mind that this was their worst Thanksgiving ever.

Chapter 30

A SURPRISE

The sun had set and was only a dim glow when Farmer heard Walter say, "They're a comin' in."

Farmer rose from the sofa, and Emile came into the room from the kitchen. Walter and Clifton faced Harold at the door.

"Pa – Ma – Harold has something he wants to say," Leah announced as she followed Harold through the door.

Farmer motioned for everyone to be seated, and then he brought in a chair from the table which he sat down with a thud. He sat down hard, folded his arms and glared at Harold – waiting for him to speak his peace.

Harold cleared his throat, and then began to nervously speak.

"When Leah told me that she was going to have a baby, I got real scared – and confused. I didn't know what you all would do. I wanted you to like me - "

"Sure a dumb way to get - "

"Let him speak, Clifton," Farmer stopped his angry son.

"I didn't know what to do," Harold continued, "so I ran away."

"Like a coward!" Clifton's remark cut like a razor.

"Yes, I was a coward. I caught rides – hopped a train and ended up in Southern California. I found work at an airplane factory making good money. I thought all my troubles were behind me, but – I was empty – and lonely. Shame and guilt haunted me at night 'til I couldn't sleep.

"One night I happened on this preacher fellow named Fuller on the radio. What he said made sense and, well, I listened again, and again. I went to his church, and it was there – I believed."

"In what?" Emile asked.

"In Christ, the church, honesty, a family, being a man, asking Leah to marry me, being a father to our baby."

"Don't use God an' the church ta try an' get in good with us, Harold," Farmer snarled.

Harold looked at them with sad eyes. "Do you think I would have travelled this distance to face you if something hadn't happened to me?" Harold asked. "I'm not the same man who ran away."

Farmer started to argue when he sensed God's Spirit stopping him.

"Be still, Farmer," the Lord spoke to his heart. "Harold belongs to Me and is My child."

"I have hurt Leah and all of you most dreadfully. I asked Leah to forgive me, and I ask the same from you. I am sorry for what I did," Harold went on. "I have proposed to Leah, and I ask for your daughter's hand in marriage."

Harold grew quiet and stared at his hands that were gripping his cap, turning it round and round. Suddenly, as though he realized what he was doing, he stopped and sat still.

"I said yes," Leah spoke softly.

"Oh, this is so mixed up!" Emile cried, burying her face in her hands.

"No, it's not, Mom! I want to marry Harold. I'm going to have his baby."

With that Clifton threw up his hands and went to the rear of the house.

Farmer studied Harold for a long time. The lad seemed more grown up, he was well dressed, he had remained calm, and he had faced them all and openly declared his love for his daughter. He had confessed his wrong and asked forgiveness. He wanted to take care of Leah and the baby to come. Farmer unfolded his arms and stood to his feet. He began to pace the floor, and it struck him that he must appear like Emile's father, Hirum Holt, the evening that Farmer and Emile announced their move to Oregon.

"What air yer plans, Harold?" Farmer asked when Harold finally looked up at him.

"I'm asking for Leah's hand in marriage, and I ask for permission to take Leah to Springdale to meet my mother. You see I bought a new car a few months ago, that's how I got here. I will bring Leah back and return to – uh – where I live. I will find a place suitable for Leah and the baby, then return around time of the spring thaw so we can get married – in your church. I work for a defense plant making more money than I ever thought possible. I will take care of her and the baby. I didn't know how strong my love for Leah was," Harold paused and took her hand, "until I saw her again, or how much I missed her."

"An' ifen I refuse," Farmer felt obstinate.

"Daddy, I'm going with Harold," Leah spoke up, "I'm going to marry him."

"How do we know you'll bring her back from Springdale, or return next spring?" Farmer questioned.

Harold looked straight into Farmer's eyes, this time not averting his own. "Because you have my word," he stated firmly.

Walter, who had been sitting cross-legged on the floor and silent until now, spoke slowly. "Harold, I looked up ta ya and admired you, but I sware ta ya, ifen you hurt my sister anymore by not bringin' her home or tellin' her you will marry her an' don't keep yer word – I will hunt ya down myself!"

"Harold, we will fix you a bed here on the sofa," Emile shifted the conversation. "Come help me, Leah."

The two women gathered blankets and a pillow, making up a place for Harold to sleep. When they were finished, Emile turned to Harold with a very stern note in her voice.

"You will sleep here, Harold, and I expect you and Leah not to do – well, you know what I mean – until you are married!"

With that, she gave Leah a look that said – "don't you dare sleep with Harold yet."

That night in bed, Emile cried on Farmer's shoulder a long time. Farmer's emotions washed back and forth like the tide. One minute he felt distrust for Harold, the next compassion. He feared Leah would be hurt more, and the thought of his little girl moving a thousand miles away left a deep ache in his heart.

Finally, Emile stopped her crying and lay still. "This sure has been a surprise," she murmured.

"You can say thet again, Emile."

Chapter 31

NEVER BE THE SAME

It was a cold Sunday morning in December. Momentarily the sun would break through patches of grey clouds to shine brightly on the snow, just to be swallowed up again and hidden from view. One of the county workers had thoughtfully graded snow off the road leading to the Church in the Woods so the members could drive to the service.

As Farmer and his family neared the church house, he reviewed the message he would deliver that morning in his mind. He was troubled. He had not slept well, and it was unclear exactly what God really wanted him to say. For once he wished it were someone else's turn to lead the Sunday morning teaching.

Folks had started talking about Christmas. The members would probably make plans after services of getting a tree and decorating the church. Farmer had considered a Christmas message, but it seemed so hard to get into the spirit of the season with so much of the world at war.

Then there was that troubling dream he had during the night. He was not sure what to make of it! Should he even mention it in his message? After all, it was just a dream – yet it had left its mark on him.

The car slid on a frozen patch of snow that covered a stretch of road. Farmer had to maneuver quickly to keep from skidding off into the buck brush. Farmer's thoughts were taken from the message as he focused on driving his automobile.

Soon they pulled up next to the church house. Something did not seem right to Farmer. He felt uneasy inside! Emile and Leah climbed out of the car talking and laughing as they did every Sunday. They hurried to the door to get out of the biting morning air. Walter in his car pulled up next to Farmer. Clifton was with him, and they both smiled and waved to Farmer as they made their way inside the church.

Farmer looked around. Little Gordie was in his Chevy coupe listening to the radio. He did that just about every Sunday for a while then would slip into the service and sit near the back on the left side.

"Won't be long in this cold," Farmer smiled, and then frowned. He felt a wave of panic when he thought about what he would say. It seemed to make no sense, just fragmented ideas and nothing to connect them. He read in his Bible hoping that God would miraculously give him a profound truth and tie all his thoughts into a powerful, organized message.

But the words in his Bible seemed to say nothing about anything. Farmer slapped it closed and climbed out of his car. Inside, the service had started with the singing of hymns, and Farmer prayed they would keep on singing.

The offering was taken, followed by Rachel who sang with a trembling voice, "It Is Well With My Soul." Now it was Farmer's turn.

He walked slowly to the front of the church and stood behind the pulpit that had become familiar to him over the years. He looked at each one as they sat waiting, and attempted a half-hearted smile.

"Well, thet was a right beautiful song, given up by Rachel," Farmer began. "But I have ta say it don't match my soul this mornin', 'cause I'm right troubled an' don't know why. Can't put my finger on it – or exactly what the good Lord done want me ta preach 'bout. Been prayin' an' readin' an' thinkin'," Farmer paused. "Jus' nothin' thet makes me any sense."

As Farmer looked into the faces of family and friends he saw each had a different reaction. Emile and Rachel covered their mouths and seemed afraid. His boys frowned; others seemed embarrassed at the silence. Ella May Brooks' cheeks turned red and she nervously adjusted her shawl.

"Heck, Farmer, life mostly doesn't make a lot o' sense," Donald piped up. "Just tell us what you're thinkin', and God will do the rest."

There were muffled laughs.

"Well," Farmer went on, "the only thing thet keeps a comin' back ta me is this troublin' dream I had me in the night, but I wasn't gonna tell it."

"Then ya shouldn't a brought it up!" quipped Joe.

"Come on, Pa!" Clifton added.

"Well, this I remember 'bout it. We was all gathered on the banks o' the Shanko River, but there was this dark fog so's we could only see out onto the water a few feet. Couldn't make out anything on the other side.

"We was standin' 'round talkin' how some folks had tried swimmin' ta the other side, but never come back. Now someone we knew an' all loved had jus' went out in the water ta reach the other side. I wasn't sure who thet person was, but knew they meant somethin' ta me an' we were all worried 'cause they hadn't come back, so's it was decided I should try and find them. The water was so cold – I woke up.

"Thet was jus' a dream, an' may not hev any – "

That instant the outside door flew open and Little Gordie who had been in his car burst into the church.

"The Japanese!" he choked. "The Japanese are bombing our ships in Pearl Harbor!"

There was a collective gasp in the church.

"I just heard it on the radio!"

"There must be a mistake," Joe Baltman spoke up.

"No! No!" Gordie protested. "I heard the news. The Battleship Arizona exploded – others sinking – many casualties – airstrips and airplanes blown up. They're attacking us!"

Confusion broke out in the church. The men ran to the cars with radios. Some of the women followed while others began to cry and pray.

Farmer frantically turned the knob of his car radio until he picked up the crackly voice of a newscaster. The terrible news was verified.

"At approximately 8:00 a.m. Hawaii time, warplanes from the Japanese Imperial Navy attacked Pearl Harbor. Reports are coming in of catastrophic loss of lives and much of our Pacific Fleet is damaged or sunk."

A few stayed by the radio in their cars, while the rest congregated back inside the church. The conversations were filled with disbelief, anger, and horror – all mixed together. When Farmer's eyes met Emile's he saw fear and worry there. A deep ache was forming in his own heart as he wondered about the future of his own boys. Maybe Washington would find a way to keep them out of the war – or maybe it could be won swiftly – maybe his boys wouldn't have to go! Suddenly his head was spinning, and he wondered where God was?

"We should pray!" Emile and Ella May both spoke at the same time. It seemed that everyone understood as soon as those words were spoken that both women had sons of eligible age for the military. By now, Rachel was beside herself and holding on to Clifton.

"I reckon thet ta be the best thing ta do," Farmer agreed, and one by one folks dropped to their knees and began to cry out to God in Heaven. But their hearts were faint and their minds distracted. The group as a whole had an unspoken desire and that was to get home to their radios to listen for every piece of news of this terrible attack, and to learn of what the United States would do next.

The time of prayer was brief and seemed like a blur to Farmer. Families scrambled into their cars, and Farmer found himself in the processional making its way out to the highway. As he drove, Emile fumbled with the radio dial. By now it seemed every station was telling about this act of war.

"We had no idea..." Farmer mumbled.

"I spoke with Harold Friday night on the phone, and he didn't think we would enter this war," Leah whimpered from the back seat.

"Farmer, will the boys have to go?" Emile asked.

"Don't reckon I know, Emile."

"Will Harold?" asked Leah.

"I reckon that depends on ifen we go ta war," Farmer swallowed a lump that formed in his throat, "but it sure don't look good."

Out of the corner of his eye he could see Emile wiping her eyes, and in the rearview mirror he caught glimpses of a trail of tears on Leah's face as she stared out the side window.

The rest of the day, they all sat around the radio. With each passing hour the news of death and destruction mounted.

"Oh, those poor boys!" Emile cried out when they told of the trapped sailors.

Clifton smashed his fist onto the table and bellowed out an oath when the newscaster reported of bombed airfields and destroyed planes.

Walter finally buried his face in his hands, shaking his head.

The women found things to keep busy and when Farmer could stand to hear no more, he walked out on the back porch to sit at the table and watch the sunset.

"Many a lad in Pearl Harbor saw their last sunset yesterday," the thought was sobering, and for the first time he felt the pain of fear strike deep inside his chest. Fear for his boys, and for countless others who would die in this awful war.

"Pa." Walter and Clifton joined him.

"Pa, I reckon we gotta go," Walter spoke softly and as a man.

"Maybe we won't go to war – maybe - "

"Pa, you know we will. After an attack like this we can't just do nothing," Clifton argued.

"Pa, I reckon we gotta go," Walter said again. It appeared to Farmer that Walter's eyes blazed in the fading sun, and his straight and steady gaze told Farmer that his son's mind was made up. In that instant Farmer felt what his father must have felt years ago, and for the first time he could understand why Franklin had kept his boys out of the Great War.

In what seemed an eternity of hushed quiet, Farmer looked deep into the eyes of his sons and felt an overwhelming need to love and protect them – and for a moment they were still his little boys, flying their toy airplanes in circles around the house. He remembered the day Walter announced that one day he would learn to fly.

He blinked, and there were two grown men sitting in front of him. Waiting for his guidance – his wisdom – wanting his permission – to fly away.

"Walter – Clifton – my sons – don't do anything yet 'til I hev time ta think on it an' pray. An' don't talk ta yer Ma 'bout this, as she is havin' a hard time of it already."

The setting sun cast a soft golden glow on Walter and Clifton as he studied their faces. His gaze moved to Emile and Leah inside the kitchen and he knew that all their lives would never be the same.

Chapter 32

SCATTERED

It was the Thursday afternoon after Pearl Harbor. Farmer, Walter and Clifton pulled up to the house. As Farmer shut off the engine, he saw Emile step out onto the porch. He dreaded facing her because he knew she was going to be upset and hurt.

"Boys, I reckon ya better let me do the talkin'," Farmer spoke under his breath.

Emile hugged and kissed each of them, searching their faces.

"Where have you been all day? I have been worried sick," Emile spoke with exasperation.

Inside the house, her eyes were still questioning and searching for an answer.

"Pa has something ta tell you!" Clifton blurted out. He could hardly contain their secret, but Walter was sullen and quiet.

Emile looked at Farmer, "What?"

"You know how I won't ask anyone ta do somethin' I wouldn't be willin' ta do myself."

"Yes."

"So's I took the boys ta the recruiter an' we all signed up."

"What! Farmer, are you crazy?!" Emile gasped, and Farmer thought she was going to faint.

"Aw, don't worry, Ma, they wouldn't take Pa. He's too old," Clifton laughed, "but I joined the Army, and they are gonna put me in the Air Corps 'cause I know about airplanes."

"Clifton – how – you- you're too young! I won't permit it! You can't!" Emile shrieked.

"Ma, I'm eighteen, and I already joined."

"How could you do this, Farmer – encourage them?" Emile was pleading.

"Emile, our boys air grown men. We can't hold them here their whole lives as much as I would want ta, I reckon we gotta let 'em do what they sees as right."

"And you would have marched off with them..."

"Yes'm, ifen they woulda had me."

Emile fell into the sofa.

"Little Gordie joined up with the Marines two days ago. He left this morning."

Emile put her hand over her mouth and cried out, "Oh, poor Gordon and Ella May! What is to happen to all of us? Both of our sons in the Army."

"Didn't pass," Walter mumbled as he eyed his hat he was twisting and folding.

"What?" Emile questioned.

"Walter didn't pass the physical. Somethin' ta do with his back. They wouldn't take him," Farmer explained.

"Oh, thank God!" Emile exclaimed.

Walter jumped up without a word, jammed his hat on his head and stomped out to his car. He kicked gravel against the house as he sped off.

Little more was said the next day, but Emile used Saturday morning breakfast when the whole family was at the table to try and ease the pain and tension. Clifton was to leave on the bus Tuesday the next week.

"We are proud of you, Clifton. You will make a fine soldier," Emile's voice broke, and Farmer knew she was trying to be brave.

"But we will still have Walter and Leah around here," she said brightly.

"I ain't gonna stick around this dried up hole of a town," Walter replied bitterly. "I done decided thet ifen I can't fight, I'll make planes so's Clifton can. I talked with Harold an' he says thet with so many men leavin' fer the military thet they's cryin' fer workers in the plants. Harold's company is makin' fighter planes, an' thet's what I plan ta do. When Clifton gets on his bus, I'll be a drivin' south."

"I'll be going with him," Leah spoke with firm resolve. "This dreadful war has changed everything. Harold has a place for us to live, and we will get married. I've spoken to him about it."

Farmer and Emile sat dumbfounded. Would all their children leave in one day?

"But, Leah, Harold said he would come in the spring, and you would get married in the Church in the Woods," Emile protested.

"Mom, I don't want to wait. I made this decision, and I won't change my mind!"

Farmer and Emile prayed for the clock to stop over the next two days; instead the time flew. All three of their children displayed an air of eager anticipation for their new adventures. Farmer and Emile found little to be excited about. Both of them wanted to impart encouragement and words of wisdom to their children, but the right words were difficult to find. To their exasperation they had an impossible time getting any of their kids to slow down long enough to talk.

Sunday service in church was lost on Farmer. His mind refused to follow the sermon and insisted on harboring depressing thoughts of loss. Walter held too much inside. Who would he talk things through with? And Clifton, who followed his older brothers every footstep, would be on his own and away from Farmer's guidance and protection. Who knew if they would ever see Clifton alive again! Farmer found himself angry with leaders of countries in far away places making hostile decisions that now affected his family by tearing his sons away.

Then there was Leah, in the passion of the moment, she had determined to go to Harold and speed up their wedding plans – thus robbing Farmer of walking his daughter down the aisle to give her away. Farmer struggled most with this decision because he felt Leah's leaving didn't have to be.

Farmer was so consumed in his own grief that he didn't consider how much the women were hurting until he observed Emile and Rachel after church, clinging to one another and weeping.

Farmer prayed for an opportunity to speak to all three of his children and for wisdom to impart something of worth to them. He knew that Emile was conducting a crash course with Leah on how to be a wife and mother, but it seemed the children avoided any in depth discussion with their father, until early Monday morning.

It was after three a.m. and a sleepless Farmer got up and went into the kitchen to make some coffee. He was working on his second cup when he heard Walter open his bedroom door.

"Can't sleep?" He yawned, squinting into the light.

"Sleep been hard to come by lately," Farmer replied.

"Me too." Walter slid onto a seat at the table and looked around as if trying to fix memories in his mind. "Pa," he continued, "I'm a mixture of excitement and anger."

"Anger?"

"I feel like a pansy! Other guys going off to war – doing something important. They are the hero's, and I get to stay home and work with old people and women."

They both stared at Farmer's coffee cup. Farmer prayed for something to say.

"Walter, when I was 'bout yer age, I heard me a message the preacher called 'Staying by the Stuff,' I never fergot it. King David was at war, and fer some reason they couldn't take all their supplies with them. The King reassigned some of his men to guard the stuff an' keep it safe. Ya know how hepped up those soldiers were when they came in from battle, but ya know what? David tol' how those who stayed by the stuff was jus' as important as those who went ta battle."

At that moment Clifton joined them.

"What's more, the King said those who stayed by the stuff shared in the glory – same as if they went to war. So, Walter, I reckon what ya do will be jus' as important as what Clifton does."

"But he'll be dodgen bombs and bullets," Walter protested.

"Heck fire, you could have a wheel or rudder fall on you," Clifton retorted.

"Ma and I sure will miss ya both and be powerful prayen' fer ya," Farmer spoke from his heart. He barely dared to look at their faces. When he did, both boys were brushing away tears.

"Pa, its right hard fer me ta leave an' its not easy." Walter was suddenly that little boy riding beside the wagon, taking off to chase a train.

"It's hard fer me too," Clifton blurted out, "and I'm darn scared!"

The three locked hands and eyes, and although not a word was spoken, Farmer knew that whatever he had imparted in his boys as they grew up would have to carry them through their difficult and dangerous days ahead. In those moments around the table, a bond was formed that would last forever.

Farmer could think of a hundred different things to say to Leah, but nothing seemed fitting. In his thoughts, all he could come up with was, 'don't understand – don't understand.' He knew that wouldn't help his daughter. Tuesday morning he made a feeble attempt at words.

"Reckon yer Ma has told ya things about marriage and well, ya know?"

"Yes, she has helped me a lot."

Farmer turned away, his heart was breaking. He struggled to turn his daughter loose, and he knew he must, for her sake. He turned back to face her.

"Leah, I reckon yer leaven' has been more weighin' on me then even on yer Ma. I've had to remember when yer Ma and' I was so in love, an' we jus' knew we had ta be together, an' it hed ta be right then. So's I need ya ta know I understand yer feelings, an' even though it pains me not ta be at yer weddin', I send ya off with all the love and prayers yer Ma an' I can give ya. Distance will never dim it!"

"Oh Daddy!" Leah cried, throwing her arms around him. He held her like his little girl one last time, regretting the years had slipped by so fast.

So it was on that next Tuesday morning in Applegate, a bus heading north with Clifton aboard, pulled out, as Walter, with Leah in his car, drove off to the south, leaving Farmer, Emile and Rachel to wave sad and lonely goodbyes.

Chapter 33

WORD FROM THE FRONTS

The telephone ringing in the dead of night jolted Farmer from a deep sleep. Emile was already up and running into the living room to grab the receiver off the hook.

"Dear God, don't let it be bad news!" he heard Emile breathe a prayer as she answered with a faint, "Hel – hello."

Farmer was up now and following Emile to the telephone. He glanced at the clock – three seventeen in the morning. For an instant he imagined Walter, Clifton and Leah rubbing their sleepy eyes, fumbling out of their rooms, curious to find out who was calling at such an early hour. Then sadly he remembered that their children were gone.

"It's Harold!" Emile announced. "Oh, my goodness, Leah had her baby! They named her Janee." Emile was relaying the details to Farmer as she picked them up from Harold.

"Leah and the baby are fine. Born a few minutes after midnight on March 25th – lots of hair – six pounds and eleven ounces – she measured eighteen and a half – oh, Harold, we are so happy and excited and so want to be there with you all!"

After Emile hung up, there was no sleeping.

"I'll look inta us makin' a trip ta California to see baby Janee," Farmer promised, but the trip was not to be – at least, not then. Rationing began in America. Gasoline, tires, butter, eggs, sugar, coffee, all became hard to come by. Gasoline supplies were cut drastically by the Government Agency. It became impossible to think of making a sixteen hundred mile trip to Los Angeles and back. They barely could buy enough gas to drive into Applegate, and if anything, the rationing would get worse. And tires? Gold was easier to obtain!

So contact with their family was confined to brief telephone calls and letters. Walter seldom wrote or called. Farmer and Emile had to find out about him through Leah and Harold. They learned that the company Harold worked for had turned down Walter because of his back. He encountered more trouble getting hired on than he should have, but finally got a job, and was renting a room nearby. Harold and Leah didn't see much of him; however, Walter was at the hospital when Janee was born.

Clifton, on the other hand, wrote often from boot camp – to Rachel, so Farmer and Emile resorted to calling her to learn about their other son.

"He'll write ten letters to Rachel to one for us," Emile was indignant. "I thought we raised that boy to do better!" Emile tried to hide a smile.

Clifton described in his letters his grueling experiences during basic training. Farmer could tell in the few letters he mailed to them that the military was changing his son.

Next he was sent to a base in Texas for mechanics school on a new fighter aircraft known as the P-38. When he completed mechanics training he was assigned to a fighter squadron somewhere in the Midwest. They had no idea where they would go from there or when. Weeks passed – Clifton wrote that they trained hard and kept busy, but were restless to be in the war!

"He doesn't know what he is asking for!" Emile cried out when she read the letter. Farmer understood what Clifton meant, but a dreadful fear gripped his heart when he thought of him going overseas.

That fear compounded late in November 1942, one Sunday afternoon when the phone rang. Farmer and Emile looked at each other, wanting to leap to the device that could bring good news, or words of tragic proportions. Farmer took the call.

"Farmer – it's your Ma!"

Her voice sounded so small and weak.

"Hello, Ma. I can barely hear ya. How's everbody?"

There was silence.

"Ma? What's wrong?" Farmer held his breath.

"It's William. We received this telegram tellin' us he's missing in action. Farmer, I don't know what that means. Is he killed? What does it mean?" Allison Trevor broke down.

"I don't know, Ma." Farmer was without words to comfort his mother.

"You are so far away – I don't even know what you look like anymore – and William may be killed! What am I to do?"

"Ma, where's Jacob?"

"Took some wheat to sale."

"Does he know about William?"

"No."

"Ma, why haven't ya tol' Jacob?"

"I don't know, I just wanted to tell you," she cried.

Weeks would pass with William's fate unknown until word came that he had turned up in a field hospital, alive, but badly wounded. He had lost his dog tags in the battle. The Army couldn't identify him until he gained consciousness – which appeared to have been a considerable time. Allison was worried sick.

"I don't understand all of this. I don't even know where my boy is at!" she fretted when Farmer called her.

"Ma, best I can tell, William is somewhere in North Africa fighting the Germans."

"This dreadful war, men killing each other," was her response.

The next call came late one night, February of 1943. It was Clifton's first and only call to them.

"Pa, our Squadron is shipping out first light of day!" his voice betrayed both excitement and nervousness. "I called Rachel and told her an' we talked. I asked her to wait for me, but Pa, I did some thinking, and I'm not so sure I did the right thing. Maybe I was selfish and not fair to her."

"Son," Farmer chuckled, "I reckon she woulda waited ifen ya asked her or not. Ma and I will watch after her, but where air ya goin'?"

"They won't tell – it's classified – but rumor has it somewhere in the Pacific. Pa, when I think about it, I get real scared!"

"Clifton, I did my best ta teach ya ta pray an' trust God. I reckon this ta be the biggest test ya will ever face. I love ya, son, an' we pray fer ya everday. Now I want ya ta talk with yer Ma."

As Emile spoke with Clifton, he could see her trying to be brave, but she was crumbling fast. When she hung up the phone, she fell into his arms and held on so tightly that Farmer was afraid to move. He patted her back and smoothed her hair, but any words of consolation just wouldn't come.

The next day, Farmer called Leah and Harold to relay news of Clifton to them. He found out that Walter had gotten a phone, so he decided to call him too. This proved to be a more difficult task than he had anticipated, for Walter never answered. He tried a morning call just before he left for work. No answer. He placed a call when he got home from work, then again at bedtime. There was still no answer. He waited and tried again on the weekend. The phone just rang and rang. By now he was concerned and contacted Leah again.

"Oh, Dad," Leah giggled. "I haven't seen Walter for some time, but I think he has a girl. Speaking of girls, you should see Janee – how she's grown and she is into everything. Was I like that? How did you and Mom stand me?"

"Ya could redo our home in a minute an' fer sure livened us up," Farmer smiled as he remembered. "Now ya have yer own..." his voice trailed off.

"Can I talk to Mom? I got a question. This rationing of shoes to three a year is impossible," then she laughed.

"Sure. I love ya, Leah, an' sure wish we could see Janee." He handed the phone to Emile who stood near listening.

"She's a worryin' 'bout her shoes," Farmer remarked dryly. Emile gave him a puzzled look.

Farmer decided to call Walter in the middle of the night. This time he got a groggy response.

"Pa, is something wrong?" fear rose in Walter's voice when he realized who he was talking to.

"Thet's what I was callin' ta ask ya."

"Pa, it's 2:30 in the mornin'. I'm half asleep!"

"Me, too, but ya never answer the phone any other time. Ain't ya ever home? Ya haven't called us on yer phone atall."

There was a long pause.

"Ya still there, son?"

There was till no sound from Walter.

"Son, I'm a sorry ta disturb ya like this."

"No, Pa, it's alright. I'm glad ya called an' I been meanin' ta call you an' Ma, I really was, but I been – not doin' so well."

"What is it, Walter?" Farmer sensed the gravity in Walter's voice.

"I been doin' a lot o' thinkin', Pa. Seems that nothin' has turned out the way I wanted it to. Ya know how fer a long time all I wanted was to join up with the Air Corps and fly a plane. Well, they wouldn't have me, so's I figure ta come down here an' help build fighter planes like Harold is doin'. Well, they wouldn't have me on account o' my dang back. No one else would hire me neither 'til I got this job."

"Well, thet's good, son."

"Not to my thinkin', Pa. Harold's over at the Lockheed plant workin' on P-38 fighter planes while I'm here at Douglas Aircraft makin' C-47 cargo planes. They probably won't even be in the war."

"Everthin's in the war, Walter. It don't sound all thet bad ta me."

"Met a girl, Pa. Her name is Karen. We kinda ran into each other at a USO show and started goin' out. Pa, I never cared all that much fer girls, but I sure fell hard for Karen. I was so happy 'til the night I was a goin' ta propose an' she tol' me she was in love with this sailor fella an' was gonna marry him. Pa, I never knew I could hurt so bad!"

"I know some how ya feel, Walter," Farmer started slowly. "Ya remember when ya were just a lad on our wagon trip to Oregon, and Ma got deathly sick in Utah, an' we were tryin' ta get ta Hurricane?"

"Yes, Pa."

"The thought a losin' yer Ma near crushed my heart flat. Couldn't think how I could go on without her an' knew ifen she died – somethin' in me would too. I hurt powerful bad 'til she pulled through."

"I didn't know all that, Pa. I don't think I will ever love anyone else – not the way I do Karen!"

"Given time – ya might – love another."

"Pa, I did somethin' I'm ashamed ta tell."

"Ya be a grown man, Walter. Ya tell me only what ya choose ta tell, but remember thet often with the tellin' comes releasin'."

"I started goin' ta bars ta get drunk an' ferget, but I hated it! Hated how I felt, what it made me do, an' I didn't ferget – just remembered! I did me a lot o' thinkin' an' came to myself an' decided I didn't want ta live thataway."

"Have ya squared it with yer Maker?"

"Ya, Pa, an' I'm a goin' on. Thanks fer listenin'."

"Yer Ma an' I love ya an' trust ya to do the proper things. We pray fer ya everday. Good night, son."

"Night, Pa – oh, 'most forgot! I've gotten some letters from Gordie. The last one came a week ago an' he wrote thet his unit was bein' transferred to the Solomons in the Pacific."

The next day Farmer stopped by Brooks' Service Station ta fill up his tank and relay Walter's news to Gordon.

"Farmer, I can only sell you two gallons today," Gordon told him after they greeted each other. "This war is hell to get gas – and other things – I pray it ends soon! You heard from your kids?"

"I got Walter on the phone early this mornin'. He's had a lot o' disappointin' things ta happen ta him. He's workin' fer a company what makes a cargo airplane 'stead o' a fighter plane. He met an' fell fer some girl named Karen who dumped him fer a Navy guy, then he went ta drinkin', but gave thet up. He tol' me thet he received a letter from Little Gordie an' thet he was goin' ta the Solomon Islands in the Pacific."

"Yes, we got that too. He was in combat inside Italy. He wrote that many of his buddies got killed in some of the battles. I don't know how much more Ella May can take – or me. We pray – all the time – and thank God, Gordie has been spared. Maybe there will be less fighting in the Pacific. What about Clifton?"

"Haven't heard since the beginnin' o' the year. His Squadron was shippin' out, but he didn't know where. Thought somewhere in the Pacific. Emile hopes ta get mail soon. We get a mite scared too Gordon, an' I know it wears on my wife. We pray, but somehow thet don't seem enough, yet I reckon I don't know what else ta do. Just wait on the mail each day – same as you all."

And wait they did. Days seemed to last longer, which turned into weeks, then months and still no letters from overseas. Farmer could hear Emile softly cryin' in the night and knew she was racked with worry and unable to sleep. Some days his heart seemed so heavy as to just plumb stop. They found themselves glued to the radio every night, and going into Applegate more often to the movies. The movies helped lift the terrible gloom and heaviness dumped on their daily thoughts and feelings by the war. However, they were more interested in the newsreels hoping to catch a glimpse of what was happening in the Pacific – or better still to see Clifton on the screen and to know that he was still alive.

It was the first of May when a car pulled up in front of the Trevor's house.

"It's Rachel in her parents' car!" Emile clapped her hands excitedly. "She must have news from Clifton!" She threw open the door and welcomed the young woman in. The stress on her face revealed something was wrong.

"I – I – I – came over – to..." she was fighting to maintain her composure, "to – to – see if you have heard from Clifton. I know you hadn't Sunday when I saw you in church, I just thought maybe..."

"Oh, you poor dear," Emile cried and folded Rachel into her arms.

"His telephone call in February was the last we heard from him," Farmer answered. "We would fer sure tell ya first."

As he watched Rachel, he had never seen such a sad and lonely woman. Like Beth before Donald came into her life, Rachel had the same look as she did when he found her on the side of the road with her suitcase that winter day in 1925.

"You are in love with our Clifton, aren't you?" Emile asked gently.

"Yes – oh, yes – a thousand times yes. I never knew how much until he left. I think I have been in love with Clifton forever, but he was always here, somewhere's close, since we were children."

Emile gave Farmer that knowing look and smiled.

"Now my love has grown up also, but I have never told Clifton. I can't bear the thought – of – something – and he never know."

"I think he knows how you feel," Emile spoke softly.

"But I can't be sure, and I worry about him so," Rachel buried herself in Emile's arms and cried as though her heart would break.

A hundred different images flashed across the backdrop of Farmer's mind as he watched the scene before him. Rachel had occupied their home as much as her own. How many times he recalled hearing a little knock on the door and opening it to a bright-eyed, sandy-haired girl who stood smiling up at him.

He saw Clifton and Rachel laughing and romping through the trees when they lived on the ranch. Ah, the ranch! How Farmer missed that place and time – especially tonight. What he would give to go back to those days and have Clifton and Rachel children again.

He thought when his kids grew up and were on their own there would be less worry, but, alas, that was not happening. The weight of worry for all of them was crushing! Farmer marvelled at how calm and in control Emile seemed. She appeared to be handling the wartime stress much better than he was. True, he knew she wept at times in the night – but so did he – often – as he prayed for each one. He sometimes sensed Clifton's fear and envisioned him dead on an island somewhere in the Pacific, crumpled up in a bomb crater. Then the icy hand of doubt would grip his heart, and he would have to turn his eyes upon Jesus Christ and trust his son's safety to his Savior.

More time passed, and Farmer knew he and Emile's nerves were beginning to unravel. They were consumed with searching the newspapers, listening to the radio for accounts of the war, attending movies they really weren't interested in just to see newsreels, praying as they never had before in their lives. They snapped at each other over minor things, and one evening, Farmer accused his wife of not being all that concerned.

"Ya don't appear ta be all thet worried 'bout Clifton, an' air calm 'bout it," Farmer remarked.

"You aren't here during the day, Farmer Trevor, to see!"

With that she turned and ran into their bedroom, slamming the door behind her! Farmer instantly realized that his flawed thinking had prompted him to make such a cutting remark. He wished he could take back what he spoke – erase it! Fix their lives!

Farmer would never forget that sunny June afternoon. He was working – concentrating on what he was doing when the form of a familiar figure in the corner of his eye caught his attention. He looked to see Emile standing in one of the large open doors. She was holding up a letter for him to see.

The whole mill was aware that Farmer and Emile were frantic to hear from Clifton. The foreman saw Emile about the same time Farmer saw her and shut down the mill operation. He motioned for her to go to Farmer. She made her way swiftly in a half run around the saws to where Farmer met her. "Farmer! It's from Clifton!" she said breathlessly as she held out the letter. "Oh, thank God, he's – alive!" she spoke with relieved excitement.

Farmer unfolded the letter with trembling hands. He wiped his eyes to see more clearly.

It was dated April 3, 1943, and read:

"Dear Ma and Pa,

They announced today that for the first time some mail would be sent out. I'll bet you been worried sick over me but I'm well.

I only have time for one letter and as much as I wanted to write Rachel , I figured I best send this to you. Please tell Rachel how much I love and miss her. I think about her all the time and wish I was there. I wouldn't want her to be here in this place. My Squadron came to an island named Guadalcanal. I think the Marines came here first and took over an airstrip from the Japanese we call Fighter One. They say that the engineers who finished Fighter One had to work under fire from the enemy. The Marines cleared out most of the Japanese ground forces, but the casualties were very high.

First of this year Fighter Two airfield was made by leveling crushed coral, then they laid down the interlinking metal strips. Our base is in the palm trees not far from the ocean. We have no buildings, just live in tents. We cover the planes with camouflage netting. That's to hide our P-38's from the Japanese dive bombers that come through. There are fierce air battles here everyday, and the planes come back in all shot up. Some of them don't come back at all! Two weeks ago Fighter Two was bombed. Two of the P-38's and a C-47 were blown up, and the worst part, one of my buddies was killed. He was a crew chief like me. We talked a long time just the night before. He was telling me his plans for after the war. He was from Wisconsin.

Here's a funny part. Before I left the states I talked to Harold and Leah. Harold told me he's making these P-38's and each one he works on he stamps a little mark into the fuselage. What he made is a small wolf's head looking up into the sky in a circle. The circle stands for a full moon. It means Moonwolf, his middle name. Well, would you believe I found his Moonwolf on all but four of our fighters. It's like a part of him is here with me. And you tell Walter not to fuss about making a cargo plane that don't count.

You tell him one of his C-47's brought us supplies and took this here letter out today.

Ma, I sure miss your cooking, and Pa, our talks. How is Scout and the horses?

Your son,
Clifton."

Emile was waiting for his reaction to the letter. He hugged her and held her tight. Tears filled his eyes as the impact of what he had just read overflowed his heart.

"I'm worried now more than ever o' the danger Clifton faces everday, Emile, but I reckon the joy o' hearin' from our boy overpowers the worries."

Farmer became aware that all the mill hands had gathered around them and was waiting word of any news received. Farmer turned to face them and held up the letter.

"It's from our boy in the Air Corps, Clifton!" Farmer shouted with a quivering half smile, "an' he's alright!"

A cheer went up that could be heard all over Douglas Landing.

Chapter 34

TWO STARS

About the time the letter arrived from Clifton, Farmer and Emile got notice of a package at the post office. It was from the War Department and contained a Blue Star Service Banner. It was on an 8-1/2 by 11 inch white field with a blue star in the center and bordered in red.

The enclosed letter told that the blue star represents one family member serving in the Armed Forces. It was to be displayed in the front window of the service man's home. The letter gave instruction that if the individual is killed or dies while serving a smaller gold star was to be superimposed on the blue one, so that a blue border is formed.

Farmer and Emile proudly hung the banner in their front window, but when they thought of having to sew on the gold star, they would have rather died themselves.

May had seen the overthrow of the Axis armies in North Africa. Word also came that the Army was sending William home to Texas. "He wrote that he was awarded medals," Allison told Farmer on the phone, "and thank the dear Lord he's coming home!"

But that seemed to be the only piece of good news. The early part of 1943 seemed shrouded in death and dismal news.

Farmer and Emile went with the Baltmans to see the movie, "Casablanca." The desperation of the characters with the war and Newsreel scenes of horrible battles in the Pacific left them all unsettled. Rachel went to the restroom when she could take no more.

Emile found Scout dead by the kitchen stove one morning in July 1943, and two months later Sunset didn't respond to Farmer's calls. He found him lying in a grove of pines, and grieved for a long time by the side of his faithful horse.

"Ya just got old an' tired, Sunset," Farmer murmured as he stroked the horse's neck and mane. "I'll fer sure never ferget ya an' how ya pulled me an' my family in that chuck wagon all those miles, an' I kept my promise ta ya, ol' man. I won't ferget ya!"

It took several weeks for Farmer to get enough nerve to tell the children that Scout and Sunset were gone. He wrote letters to each of them. Walter took it the hardest, Farmer thought, and he wasn't even sure if mail was getting to Clifton.

Just before the first snow, Michael O'Malley passed away from liver disease.

"I told him that all the drinkin' he did would put him away, but he was a dang fool not to listen and now I'm lookin' after this store by myself!" Molly spoke in her usual gruff manner to Farmer. He had stopped by as soon as he heard.

"Won't be quite the same, not seein' Michael here. Molly, how can we help ya?"

"Jus' come buy my goods and keep me in business," Molly joked then quickly turned her head.

The funeral service was at the Catholic Church in Applegate. As Farmer walked by the casket and looked in the face of a friend he had known for years and witnessed to, he remembered how Michael had given from his store and heart when times were so rough in the Depression.

"Will we ever see any happy times again?" Farmer wondered as he and Emile drove back into the mountains to Douglas Landing.

Thanksgiving quietly came. Not the festive holiday it was meant to be. True, there were lots of things to be thankful for. All their children were well – as far as they knew. William had arrived home in Holt, Texas back on the old farm. Today, Farmer and Emile had a bountiful table to share with good friends. Several joined them for dinner. Molly came and was glad to not be alone; Donald, Beth and Beverly Ann brought Rachel with them.

"Mom's got some kinda sickness, and Dad stayed with her," Rachel announced when she bounded through the door. "Have you – heard from Clifton?"

"No," Emile replied. "We hoped that you had."

"Only one letter in June that he sent you. I haven't gotten any. Some days I think I will just die if I don't get a letter!" Rachel spoke in exasperation.

"What about that new boy who came to town workin' with my Pa, who wants to date you?" Beverly Ann teased.

Rachel turned red and snarled up her nose, and everyone laughed.

"What are your Mother's symptoms?" Dr. Put, who also had come for Thanksgiving, inquired of Rachel.

Farmer stood listening to his friends' conversations and watching them. His mind wandered to two years ago on Thanksgiving when Harold showed up on their front porch. How he wished Harold would again with Leah, Janee and Walter. Once he walked over to the window and looked out – half expecting to see a strange car pull up and stop, loaded with his family.

Emile broke his thoughts slipping her hand inside his arm like she always did.

"Farmer, what's wrong?" she whispered.

"Nothin', just rememberin' two years ago when Harold broke inta our Thanksgivin' - " his eyes grew misty – "and missin' our kids."

"I know," she nodded. "It's time to eat."

Thanksgiving Holiday gave over to the weekend. Farmer and Emile went to church Sunday morning. They had a visiting Preacher from Springdale. Part of the morning collection was gasoline ration stamps so the man could drive back home.

Joe and Sally were in church as well as Rachel. Sally was feeling better. Joe spoke to Farmer on the way out.

"Rachel tells us you've had no news of Clifton. You all must be at your nerves' end. Rachel worries terrible like so I know it must be hard on you an' Emile."

"Joe, it's most hard on Clifton's Ma, an' there be days I reckon I can't take no more. Evertime a car pulls up or the phone rings, we be afraid of bad news. We go to the Post Office everday hopin' fer a letter – terrible scared there might be news of Clifton's - " Farmer couldn't go on.

"Well, as for bad news of that sort I hear tell, Farmer, that the military contacts the family in person – so I guess that means you won't hear it on the phone or by letter," Joe placed his hand on Farmer's shoulder with a look that said a volume in friendship. Nothing else needed to be said, and they went their ways.

That afternoon in their home, Farmer was trying to get some updates in the news. He had just listened to the "Old Fashioned Revival Hour" – the church where Harold found the Lord. As he turned the dial he heard Emile.

"Oh, dear Lord!"

He turned to look. Emile had turned pale and was pointing out the window with a shaking hand.

Farmer jumped to the window. He felt his heart stop! Outside was a military vehicle with the big star painted on the door.

Emile began to whimper, "No, oh, God, no, not Clifton!" Farmer tried to help her, but his own fear and grief paralyzed him. He saw a soldier in uniform with a paper step upon their porch. He froze. The very thing they feared most, their worst nightmare was coming true.

The knock!

Emile sat up holding out her hand. She seemed blind – dazed. He didn't want to answer the door – but he had to – had to know. A flash of his boy's dead mangled body on some lonely island in the Pacific ripped across his mind. He shuddered, and then stood back up.

Another knock!

His knees turned to water, and he grabbed the arm of the couch to right himself. Emile clung to him as they made the long walk to the door. Everything seemed in slow motion. He opened the door to face a young soldier who had removed his hat. Emile covered her mouth making a whimpering sound.

"Mr. and Mrs. Brooks?" the soldier began.

"What! Wait! No! That's not – us... they live - " Farmer pointed down the street.

The soldier stiffened up and his face got red, then softened.

"I am very sorry. In such a small town I never thought there would be two – on the same street. I just thought... I apologize for bringing you distress."

Farmer and Emile stood stunned and drained watching the military vehicle drive slowly down to the Brooks' home.

"Little Gordie," Emile gasped. "Oh, dear God!"

As quickly as grief had overtaken them for their own son, now it turned towards their friends.

"God help them," Farmer breathed a prayer.

They could see the soldier get out of the car. Gordon and Ella May were already out of their house. The soldier talked to them and handed them the envelope he was carrying. He stepped back, saluted them, and turned to leave. Ella May fell to the ground holding onto Gordon's leg. Soon he was down with her trying to hold her as the soldier drove away.

"We must go to them!" Emile cried, and they took off running down the street. When they went into the yard, all they could hear Ella May say over and over was:

"Not my Gordie, not Little Gordie, not him; there must be a mistake!"

Gordon was trying to console her but was overcome with his own grief. Farmer and Emile sat on the ground, the four of them holding each other. After the tears stopped and they were spent, they got up and went inside.

In tragic times sometimes the best thing a friend can do is just be there. The closeness does the talking, and no words needed spoken for a very long time. They just sat still, remembering...

Finally, Gordon spoke. His voice filled with sorrow, he read from the letter he had been given.

"It says," he began slowly, 'that Gordie Brooks, a U. S. Marine, was killed in action in the Gilbert Islands at the Battle of Tarawa.' I think Ella May an' I would like to be alone."

On September 24, 1917, when the Blue Star Service Banner was adopted, the following statement was read into the Ohio Congressional Record:

"The world should know about those who give so much for liberty. The dearest thing in all the world to a father and mother – their children."

Two stars remain in the front windows of two homes in Douglas Landing. The star in the Trevor's window is blue. The star in the Brooks window has turned to gold.

Chapter 35

HAPPIER TIMES

"What would ya fancy fer Christmas?" Farmer asked Emile at breakfast before he left for the mill.

"Clifton home safe!" she answered without hesitation.

That afternoon when he left work Farmer stopped by the Post Office on his way home. The box was empty.

"'Nother day o' not hearin' from Clifton," he sighed.

Snow had been falling since three o'clock. The temperature was dropping, and the wind that had picked up cut through his coat. Snow was drifting, making it more difficult to drive. When he reached the house he saw the Baltman's car. He slid to a stop, and before he could get out of the car Rachel came running out of the house into the snow.

"I got a letter from Clifton!" She was jumping up and down waving the letter. "Hurry, Mr. Trevor, come read it! I am so happy I'm crying, laughing and dancing all at once!"

"Reckon thet's the best news I've heard in the longest time. Get inside, girl, it's freezing out here," Farmer rushed up on the porch where he was greeted by Emile.

"You read the letter?" he asked as he kissed her. She grinned.

217

"I'm the happiest woman alive!" Rachel gushed holding the letter out to Farmer.

His hand shook then steadied as he read. The letter was dated September 29, 1943:

"Dearest Rachel,

I have so much to tell you, but most I will keep 'til I see you, because it will be for your ears only, and knowing you, you'll make sure my Ma and Pa and everyone else reads this letter.

I must tell you though how lonely it gets here. We keep mostly busy, so busy we fall on our cots and are dead asleep. But there is time to think, usually in the night when I can hear the sound of the big guns on the Navy's ships – or the roar of airplane engines flying overhead. That's when I think of you and dream of when we will be together. Sometimes my longing for you gets – as my Pa says – powerful strong.

I've started getting your mail, and yes, letters from my Ma and Pa. One from Walter, and he's not much to count on for writing. Leah and Harold seem to be doing fine. They sent a picture that Janee – scribbled. Let's see, I got a letter from Beth Parrigan and several from Beverly Ann. I also got one from Mrs. Brooks asking if I might have run across Gordie. I don't know where he's at.

We have two airfields here. Fighter One or Henderson Field, as it's called, is the Marine Base. I'll tell you something about that in a minute.

Fighter Two is our airfield where our P-38's are based. Something mighty important happened in April right after I wrote Ma and Pa. Intelligence reports came in of a big Japanese Admiral flying through on Easter Sunday. One of the P-38 squadrons took off to intercept the Gym Betties, and, dang it, if they didn't shoot them down – Admiral and all. Maybe you've heard about it?

But a funny and strange thing happened to me that I gotta tell you about. The Marines on Fighter One had 'Wildcats,' but a few months ago some newer planes, Corsairs and Hellcats started coming in. The Marines were low on supplies and men. They asked if they could borrow some of us to be crewchiefs. I told them I had worked on a engine like theirs – only smaller, so I got sent over to the Marine side. They put me on one of the old 'Wildcats' that would hardly run, and they were terrible short of parts.

The fighting in the sky was fierce everyday and some nights. The Japanese were bombing our fields and we were losing planes in the air. They needed every available plane and my pilot, a Lieutenant Alderman, was in a hurry to get into the battles.

I remembered something I learned from my folks about praying, and I prayed my heart out while I worked long hours on that fighter. I felt the Good Lord showed me things to do to make the engine run better. When I finished, that plane was still a Wildcat, but it roared like a tiger.

Every time Lt. Alderman flew a mission I told him I was praying that the Good Lord would keep that plane flying no matter what. He just smiled an' said, 'Good!'

Well, not long after that my Wildcat was flying in a formation when a pack of Japanese Zeros came out of the clouds with the sun behind them. They were all over the Marines. Lt. Alderman could barely see for blood and sweat. The wings were riddled and bullet holes were in the engine, but my Wildcat kept on running – it wouldn't give up.

Alderman said the Zeros spent their ammo on him and came alongside – amazed he was still in the air. They peeled off and left. The plane came back and landed – engine still going – but it will never fly again. The guys say it was a miracle. I tell them the Lord kept it flying. Prayer power!

It is late, and mail goes out at dawn. I love you. The fighting has moved from here. I think we are safe now.

Clifton."

Letters from Clifton became more frequent and arrived faster in 1944. It appeared to him that he would wait out the war at Fighter Two on Guadalcanal. Anyway that's what he kept repeating in his letters, and Farmer could see the tide of war turning in favor of the Allies.

Walter and Leah telephoned more often in '44 as well. Two of those calls ushered in life changes, although Farmer and Emile didn't detect it. They were too busy keeping up on the war news and praying for it to end, and for Clifton's safety, to be able to look that far into the future.

The first of the two calls came on a lazy summer Saturday afternoon in June. Emile was at O'Malley's doing a little shopping. Farmer had just walked in the back door from tending the horses when the phone rang. It was Leah.

"Hello, Dad."

"Well, hello yerself. Reckon it sure be good ta hear yer voice. How air y'all?"

"We have had a wonderful an' interesting three weeks. I wanted to tell you and Mom about it."

"Well, she ain't here, but I reckon I can be ears fer both o' us."

"Dad, you are so silly!" Leah laughed.

"You remember I told you we live near one of these movie studios."

"Yes, I recall ya tellin' thet."

"I was walking on the sidewalk with Janee by this studio when this big fancy car showed up – turned around to come back. I was a little nervous and told Janee to hurry along. This car passed real slow, then stopped ahead of us and the rear window rolled down. I stopped walking, and then the car backed up to where we stood. I was really feeling scared, when this man in the car said not to be frightened. He wanted to talk to me about using Janee in his movie. He gave me his card and told me to bring Janee to the studio the next morning."

"Well, Leah, was he who he said?" Farmer questioned.

"He was the director of the picture. He did some photo tests and said Janee was very photogenic – a natural."

"Reckon I coulda tol' ya thet!" Farmer smiled.

"Dad, Janee did very well and loved it! It was a movie of the pioneers going west. Janee played the daughter of one of the families in the wagon train. It wasn't a big part, but the pay was good."

"Leah, thet's most excitin' news. Yer Ma will be most glad ta hear it, an' we will fer sure go see the movie. What they callin' it?"

"They haven't titled it yet. Probably come out next spring. Pa, as I watched them filming the story, it made me think of our family travelling from Texas in a chuck wagon. I can't believe you and Mom did that. Wasn't there any cars?"

"There was, but we couldn't afford ta buy one, and the roads were not near finished yet. Ya can be sure thet gasoline was near as scarce as it is now."

"In the movie, they said they only made about twelve miles a day, and travel was perilous."

"Thet be about right."

"Didn't we get tired, and restless, bored to tears and frightened?"

"Don't reckon ya knew much about it."

Leah burst out laughing as she realized what she had said.

"Anyway, Dad, Janee made a pretty good little pioneer girl."

"Takes after her Ma," Farmer joked with seriousness.

The second of the two calls came from Walter late Thanksgiving evening. Emile took the call and spoke with Walter awhile. When she handed the phone to Farmer there were tears in her eyes. She smiled.

"Pa?"

"How ya be, Walter?"

"I'm a missin' everbody and everthing tonight. It was a lonesome Thanksgivin'. I missed bein' there with you all. I miss Ma's Thanksgivin' dinner; I miss Gordie; I even got to missin' ol' Scout."

"We miss 'em too, son."

"I know Gordie's in Heaven, but do you think Scout is there too?"

"I don't rightly know fer sure, Walter. I never reckoned animals ta be there since the Bible says they got no spirit like we do."

"That would be sad not seeing Scout or Sunset ever again. I miss the trees and mountains. 'Course we have those around here we can drive to.

"Say, have ya been hearin' about how good a job these C-47's are a doin' in Burma? An' I'll bet any amount o' money they will carry our men into Europe!"

"Yes, Walter, I've been a hearin' those good reports, an' ya did a good job a buildin' those planes, Walter. Ya put a stamp on 'em like Harold?"

"Na! They have me testin' each one. I take it out to the runway and back. I've learned a lot about the plane. Pa, I just know I could take one off."

"What?" Farmer was shocked. "Don't ya be a doin' thet an' get yerself in trouble – or even worst – hurt bad!"

"Aw, Pa, I was only foolin'. The easiest is takin' off. Landing is the hard part, but there is somethin' I got from Clifton. I pray the Lord keeps each of the C-47's workin' an' flyin'."

"Good idea," Farmer was sensing that Walter had something he wanted to talk about and was working his way to it.

"Another thing I'm prayin' about, Pa. This fella thet's a part of a new airline starting up in Alaska was tellin' me they need pilots for these C-47's they is gonna be buyin' in a most terrible way. He says that his company will train me to fly if I will come work for them, but as I think on it, I have a good job here. What should I do, Pa?"

"Son, do ya remember thet first airplane ya saw just outside of Amarillo? Thet did something ta ya an' ya never got over it."

"I knew then I wanted to fly, Pa! But now I'm scared to try it! I think about my back an' how foolish to leave a good job here. I just got a promotion an' the money – more then I coulda dreamed of."

"Walter, it wasn't easy fer yer Ma an' me ta uproot an' leave our home in Texas. We sure had a lot thet spoke against it. It comes ta the end a doin' what God tells ya ta do."

"Pa, I'm a thinkin' thet I'll just wait on it," Walter concluded the call.

New Year's Eve there was supposed to be a gathering at the Church in the Woods; however, a strong snowstorm blew in making it difficult and hazardous to drive. The meeting was cancelled. Instead, Farmer and Emile bundled up and trudged down the street to the Brooks'.

The evening was spent visiting, playing some board and card games. Gordon and Ella May taught them a new one called, "Rook" that they had just purchased in Applegate. As midnight neared the four ate popcorn and drank hot cocoa and coffee. The Brooks were pleased that Farmer and Emile had come to share New Year's Eve with them, but Farmer and Emile both knew that the friendship they once enjoyed was changed. Both families had struggled in the Depression; both lost their ranches, both sought out work. But in the death of Gordie, Gordon and Ella May had gone on alone.

Emile asked Farmer about it a few months after Gordie's loss.

"Am I just imagining, or do the Brooks seem cool towards us, Farmer?"

"I reckon them ta be a mite angry, Emile."

"Hurt – grieving I can understand. Why, angry? At us?"

"Think on it. We hev us two boys, both still livin'. They had one, an' he was taken. I reckon thet's somethin' they be wantin' ta ask the Lord about an' why He done thet."

"Oh, dear!" had been Emile's response.

As 1945 was ready to make its entrance, the Brooks and Trevors prayed the New Year in. All four felt the touch of God on their hearts and many of the prayers were tearful as well as hopeful. Farmer hurt for his friends, and he felt there was some healing and closure that took place in Gordon and Ella May that night.

Emile's prayers were filled with longings and wishes, which stirred deep feelings in him. They ran to their house through the snow and icy cold, but that failed to diminish what had stirred inside of him. Those feelings grew stronger. He remained silent even while Emile recalled the events of the evening. He didn't say anything until they had snuggled into their bed and gotten warm.

"Emile, hearin' yer prayers tonight made me ta understand how powerful we miss our families. I mean our children, an' little Janee who we ain't never seen, an' yer Ma an' Pa an' sister..."

Emile let go! It was like a dam burst! She wept loudly, and Farmer could not hold back his own emotions as those deep feelings poured out. Finally they both quieted down.

"Gordon asked me tonight when ya an' Ella May was in the kitchen ifen we wanted ta buy Little Gordie's Chevy. Said they can't bring themselves ta drive it, an' it's near brand new as Gordie bought it new right after Walter got his Ford. He really wants us ta have it.

"I was thinkin' – an' it hit me in prayer – ifen we get thet car, I have me some time comin' at the mill, and gasoline be gettin' more plentiful, an' we been savin' our money..." Farmer paused, making sure of what he was about to say.

"Appears ta me thet a vacation trip ta California to see Walter and Leah, Harold an' little Janee – then on ta Texas ta see yer family an' mine be long overdue."

Emile sat straight up in bed.

"Oh, Farmer! Do you think we can? Is it possible? Am I dreaming?!"

She started bouncing up and down in bed, clapping her hands in joyous laughter.

"Oh, that would be the happiest of times!"

"It's settled then! We'll be makin' thet trip soon's the spring thaw comes."

Emile threw herself into his arms!

Chapter 36

TWENTY YEARS AGO

"Emile?"

Farmer shook Emile from a sound sleep.

She stirred.

"Emile!" Farmer called again. "I'm so all fired up. Let's leave now!"

Emile turned making a sound something between a groan and a "what?"

"I'm a feelin' that same excitin' way I did when we left Holt. Been a tossin' an' turnin' an' can't sleep, so's I reckon I can drive better'n thrashin' around in bed!"

"What time is it?" Emile muttered, not sure if she was actually hearing Farmer or dreaming it.

"It be one twelve, an' I think I've been countin' every minute."

"Farmer Trevor! You are dreadful!" Emile turned away from Farmer pulling the quilt over her ear.

"Darn," Farmer thought as he lay looking at the ceiling. It was quiet except for the slow ticking of their clock. Then he heard the 'whooo' of an owl out back in the trees. Later, Wind clomped the ground and snorted. The sounds took Farmer's mind back to when they had migrated to Oregon.

It was exactly twenty years ago Farmer, Emile and their children left the farm in Holt, Texas, to travel west in a chuck wagon.

"Twenty years today, March thirty-first!" Farmer mused. He couldn't believe how the time had slipped by so quickly. Twenty years since he had seen his family. His Ma must be looking old. And he had never laid eyes on Jacob's boy who was near grown up. Then there's William, and Pa's grave, and the old house where he and Emile started their life together and their two boys took their first breath.

"Sixteen years since Emile seen her folks an' her sister Susan an' husband Andrew," Farmer calculated as memories of the Holt's visits in the late twenties made their way into the forefront of his thoughts. He could picture Hirum walking along Cold Creek early in the mornings, and recalled the laughter of Emile and Susan and the children...

He smiled ta again hear Leah's little voice as she played and babbled near the big fireplace.

"Now she be grown an' has' a baby o' her own what we ain't never seen!" Farmer exclaimed, overcome with emotion. He felt Emile move and turn her face towards him. He lay still, hearing her breathing and the ticking of the clock.

Suddenly, she jumped up giggling and started tickling his sides. Farmer tried to ward off her fingers from his body, but he was laughing so hard he felt weak and helpless. He finally dove out of bed to escape. She sat in bed laughing and pawing at him like a playful cat.

"Twenty years ago we waited until dawn, Farmer, and I do recall we wrestled and laughed. Yes! Let's do one thing different this time! Let's leave now!"

Chapter 37

CALIFORNIA, HERE WE COME

Farmer and Emile left while it was still dark, early that morning, March 31, 1945. They had no idea what lie ahead or what events would unfold as the eastern sun rose upon them. They were simply two brave pioneers returning to the place of their birth and their roots. Their chief objective- seeing their children and granddaughter, and the family they missed and loved.

Farmer was confident the time was right. He had felt the leading of the Lord to make this trip - just as he had when they traveled to Oregon. Everything seemed to fall into place. They bought Little Gordie's Chevrolet; it was in new condition. Farmer asked the mill for three weeks vacation and was granted it. He and Emile had been saving, and there was ample money for the trip to Texas and back. Gordon Brooks told him that gasoline was getting easier to come by each week that passed.

Donald Parrigan questioned the timing.

"You think you oughta wait 'til the war's over?" he asked.

"I reckon this war is windin' down, Donald. Everday we see the battles turnin' ta our side. Don't reckon ta see it last through this year. Our troops be knockin' on Hitler's door, an' Clifton tells us there be talk o' shippin' out ta the States," Farmer responded to Donald's concerns.

"Well, anyway, I'll be like a horse a waitin' in the barn if you need anything. Thinkin' on horses, who's a carin' for yours?"

"Joe tol' me he would drop by - but ifen he can't, he'll call ya, Donald, an' I appreciate it."

All these thoughts replayed in his mind until he became conscious of the grey outlining the trees and mountains towards the east. The route into Applegate and over the pass on the Greenspring Highway on which they had arrived in their wagon twenty years before was familiar to them both, but wider and paved now.

The headlights searched out the curves as the road wound higher and higher in Northern California approaching the base of Mount Shasta. Patches of remaining snow illuminated bright for a passing instant when hit by the Chevy's lights. When the grade steepened, Farmer downshifted and could feel the vibration of the road and engine in the steering wheel. For an instant he was no longer holding the wheel but a set of reins urging Sunset, Wind and Dusty out in front of him up the grade - then he was back to 1945 in their automobile.

He glanced over at Emile. She had fallen asleep and looked angelic and peaceful as her head rocked to the motion of the car.

"Look, Emile, behind ya! The sun is crestin' the white top o' Mount Shasta an' is a sight ta see. This be the dawnin' o' the first day o' our travel, an' I reckon we'll go back a mite faster'n we travelled out here."

And they made good time. Farmer had told Emile in the darkness of early morning that they would "stop by light of day for breakfast if the eatin' places ain't too few an' far apart." To their surprise towns were numerous and cafés and gasoline stations plentiful. The highway dropped down into a river canyon and followed along the railroad. The couple stopped for a quick cup of coffee and breakfast in the downtown of a railway stop called Dunsmuir.

Farmer and Emile kept a steady pace until around ten o'clock when Farmer couldn't stay awake. Emile took over driving for awhile, and Farmer slept. They had left the mountains and forest stands behind and had driven out into flat farmland. When they got near Sacramento Emile pulled over.

"Farmer, wake up!" she took his arm. "We are near Sacramento, and there is too many cars. I get frightened!"

Highway 99 passed through the city near the State's Capitol building. Emile insisted they stop so she could take a picture with the new camera they had purchased from O'Malley's.

"Stand right there so the Capitol dome shows up behind you."

Cars and trucks blew their horns as they pressed by. Farmer grabbed for his hat.

"Emile, I reckon we ain't in Douglas Landing no more," Farmer teased.

But they were both too anxious to reach L.A. to spend much time sightseeing. They drove hard all afternoon passing through one town after another. They finally gave out in Bakersfield and found a hotel where they, as it would seem, died to the world.

Early next morning right after sunrise Farmer came waltzing into the hotel room where they were staying. The thud of the door woke Emile.

"Where have you been, Farmer?" Emile squinted at him.

"Found a phone and called Harold and Leah."

"Oh, Farmer, you called them - this early?! You had to wake them up! They will be wishing us away before we ever get there."

"No sense ta thet, Emile," Farmer laughed as he plunked down on the bed beside her. "I reckon they be right anxious fer us ta get there. They be stayin' outa church so's not ta miss us."

"But - it will take longer than that to - "

"Harold says we be three hours outa Los Angeles - so ifen ya don't dally, woman, we be there for lunchtime."

Farmer grabbed Emile's foot, pulling her from under the covers. She screamed, started kicking and hitting at him with the pillow. He burrowed under her barrage, coming up nose to nose with her. As quickly as the wrestling match had started - all struggle ceased. They kissed each other with a kiss deep and full of meaning. It expressed their mature love for one another, excitement to see their children and multitudes of memories of life!

Emile put her hand on Farmer's face; looking into his eyes she smiled a smile Farmer recognized as one meant just for him.

"We keep this up we will never get out of this hotel, Farmer Trevor - my man," she giggled.

Soon the pair was back on the road, eagerly absorbing anything they could look at.

"Harold gave me directions ta their place - I wrote it down."

"Oh, Farmer! I can hardly contain myself. I feel I will burst if we don't hurry! I'm so looking forward to seeing our little Janee."

Farmer's thoughts turned to their granddaughter. He tried to picture how she would look - how she would act.

"Wonder ifen she'll take ta us - ya know - right off?" Farmer queried.

"I'm sure she will, Farmer. We aren't exactly strangers to her. We have spoken on the phone; we have sent pictures back and forth this last year."

"Just wonderin', I reckon…"

Soon they were climbing a steep grade that wound up a canyon pass that had become known as the "Grapevine." The name was descriptive of a road twisted and turned like a vine. Harold had warned of this particular stretch of highway.

"Downshift into lower gears to keep your motor running faster, or you will overheat," he had advised, and Farmer now heeded that wise counsel. They passed car after car dead on the side of the road, hoods up, steam and heat rising from an engine underneath that could stand no more.

"Oh, these poor people!" Emile cried aloud as they passed stranded travellers standing beside their vehicles. "It reminds me of that family we helped with water on the desert. Do you remember them, Farmer?"

"Reckon I do, Emile."

For the next two hours the highway made its way through grass-covered hills of velvet green born from spring rains. The road dropped into little valleys and flat areas to climb again, but mostly Farmer could tell they were getting ever lower in elevation. But where was L.A.?

About the time they were wondering if they were on the wrong highway, they passed a marker - "Los Angeles 40 miles."

"Heck, Emile, we still be near an hour away," Farmer grumbled.

Suddenly, the canyon passage they had been driving in opened up to reveal scattered homes. As they drove on, the number of houses increased, and they got closer together. It dawned upon Farmer as they began seeing different names of cities that Los Angeles was comprised of many smaller communities and that L. A. was indeed spread out the forty miles.

The Los Angeles basin was lush with trees, bushes, flowers and grass. They could see construction everywhere; homes, businesses, new roads.

"I reckon people and cars be as thick as ants on a peanut butter an' jelly sandwich at a church picnic," Farmer laughed out loud.

"There's more than I can take in!" Emile gasped.

Farmer soon got his first taste of driving in Southern California. The rush of traffic would not allow him the luxury of Sunday driving - looking at the sights. The fast pace and blaring horns of impatient drivers rushed him along quicker than he cared to drive. Soon the beating of his heart matched the speed of the traffic, and he pulled over to check his directions to Harold and Leah's house. He sat there a moment settling down. He watched the people on the sidewalks and in the cars. Never had he been in a city that had the life and energy of this one. It was so strong he could feel it. He wanted to inhale it - chew on it - keep up with it!

The eager travelers got lost several times and had to inquire for help. Finally, they found the street that their children lived on.

The street was lined with tall palm trees, the tops fluttering slightly in a gentle breeze. The homes were different sizes, shapes and colors. All of the yards were neatly trimmed, splashes of bright-colored flowers bordered walls and porches.

Farmer noticed as they drove slowly down the street that Emile could not sit still. She was pointing and calling out house numbers.

"Here it is!" she screamed.

Before he was stopped and had the engine shut off, he could see his family pouring out of the house. Emile was out in a flash and into their arms.

Farmer had told himself he wouldn't cry, but the sight of Leah and Harold - and Walter was there - he couldn't hold back. He wiped his face as he joined the group. There was a mingling of sobs and laughter.

Leah turned to him. What a beautiful woman she had grown into. She so favored her mother.

"Oh, Daddy!" She hugged him, and Farmer held her tight and patted her back.

"I've missed you so," he heard her whisper. "Me too, Leah! Let me look at ya!"

"Pa, can't tell ya how good it is to see ya!"

Farmer let go of Leah to look into the face of his oldest son. He was a grown man and held himself with a confidence Farmer had never seen before. He was still the tall, lanky figure he had been the day he drove away from Douglas Landing - yet different.

Farmer grabbed his son's hand and pulled him into a bear hug.

"Been a long time, Pa!"

"Too long, Walter, but we be powerful glad ta see ya now!"

Harold, who had been standing to the side, finished greeting Emile, then held out his hand to Farmer. Farmer pulled him also into a hug.

"Harold, I hardly know ya, but reckon ta make up fer lost time - Son."

Farmer felt a shock go through Harold as he stiffened, then sorta collapsed against Farmer. The young man did not speak, but Farmer saw him hurriedly wipe his face.

Everyone was talking at once, laughing, hands and arms in wild motion to accent what was being said, when suddenly Emile and Farmer were aware of a little golden-haired girl standing quietly on the walk - taking in the scene before her.

Emile approached her and squatted down.

"I'm your Grandmother Emile."

"I'm Janee," she presented her hand as if to shake hands.

"I am so happy to meet you, Janee, but can I hold you?"

"Pleased to meet you," and she did a curtsey.

"But can I hold you?" Emile asked again and held out her arms.

"No!"

Then she eyed Farmer up and down - put her hands on her hips and spoke in a strong voice, "And who in God's green earth are you?"

From that moment on she had captured her Grandpa's heart.

Chapter 38

VACATION TREATS

The rest of that week was filled with fun and adventure. There was so much to see and do. Mountains rose high off the floor of the basin on one side, the Pacific water glistened to the west. It was on the beaches that Janee really warmed up to her grandparents. It soon became evident she loved Emile with a great love, but she adored her Grandpa Farmer. She tagged after him wherever he went. Janee was put out the morning Farmer went with Harold to his work to see some of the planes. She was furious when she woke up and discovered her daddy and grandpa were gone. They both fell under the fiery indignation of a three-year-old upon their return.

"Why couldn't I go?" she demanded through her tears, then ran to her bedroom plopping herself down on a little chair. She had her face buried in her hands when Farmer crept into the room. Soon the two of them were laughing and teasing - bantering each other back and forth jokingly.

That evening Harold and Leah took Janee to see the recently released Disney movie, "The 3 Caballeros." Farmer and Emile were invited to go along, of course. "This movie came out in February," Leah explained, "but we waited 'til you were here to see it."

Dinner reservations had been made for the group prior to the movie. Farmer was concerned about how Janee would act at an eating establishment, especially one this nice, as well as in the movie, as he remembered how loud, bold and active Leah was at three.

But Janee sat in her chair very ladylike. He was even more amazed when she gave her own order.

"I'll have a child size plate of steak with mu - er - mushed potatoes and green beans," she said politely.

"And to drink, Miss Janee," the waiter appeared to know her well.

"A glass of milk, please."

Emile silently clapped her hands. "Very good, Janee, I am so proud of you!"

His granddaughter was equally as well behaved in the movie, and Farmer found himself watching her from the corner of his eye. She became absorbed into the movie, taking her eyes from the big screen only briefly to look over at her folks or grandparents.

Farmer would see her frown, and then smile; many times she giggled and laughed out loud. She was talkative and wiggly on the drive home. She seemed to run out of steam all at once and fell asleep in Emile's arms.

Farmer was awake when he heard Harold leave out of the house the next morning before the sun came up. He went into the kitchen and poured a cup of coffee from the pot Harold left. He walked outside when it got light, but the sky was grey and the air damp.

Farmer drank the rest of the coffee and was making another pot when Leah came down the hallway from her bedroom.

"Mornin', Leah," Farmer spoke huskily. "Been some time since I been able ta greet ya like this."

Leah smiled and nodded.

"I reckon we be havin' rain today," he went on, looking out the window.

"Oh, no, Pa, this is overcast from the ocean. It'll burn away as the sun gets up. We have to go to work this morning. You and Ma must come!"

"Didn't know ya had a job," Farmer spoke with surprise.

"Not me - Janee! She's doing a movie part. You must see her!"

That morning, Farmer and Emile were thrust into the fascinating, strange and exciting world of the Hollywood movies. Farmer and Emile had never remotely dreamed they would ever be a part of a moving picture. They had never even entertained a thought of any involvement apart from going to a theatre. Yet here they were on a stage where one was being filmed, and their granddaughter was in it.

Leah introduced them to the director. She had already told him of her parents visit. He welcomed them warmly, then turning to his cast and crew, "Before we start shooting, let me have everybody's attention. Listen up!" the director shouted.

Everyone stopped and gave him their attention. The set grew still.

"We have two very special guests with us today. Janee Stemper's Grandfather Farmer and Grandmother Emile drove all the way from their home in Oregon. Make certain they are treated in the style fitting this studio. Now, let's get to work!"

Suddenly everyone came to life and the sound stage became a flurry of activity. Each person had a task to do and a place to be 'til the motion fell into some kind of organization. While this was happening a man approached Farmer and Emile as Leah took Janee off to a dressing and make-up room.

"I'm Edgar, the floor director," he spoke with polite promptness. "We have some chairs over here where you can see what is being shot. When you hear, 'Quiet on the set,' please don't speak or make any noise. The microphones can pick up even a cough or something that's dropped, even footsteps. When the director calls 'Cut,' then you can talk or move around. Janee is scheduled for the third scene this morning."

Leah joined them directly. Farmer watched with fascination as the filming began. During breaks, Leah introduced her parents to some of the actors and crew. They all seemed to find Farmer and Emile colorful and interesting people.

"Your Granddaughter Janee is very talented. She will go far in Hollywood," one of the main characters remarked prophetically.

"They are ready to do Janee's scene," Leah motioned them back to their seats.

"This is a movie about the war?" Emile asked.

"Yes, Mom, actually about when it ends. Janee has never seen her father, who has been a soldier overseas all this time. He comes home to surprise his family. Janee comes to the door. She asks, almost afraid that he is someone else - 'Are you my father?'"

"Oh, how sweet and sad!" Emile exclaimed.

"Quiet on the set!" came the command.

"Ready. Camera rolling."

"Action!"

A soldier makes his way through a small picket gate. He drops his duffle bag on the walkway and hesitates - then knocks on the screen door. A beautiful little girl, Janee, comes to the screen door, looks out and pushes it open. The soldier steps back to look at her. She places her hands on her hips and demands loudly, "And who in God's green earth are you?"

Leah gasped! The soldier seemed taken aback, but recovered quickly.

"Alice, I'm your father."

Then Janee, as though living the part cried out, "Oh, it is really you! I was scared you were just a stranger."

She held out her arms and wrapped them around the soldier's neck when he dropped to his knees to hold her. "I wished you home, Daddy!" you could hear her say.

"Alice? Who is it?" a voice could be heard from inside the house.

A long moment of silence, then, "Cut!"

Leah was furious!

"That wasn't how she was to do that scene," she fumed.

Farmer touched her arm to soothe his daughter, "I reckon she played the part as she felt it."

"She knows to follow direction!" Leah shook her head.

Everyone waited for the director's next order. They all expected a call for another take and instruction for Janee to do it the way she learned. The director sat thinking; then he stood up.

"Beautiful! He exclaimed. "Keep it." Everyone on the set clapped for Janee who did her little curtsey.

"So beautiful!" Emile spoke softly as they watched a brilliant golden sun dip into the blue water of the Pacific. Janee ran along the waters' edge in the sand with her dad. She wore Farmer out trying to keep up with her. He plunked down on a blanket next to Emile.

"I could never o' dreamed this sight up in my head," Farmer mused. "Ain't this somethin' ta behold."

"Perfect ending to a day at the studio. I'm glad the children brought us here," Emile added.

Walter, who had joined them at the beach, started a small bonfire. Finishing that task, he walked barefooted to Farmer and sat down beside him.

"Never did like shoes much, did ya, Son?"

"Naw, Pa, only if my feet was freezin'."

Emile got up to go help Leah. They began cooking over the beach fire.

"Ya be happy, Walter?" Farmer queried. "Seein' as how what ya dreamed of didn't work out."

"I think the path God has set me on is far better'n the one I dreamed up. He needed me here makin' the planes that would help in the war. Funny, some o' my planes have flown the Burma hump. Some made it, some didn't, but a part o' me was right there - fightin' too."

The firelight illuminated Harold and Leah's faces. Janee played in the sand nearby. Emile turned and smiled a smile at him that said, "I love you."

"But ya have no-one, Walter."

Walter knew the meaning of the words and dropped his head suddenly.

Farmer instantly wished he had not uttered them.

"Son, I reckon thet be none o' my business. Take what I said an' fling it out in the ocean!"

"I loved once... with a powerful love," Walter spoke carefully and his words were labored. "The hurt in my heart went as deep as the love I bore. Pa, I don't know if it's in me ta ever love like that again, or to be hurt...so much.

"Anyway, Pa, ya and Ma need ta be up early in the morning. I have a surprise!"

That night, after eating around the fire, Farmer walked alone along the sandy beach. The waves were not large, but he marveled at the power and force of the ocean. Each wave illuminated fluorescent in the starlight as it broke and crashed onto the shore. As he gazed out into the expanse of water and stars two thoughts crossed his mind.

Somewhere in all that water was an island and on that island was his son. Being with his other two children the last few days caused Farmer to realize how much he missed Clifton. His wish and longing to see his military son welled up in his heart and lifted into Heaven as a prayer.

Heaven... He looked into the sky, bright and twinkling with countless stars. How far away that mystical, wondrous place seemed. Farmer had been too busy living to think much of dying and Heaven. Right now, Farmer felt God had blessed him beyond measure.

True to his word, Walter pulled up at Harold and Leah's place before Farmer had his second cup of coffee.

"Gosh, Ma, ya gotta hurry!" Walter implored when Emile wandered out of the bedroom.

After a frantic scramble to get ready, Farmer and Emile were piled into Walter's car and driven across town.

"My lands, Son, you children have kept us going at a pretty fast pace!" Emile exclaimed as she gripped the door handle.

"We only got you an' Pa a few days an' gotta get the most outa our time," Walter laughed back.

Several miles through city streets brought them to a small airport. Walter stopped the car in a parking area by a hangar, and he got out.

"What are we doing?" Farmer asked, thinking they would tour the hangars and planes.

"Taken ya for a airplane ride," Walter tried to act nonchalant.

"Oh, Walter, I don't know," Emile pulled back.

"Come on, Ma, you'll love it!"

"Who's gonna be the pilot?" Farmer quizzed.

"Me!"

"What?" Emile looked shocked, and Farmer couldn't believe what he was hearing.

"Ya remember me telling ya all about this airline company in Alaska wantin' pilots and willin' ta school 'em. Well, I took them up on their offer an' so far have my pilot's license. As soon as I qualify for their larger plane, I'll be a headin' for Alaska."

"Alaska? Oh, Walter!" cried Emile.

Walter seemed not to hear his mother as he led them to a small private plane parked on the ramp beyond the hangar.

"Wouldn't reckon there ta be thet much travelin' in Alaska," Farmer was trying to understand what Walter was figuring to do.

"The airline has government contracts on the west coast to transport troops and families when the war ends. I'll be busy sure nuff."

"Oh, Walter, do you think the war will end soon? Do you?"

"'Course, Ma. We are breathin' down Hitler's back, and the Red Army is bangin' at his door."

Walter situated Emile in the back seat and set Farmer up front with him. He removed the wheel chocks, climbed in and started the engine. Farmer watched with admiration as Walter maneuvered the plane down a taxiway to the end of the runway. He faced into the wind, and the engine burst into life, speeding the plane along the smooth hard surface, the tires making a singing noise. Then it happened! The plane did a slight bounce, the tire noise ceased and the ground dropped away beneath them as they rose past the end of the runway, up, up, over rooftops!

Farmer heard a faint cry from Emile, and looked back over the seat at his wife. She was pale, her face scrunched up, and she had a firm grip on the armrest.

"Ya alright, Emile?"

"Ma, you'll be fine," Walter laughed before Emile could answer Farmer. "Look there! The beach where we were last night."

The whole western horizon was ocean. Water stretched before them as far as they could see except for some islands.

"That's Santa Catalina Island," Walter pointed out, "and ta the north is the Channel Islands."

Walter turned the plane inland from the beach.

"Los Angeles sure is growin'" he went on. "It's all these small towns that are growing together to make one gigantic city. There used to be lots o' orange groves - see! There's some down there! But they are givin' way to land buyers to build more homes - more highways."

Farmer watched houses and lands pass underneath as the plane gained altitude to fly over the San Bernardino Mountains. Soon Farmer could make out rugged canyons filled with brush and rich forest at higher elevations. A glint of sun reflecting off water gave away the presence of a lake. In a few minutes Farmer caught sight of not one, but several small lakes.

Walter turned the plane east and came over a long desert-like valley.

"See that ribbon running along there?" Walter pointed out.

Farmer could see a line that wiggled along the floor of the valley and dots moving on it he could make out as automobiles.

"Yes," he answered.

"That's the highway that goes to Texas."

"We'll be on that?" Emile exclaimed from the back.

"Shore nuff, Ma."

Farmer became lost in his thoughts as the plane slid smoothly across the sky. He absent-mindedly watched out the window not really seeing. He thought of many things past. He thought of how the children made his and Emile's visit such a wonderful time, filled with special treats. He hated to see it end; an ache filled his heart. Then his thoughts turned towards the long drive that lay before them, and he began to feel that stir of excitement, the urge to be back on the road. He came back to the present when Walter began their descent.

"Ya be doin' what ya always dreamed o' doin', ain't ya, Walter?"

Chapter 39

THE MOTHER ROAD

The highway weaved its way up the rocky Cajon Pass and eventually leveled out into the high desert above. The travelers passed through the towns of Victorville, Oro Grande, Helendale, Hodge and Lenwood. An hour beyond to the east lie Barstow where Farmer and Emile stopped to gas up the car and eat a bite of lunch. One would have thought the couple would be jovial, excited to be on their way, but their meal was eaten mostly in silence. The sadness of leaving loved ones made conversation difficult.

The road now went straight into the desert lined on both sides by rugged mountains. It cut a straight line across the desert floor until it disappeared in the distance, obscured by waves of heat rising from the parched land. It was still early in the year, but already hot. Farmer could feel the sting in his throat and nose that he remembered well from desert travel twenty years before.

Emile grew tired, fluffed a pillow to lay her head on, and was soon sleeping - leaving Farmer to his thoughts. How many times had he already rehearsed the events of the last two days over in his mind?

On Thursday, Farmer began to notice a brooding sadness creeping over everyone as they realized the next day there would be a parting. Everybody avoided any discussion of Farmer and Emile driving away the next morning. Only Janee seemed untouched by the grey sadness that suddenly settled on the family. There clearly was no festive spirit any longer, so when Walter arrived they ate quietly around the large radio Harold and Leah had in their living room.

Late that night Farmer and Emile said tearful farewells to Walter as he needed to be up early for work the next morning.

"Sure ya can't stay an extra week 'til Friday the 13th?" Walter teased, half laughing, half crying after he hugged his mother. "Just ta prove it ain't unlucky."

"Reckon the Lord ta care fer us all," Farmer's voice broke as he hugged his son.

The next morning was not any easier. Farmer was up early to tell Harold goodbye. The womenfolk were still asleep. Farmer gripped Harold's arms before he reached the door.

"Harold, I reckon ya made me rethink everthing I ever thought 'bout ya. I know I can't replace the Pa ya lost, but Son, I'll do the best I can."

Harold looked straight into Farmer's eyes. Farmer saw a different person from the one he first met at the airfield in Douglas Landing and knew God had done a work in this young man.

"Thank you - Dad," Harold spoke in his quiet manner, but the message of his heart rang loud and clear. The two men gave a parting handshake, and then Farmer grabbed the back of Harold's neck to pull his head against his chest where he held him firmly for a moment. Words could not convey what was said in that gesture. Farmer felt Harold's body shake and both men wept.

The parting with Leah was even harder. She clung to Emile a long time. Both tried to reassure each other that they would see one another again soon - but seemed to sense - there was no promise.

"We sure had us a time, Daddy," Leah smiled through her tears.

"We surely did. We surely did," Farmer whispered as he remembered.

Then he thought of Janee. Five days with her had made precious memories, never to be lost. The night before, she observed the goodbyes with her Uncle Walter without showing any emotion or concern. Now as Emile and Farmer held out their arms to her, she held out her hand.

"Oh, Janee, can't you give your grandmother and grandfather a hug and kiss goodbye?" Leah implored.

Again Janee stuck out her hand - this time more firmly. Finally, Emile and Farmer shook her little hand.

"Pleased to have met you," her child's voice conveyed refinement and politeness.

They waved to Leah and Janee who were standing now inside their yard. Farmer helped Emile into the car and closed the door. Suddenly, Janee broke into a run to him wrapping her arms around his leg.

"Please don't go! Please don't go, Papa!" she cried.

In a flash, Emile was out of the car holding and kissing Janee. For an instant it was like Leah at that age all over again.

"We have missed so much of your life," he heard Emile say.

Farmer could still see Leah, holding Janee as they drove away. Each mile drug under the car, and he felt that they were leaving a part of themselves back there. When they passed over the Arroyo Seco Bridge in Pasadena, a wide chasm lay between them and their loved ones. An ache and pain filled his heart with a bittersweet feeling he feared was more than he could bare. He knew Emile felt it too!

The highway rolled under the steady hum of the tires. His thoughts turned to the second phase of the trip they had embarked on. Flagstaff, Arizona would mark the spot where they would start retracing the route they had traveled in the chuck wagon twenty years ago. How much had changed? Would they recognize places? Excitement began to stir, and the ache he had felt before gave way to thoughts of adventure. He knew the ache would always be there, to return ever stronger in dimension when precious memories of this trip were rekindled. It would return with every letter, phone call or picture they looked at. But for now there was family to see in Texas!

Mile after mile of desert approached, sweeping past. The view out of the windshield reversed into the rearview mirror. The open windows no longer offered relief from the rising temperature. Farmer looked over at Emile who was sleeping. Beads of sweat dotted her face. Farmer felt impish.

"Emile, ya be missin' out on all the beautiful scenery," Farmer tugged at her leg.

"Nothing but sand and brush," she muttered.

"Ya gonna sleep all day an' keep me up all night," Farmer pulled her arm.

"You can sleep peaceful in the car; I'll stay in the room," she smiled but never opened her eyes.

Farmer turned the heater on. It took Emile about two minutes to come up for air.

"You are a terrible man, Mr. Trevor!" she exclaimed, hitting his arm. "You are mean."

Farmer laughed as he turned the heat control off.

"We be comin' ta a place called Amboy. How 'bout we get somethin' cold ta drink?"

"Oh, please," she blotted her face.

At Amboy, they were told the most grueling part of the desert was ahead all the way to the Arizona border.

"In the summertime most folks don't drive during the day - only at night," the attendant told Farmer as he filled the gas tank. "However, it's still early in the year. You shouldn't have no trouble, but I would advise you getting a couple of canvas bags full of water. Hang 'em on your bumper."

Emile came from inside where she had used the restroom and purchased cold soft drinks.

"Thet fella tol' me thet the worse part o' the desert be ahead o' us, but this time o' year it ain't so hot," Farmer remarked as they pulled out onto the highway.

"Oh, Farmer, remember how dreadful the heat was when we traveled in the wagon? There were times I thought I was going to die!"

"He also tol' me thet ifen we drive steady we could make Oatman, Arizona tonight."

The rest of the afternoon was spent in conversation to pass the time. Words that seemed locked up in thought in the morning now flowed freely. They were glad to drop down into the Colorado River Basin and cross the steel span bridge because it meant the horrible Mojave was behind them, and they were in Arizona and that much closer to their destination.

The sun had set behind them, and darkness fallen when they reached Oatman. They were surprised to see a herd of burros wandering down the highway in the middle of town. The Oatman Hotel had room accommodations for the weary travelers.

"Remember the actor who starred in 'Gone With The Wind,' Clark Gable? Well he and his new bride, Carole Lombard, stayed upstairs in one of our rooms on their honeymoon night," the man behind the big wooden counter smiled.

"Reckon we'll take thet room," Farmer drawled. Emile giggled.

"Haven't had no one stay in that room since 1939 - the night they stayed in it. Some say it's haunted now."

Farmer and Emile were too tired to care whether Clark and Carole were hanging around. They didn't much believe in ghosts.

The sun greeted them the next morning as they climbed the steep and treacherous grade up to the summit of Sitgreaves Pass.

"Any ghosts scare ya last night?" Farmer asked dryly.

"No, but this road is scaring me. Sharp curves and cliff drop offs - I'm holding on so tight my arms and hands ache!"

A sign on the side of the road announcing an upcoming filling station caught Farmer's eye. The sign read:

"Tow your car to the top."

Farmer pulled into the station.

"You aren't going to...?" Emile was wide-eyed.

"Naw!" Farmer answered before Emile could finish. "Reckon both us and the Chevy could do fer a rest."

They stretched and walked around a bit. While Emile went inside the small gas station, Farmer struck up a conversation with the tow truck driver.

"Mighty steep grade," Farmer remarked.

"Yes, but the worst part is down the other side."

"Thet be hard ta imagine! I think my wife left finger marks on the dash an' door."

The man laughed, then continued, "That's why I tow or drive some travelers over the top. There were families that lost their lives coming during the Depression. They lost their wits and their control and plunged over the side. When you go down, look into the canyon an' you'll see car and pickup remains."

"Can I drive it?" Farmer asked.

"Sure. Ain't that hard. Pump your brakes - don't hold them down steady, or they'll get hot, and you'll lose 'em - and that would be bad. If you do, use your emergency brake to get stopped, and let your brakes cool."

Farmer didn't share the conversation with Emile for she was nervous enough, but he thanked God for the information he'd been given.

The descent down into Kingman became so dangerous that Emile had to cover her eyes.

"Oh, Farmer, do be careful," she cried out on many of the hairpin curves.

"Not the Lord's time fer us, Emile!" Farmer tried to ease the tension with humor, but he clearly was having a difficult time. Even as he joked he could see rusty skeletons of cars down the side of the mountain. Both were relieved to finally reach Kingman.

That afternoon they made the trip off of Route 66 to see the Grand Canyon. Twenty years before, they had not traveled that far, but had vowed to do so when they came back. They stood in awe of the enormity of the chasm, which the Colorado River had cut into the earth.

"I think God must have helped the river do its carving, then He splashed the finished work with sun and shadow," Emile murmured.

Night was upon the two when they passed through Flagstaff and stopped in Winona. They found the grove of trees and the remains of the cabin they stayed in twenty years before. New business buildings and homes had grown up in its place. As they gazed at a few scraps of lumber collapsed on a foundation illuminated by the headlights of their car, they both remembered what had taken place there - how sick Emile was, and the good doctor from Pasadena who helped them.

They found lodging that night in Winona and were on their way again early the next morning.

The entire route was paved, like a black ribbon laid out across the country. Travel was increasing as the war was nearing its end. License plates from different states could be seen in passing. Farmer and Emile made a game of it. Farmer checked the plates of cars passing them from behind, and Emile did the cars coming at them from the east. The farther away from the cars home, the more commotion

Farmer and Emile raised, like when a car with New York or South Carolina passed. They spotted cars from Indiana, Mississippi, Iowa, Oklahoma, Arkansas, and they hollered when a Texas one passed.

Some folks were friendly and waved from their open windows. Traveling on this highway became an experience.

Not only was the road fully paved, but also the towns along its path had flourished. Most all had grown; only a few had not.

The same sinister feelings of a boding death came on them as they drove through Two Guns. This town had not experienced growth enjoyed by others along the route.

Farmer and Emile tried to find things they remembered, but since there was so much change, they were confined more to landmarks and the landscape.

Establishments where travelers could eat and sleep appeared countless along the road. Service stations were in ample supply. Many tourist curio shops were in business, many others were being built, population was exploding and jobs seemed plentiful. It was like all of it drew life from the highway that crossed a large part of the nation.

With each mile memories came back. They got excited when they drove through a town and discovered a café or shop that they recognized from their first trip.

The new route no longer went through Santa Fe, but struck a more direct path from Albuquerque to Santa Rosa. The travelers were amazed when they drove into Tucumcari at how much the town had spread out along both sides of the highway. They drove the length from one end to the other of Tucumcari to take it all in.

"You saw this growth - this nation on the move long ago, didn't you, Farmer?" Emile spoke with admiration.

"I reckon I could see it in my spirit even when I was a lad. I knew it was comin' - and by golly, Emile, we was a part o' it."

"Oh, look, Farmer! The cabins we all stayed in is still here! We must stay here!" Emile squealed, pointing out the window and clapping.

"Yer right. Those be the same, 'cept they done some redoin' over the years."

That night as they lay in bed they recalled a hundred experiences from their travels in a chuck wagon. Spending the night in the same cabin brought memories and visions of their boys and people they met in Tucumcari so many years ago.

"Tomorrow, we be home ta Holt by evening, Emile."

"I can't wait," Emile purred as she snuggled her head against his chest.

Sleep did not come readily to Farmer. His thoughts drifted back to Southern California and his family. An incident that happened the morning before they left came back to mind. He had not paid much attention to it at the time, but now it held more significance.

Leah had driven them to the beach in Santa Monica. She parked the car in a space on the road that ran along the beach. She pointed to a highway that dead-ended at the beach.

"A road was made that started in Chicago, and right here is where it ends. It is numbered as Route 66. You and Mom traveled it in its infancy - now you will travel a road that's been finished. It's called 'The Mother Road.'"

Chapter 40

FAMILY REUNION

The drive into Holt was like going back in time. The main street was paved, but the road out of town for miles was still graveled. A modest filling station and small restaurant stood out in sharp contrast from the rest of the unchanged town. Hatchet's Mercantile was dark and boarded up, the faded sign barely readable.

Farmer and Emile had argued over which family to see first. Farmer insisted they see Emile's people before his.

"It's been longer since you've seen your mother and brothers!" she retorted loudly.

"Reckon I'm gonna be boss over this one," Farmer tried to keep from laughing, but straightened up fast when Emile came right back at him.

"Don't give me the stuff about, 'Wives submit to your husbands,' Farmer Trevor. If you pull up in front of my parents' house, I'll - I'll lock the door. I'll sleep in the car, I will!" She turned her head away from Farmer, looking out the door window. He couldn't tell whether she was teasing or serious.

Finally, they reached an agreement on the plains of Texas, west of Amarillo. Farmer won out that they would spend that night at the Holts and drive out to the Trevor's and surprise them the next morning.

"Can't believe it took us the better part o' travel from Tucumcari ta Amarillo ta figure this out - ifen ya jus' woulda listened - "

"Hush!" Emile snapped at him.

The morning the Trevor's left Holt in the chuck wagon, the sun was rising to their backs. This time the sun was setting behind them as they drove into the rural town. They could not have known the prophetic symbolism of those two moments.

Farmer stopped the car in front of the Holt's house. It appeared dark.

"Oh, dear," exclaimed Emile. They both approached the front door, and she knocked. Waited. Knocked harder. They were about to return to the car, figuring no one was home, when the door opened to reveal a silver-haired man leaning on a cane. He had lost so much weight, his clothes hung loosely on his limbs. He spoke with the familiar attorney-bred bite Farmer remembered so well. No doubting, this was Hirum Holt.

"Well, now, just look at you, daughter, coming home after all these years! If I'd known you was taking so long, I'd never have let you go." Hirum broke into his deep, growling laugh that switched to coughing.

"Come in; come in," he motioned them through the door. Emile hugged him with the reserve and respect she had learned when she lived at home.

"Emile, I'm too old to worry about formality. You can do better than that. I want a real hug from my daughter!" Hirum grumbled.

Emile let out a sob and hugged her father tightly, kissing him on the cheek. "I've missed you so," she whispered.

"Farmer, my boy, get in here!" the old man waved him into the house.

"Your mother and sister just went to the food store to get a few items they are needing. They will be most upset, missing your arrival and all," Hirum continued.

"Oh, Susan's here?" Emile asked, overjoyed.

"Been here four days, afraid she would miss a minute with you. Between your sister and mother, I was understandingly concerned they would wear through the floor, walking to the window to look out - pacing the floor - looking every five minutes out the window. I believe they wore out the glass as well!"

"Oh, Father, you exaggerate!" Emile laughed.

A commotion could be heard outside. The door flew open, and the room was filled with squeals and laughter. There was a flurry of hugs and kisses! In the midst of it, Hirum caught Farmer's eye.

"Ever see the likes of it?" he winked and smiled.

Farmer braced himself for the affection that would come to him in a moment. It did! Susan held him a long time; she was crying.

"We are so proud to have you here! I've been beside myself wishing the time to hurry so you all would get here. And here you are!" She stepped back.

"Let me look at you and Emile," she eyed them. "My, you both are still so young."

"Ha!" Emile laughed.

Vivian gave Farmer an affectionate hug.

"Welcome," she said, and her voice conveyed a love and acceptance she would have for her own son.

"We saw your car drive through town," Susan gasped, still trying to catch her breath from all the excitement. "We ran all the way to the house!"

"Lands, yes!" Vivian agreed.

"Is Andrew here?" Emile asked.

"No, he had a court hearing today. He hopes to wind it up by tomorrow. He will be here by Thursday, he thinks," Susan replied.

The women never slowed down in their talking the rest of the evening. There was so much to catch up on. Hirum and Vivian wanted to know all about the grandchildren, and that topic dominated the conversation around the dinner table.

"What have you heard from Clifton? Tell us about your visit with Walter and Leah. We want to know all about Janee. How's Harold?"

Emile, first thing dug out pictures she had brought.

While the women were in the kitchen, Hirum sat down by the fireplace in the living room and motioned for Farmer to join him.

"I'm pleased at the accomplishments of the grand-children. You say Walter is a pilot?" he began in his gruff voice.

"He will be flying a passenger plane fer an Alaskan outfit when he finishes all his schooling."

"Always wanted to see Alaska," the old man said thoughtfully.

"And Clifton, he works on airplanes - like Harold?"

"Yes."

"One spent the war at home and the other in the Pacific..." Again Hirum spoke thoughtfully. "When will Clifton come home - the end of the war?"

"He wrote thet there's talk o' shippin' back ta the states soon."

"War with Germany is nearing its last gasp," Hirum growled, "but Japan will hold on longer. That Janee in the movies is hard to believe. Susan and Andrew went to a picture show in Dallas to see the western pioneer movie she starred in. Said her name was at the end."

"Leah tol' us it was a small part, I reckon not a star - yet."

"She is a star to me," old man Holt spoke gruffly - his eyes blazed along with the fire that was crackling in the rock fireplace. Both men sat in silence for some time, lost in thought, staring at the jumping flames.

Hirum ended the silence.

"How's your ranch? Have you been out there lately?"

Farmer dropped his head. He could feel his face flush hot.

"Haven't hed the heart or the stomach to go back, the losin' of it was most painful, tol' myself I'd not step foot on the place 'til I could buy it anew."

"I truly did like it out there. I found it to be one of those rare places I could be at peace. I did grieve with you when you lost it."

They spoke of the terrible Depression, and the dreadful war. After Hirum fell asleep in his chair and awoke with a start, he excused himself and walked slowly with his cane back into the rear of the house. Farmer made his way into the guest bedroom where he had deposited their luggage. He undressed and climbed into bed, but sleep did not come. His mind was full of memories triggered by the evening's conversations. Then there was the anticipation of again being with his family that made sleep evasive.

He was conscious of the women talking long into the night. He could make out much of what was being said.

He heard Vivian tell Emile, "Farmer's mother has had such a rough time. She is so anxious to see you all!"

Then he heard her continue with, "Does he know about William?" but voices got low, and he couldn't make out the rest.

After Vivian tired out and said her goodnights, Farmer heard some conversation between Emile and Susan.

Susan said, "I so love and miss your children. All these years I have envied your having them."

"All these years - you've never had children," Emile replied gently, undoubtedly touching a very tender spot, as nothing was said for a long time.

"We can't have any children." Farmer could barely hear Susan. "We tried - tried so hard - God knows how we tried - we wanted - "

Farmer did not hear anymore, nor could he see the scene unfolding in the other room, but he knew Emile and knew she was ministering to her heart-broken sister.

"I declare!" Farmer bellowed out as they neared the farmhouse where he had been born and raised. "Ain't nothin' changed here 'bouts in twenty years 'cept they got tractors in the fields 'stead o' horses. Why, the roads still be dirt and rutty as ever!"

Emile laughed. "Well, Farmer, that may be so, but aren't you glad to be back?"

"Of course, but I reckon it sure nuff makes me glad we left!" They both laughed, happy to see the old Trevor farmhouse come into view. Before they got up close, someone walked out onto the porch. Farmer recognized William. He walked stiff on one leg and hobbled down the porch steps to the ground. Suddenly Farmer made out that where a left arm had been was a stump.

"Oh, dear God!" Emile caught her breath. "William is crippled! Mother told me last night that he was wounded in the war, but said nothing of this."

Farmer looked at his brother, the old familiar house, then his mother appeared in the door. Twenty years of dammed up emotion flooded over him like a giant wave. He slid the car to a halt, jumped out, and stumbled, half blinded, into William. Farmer grabbed his brother and pulled him close. An instant later his mother Allison was there, and he swooped her into the hug. He blubbered, not knowing exactly what he was saying. He only was aware of a great joy and happiness that filled his heart. Any composure he might have had stayed in the car.

Farmer was shocked at how old and frail his mother looked. Long hard Depression days followed by the war had taken a toll and left its heavy mark on her.

Allison went to Emile and greeted her warmly and lovingly. "We must call Jacob and Dorothy right away," she spoke through her tears.

"Ya mean ya got a telephone?" Farmer quipped.

"Got us a tractor and truck too!" William laughed, teasing. "See, we ain't as backward as ya think, Farmer!"

Farmer laughed, and then grew serious.

"I didn't know ya lost an arm, William."

"Heck! Lost me a leg too," he hiked up one pants leg to reveal a portion of an artificial limb.

"Why didn't ya tell me?"

"'Twas done. No sense cryin' 'bout it. Still got one good arm and leg. I can 'bout run on this thing. Bet I can out-race ya, brother."

Farmer didn't acknowledge William's joke, but went on, "How'd it happen?"

"Got in a fight with a round from a tank an' I lost." William looked at Emile. "Emile, didn't ya teach my dang brother nothing atall?

Emile snickered, "I can't handle him!"

"Stop all this depressin' talk," Allison scolded. "You all come on inside! I've got coffee on."

Later that day, Jacob and Dorothy came over. They all went over to the house where Farmer and Emile had started their marriage. Jacob and Dorothy were pleased with how they had fixed up their home and anxious to show every room. When Farmer looked in their old bedroom, thoughts of times he and Emile made love there flashed across his mind. He caught Emile's eye and smiled, but he wasn't sure she understood what he wanted to say. Then there was the other bedroom, and images of two young boys being tucked in for numberless nights. It wasn't memories of the house that filled his mind, but of the family who once loved and lived there, and the incidents that happened to them. Anyhow, it was all very different now. It belonged to Jacob and Dorothy.

When school let out Jacob and Dorothy's boy, Sidney Dean came in. He was almost 18, in the last year of high school, had his own car and was definitely independent!

He was a jovial lad and a kidder. Though a plain looking young man, he seemed to have a keen mind, eager to learn. He reminded Farmer somewhat of himself when he was young.

Sidney was anxious to enter into discussions with the men and had hundreds of questions for Farmer as they sat around the table.

Allison and Dorothy had been saving for a huge home cooked meal when Farmer and Emile got in. Emile helped finish the cooking, and the family ate at Dorothy and Jacob's house. Supper had just begun when a knock on the door was barely heard above the chatter and the laughter. Dorothy answered the door and let a woman in. William got up to greet her, and they kissed.

"This here is Phyllis Doyle," William introduced the woman to Farmer and Emile.

"Oh!" exclaimed Emile, "We went to school together. You were in first grade when I graduated. I know you! You were just a little girl."

"I don't clearly remember you," the woman spoke slowly as if trying to recall.

"Phyllis and me have been datin'," William beamed with pride. He went to retrieve an extra chair.

Phyllis was not attractive, as some would count attractiveness, yet she shyly flashed a beautiful smile as she made quick eye contact with everyone seated at the table. "She can't be half bad," Farmer thought, "she bein' willin' ta love and stick with a man all crippled up from the war!"

"Well, little brother, I reckon ya be fulla surprises today," Farmer spoke with his Texas drawl, after Phyllis and William were seated at the table.

"Wouldn't be no surprise, big brother, if you hadn't moved so clean far away to Oregon," William spoke good-naturedly.

Everyone laughed and then grew quiet, as William, without realizing it, had struck a tender cord. Farmer could see that Emile was deep in thought when his mother raised her hand to speak. He remembered her doing that familiar gesture back when he was a youngster.

"Let me - " Allison cleared her throat. "Let me have your attention. Her voice cracked and quivered, full of emotion. She turned her head, waved everyone off, wiped her eyes and started again.

"When your Pa was alive and something wonderful was happening or had already done so, he would say - "Let's tell 'bout it!"

"I remember that!" Jacob exclaimed. Farmer, too, recalled those times around the table. Some of the few pleasant memories he had from early home life!

"An' this has been a most wonderful - having Farmer and Emile back with us - after so..." Allison couldn't go on.

"Hear - hear -!" William banged his fist on the table making the women jump.

"Ma said tell 'bout it," Dorothy snapped with a flash of her eyes, "not beat it up!"

Everyone laughed except Emile. She slowly raised her hand to speak, and the attention turned on her.

"When I was a little girl, I met a little boy with a restless nature named Farmer Trevor. I loved him, and when we grew up, I gave him my heart." Emile gave Farmer a smile and look that spoke volumes.

"I knew he had this wild and crazy dream to fly away to the west and have a cattle ranch. The day came when that dream came true, and I have never for one instant believed that was the wrong thing for us to do. But who could have foreseen the years of a dark and dreadful Depression and the terrible war coming right in on its tail. Times so troubling to make travel impossible - times that prevented my mom and dad from making further trips to Oregon - you folks from any at all - us from seeing you - 'til now.

"Who could have seen the years pass by that would rob you, Allison - Ma, from watching your grandchildren grow into men, or being there when Leah was born, or even layin' eyes on your great grandchild, precious Janee.

"And you, Dorothy - Jacob, we didn't get news of your wedding 'til you were already married. And we missed out on eighteen years of your Sidney Dean living and growing. And you, William, we should have been here to welcome you home from the war, to be proud for you and to thank you. All this isn't anyone's fault - who could have known? Just sad, and I'm sorry for it…"

The group sat stunned and moved. Jacob broke the quietness.

"Heck, Emile, now you got us all a bawlin' like a bunch o' wet-nosed kids!"

Everyone broke out in laughter, except for Farmer, who now raised his hand to speak.

"My wife be powerful amazin'," he spoke with great respect for Emile. "She put inta words what a lot o' folks be thinkin', but our circle here tonight is not complete. I be a missin' our sister Stella."

Everyone dropped their heads.

"Where is she? Is she well?"

No one answered.

"She's not been mentioned one time since we first walked in Ma's house - nor here. I see no pictures o' her on the wall. Be she alive or dead?"

Allison broke down and wept!

Farmer looked at Jacob for answers. He could not understand any reason for secretiveness.

Jacob's face was pained. He looked off into the distance. Everyone shuffled around nervously.

"What?" Farmer questioned. "This is tell about it! I'm her brother! Why can't ya tell me?"

"'Cause it's painful!" Jacob shot back. "She ran away when she was nigh unto fifteen, and caused a heap o' trouble. She fought Pa like a caged animal. We would hear tell o' things she was doin' in Dallas. Ma thinks Stella was the death o' Pa - that an' ya -."

"Stop it Jacob!" Allison would hear no more.

The conversations went to lighter topics. After dinner was cleared, the men engaged in a lively game of Dominoes around the table. The women took part for a short time, but they had far too much to talk over, so they retired into the living room.

After the women left, Jacob and William disclosed some information about Stella. It was four years since they had heard from her. The last letters were returned unclaimed. They thought she was still in Dallas. Later Farmer excused himself and made a long distance call to his brother-in-law, Andrew Neilson.

The next few days were filled with laughter, fun and visits - mostly with family. Many people who Farmer and Emile had known either had passed away or moved during the Depression. Farmer felt a sense of sorrow and loss every time he passed the old Hatchet's building. He could picture her inside the store. He missed this woman who had been a longtime friend, one who influenced his life.

Farmer and Emile stayed at the Holts and shuttled back and forth from their home out to Farmer's Ma's farm. Farmer even came over and helped Jacob and William plow one of their fields. Andrew arrived from Dallas on Wednesday.

"I found where she lives!" Andrew added in a low voice when they greeted each other. He slipped a piece of paper with Stella's address into Farmer's hand.

Thursday turned dreary and grey.

"A northerner is blowin' in," Farmer's Ma remarked as she pulled a curtain aside to look out the window. "Been so special havin' you here, Farmer. I'm feelin' the sadness settin' in and dreadin' your leavin'. And you picked Friday, the 13th to go. I pray no evil befalls you." She turned to give Farmer a kiss and a hug.

To make matters worse, Hirum Holt announced later that night when Farmer and Emile came in that President Roosevelt had died that afternoon in Georgia. They all stayed up late listening to broadcasts and talking. Phone calls came into the Holts' - even Leah calling to ask if they had heard the tragic news.

Farmer and Emile drove away from Holt, Texas in the rain, April 13, Friday, 1945. They made Dallas in three hours, and after getting lost several times and seeking directions, they pulled up in front of a small rundown house on the outskirts of the city. They both went to the door, and Farmer knocked with trembling hand. There was no sound from inside, and Farmer knocked several times. Finally, the door cracked slightly. Farmer could not make out who was on the other side.

"Stella?"

A pause.

"Farmer? Is that really you? Oh, Gawd, it is you!" The door opened, and Farmer and Emile entered into a dark room. Farmer could not see his sister's face. She turned away. The smell of booze and rank stale cigarette smoke mixed with body odor was so stifling Farmer could hardly breathe. Emile had her hand over her mouth and nose.

"Aw, nooo - nooo - aw nooo, oh, Gawd, Farmer, I don't want you to see me like this," Stella muttered; it was obvious she was half drunk. She stumbled around the room, making feeble attempts to pick up.

"Maybe if we let some light in and open a window," Emile suggested, stepping towards a near window.

"No!" shrieked Stella. "No," she toned down. "No light - no air." She came closer to Farmer to see his face. He could smell liquor as she breathed on him.

"Well, well, well, if it - isn't brother Farmer an' - an' sister Emile. You come all this - this way - just to - preach - to me - about my sins."

"No, jus' wanted ta see ya, Stella," Farmer answered.

"Then let's - celebrate!" Stella laughed. "Have a drink with me."

Farmer didn't answer, and Stella waited for his reply.

"It's been a long time, Stella. Jus' came ta visit ya."

"You didn't have to move away. You coulda stayed, but nooo - you were too high and mighty. You always thought you were better'n other folks."

"Pa an' Ma never raised us like this," Farmer retorted.

"Don't talk to me - 'bout - Pa - Ma!" Stella exploded. "Ma was a spineless weakling - 'Yes, Pa! No, Pa! Do what your Pa says!' An' - Pa... He was a cruel tyrant - bad as Hitler, and may his soul burn in hell, the hypocrite!"

"Don't say that!" Emile implored.

"Why not? It's true! He ran you off, same as me. I'm glad he's dead."

"Stop it, Stella!" Farmer raised his hand but Emile grabbed him.

"Don't!" she said sadly.

"I thought ya had the Lord in yer heart?" Farmer questioned.

Stella laughed loudly, dramatically, in their faces until the laugh degenerated into a hoarse hacking cough.

"What's He ever done for us? You went your way, and I went mine. I'll surely be in Heaven 'cause I've already lived in hell."

"Ya don't have ta keep on this way. It can change - ya can change!" Farmer pleaded. "The Good Book says hell is fer those who reject Christ."

Again Stella laughed that long mocking hoarse laugh. This time she stepped more into the light where Farmer could make out her features. Stella was thin - her face splotchy red and drawn. Her hair was ragged, her body and clothes were dirty. Years of drinking, smoking, men, and Farmer could only guess what else had robbed her of her youth and beauty. It was hard for him to find anything of the sister he once knew.

"Well, old brother, Farmer," her words were slurred and sarcastic, "if you believe all that rot then this is what I have to say - to say. I'll have one big reunion in hell, and we'll be - having us - having one hell of a party."

"Won't be no reunion or party there," Farmer remarked with heavy heart.

Little did he know how prophetic his words to his sister were, or that they would be the last ones he spoke to her in this life.

Chapter 41

DIFFERENT PATHS

The next six years brought many changes. Most were welcomed - some left mixed feelings - a few were painful. Such seems life!

Shortly after their return from Texas, news came of the surrender of Germany and the end of the war in Europe. August 7, 1945, the radio was filled with word of a super bomb that had been dropped on Japan. By August 14th our enemy in the Pacific gave up, and the world was again at peace.

It was early in 1946, when Clifton surprised them with an unannounced homecoming. He promptly proposed to Rachel Baltman, and they were pronounced husband and wife during a small but beautiful wedding at the Church in the Woods. The church's new pastor performed the ceremony.

"My first wedding here!" he beamed happily.

"Don't get yourself in a sweat, preacher," Donald Parrigan slapped him on the back. "Small as we are could be your last."

Later that same year, Alaska voted for statehood. Walter, Clifton and Rachel were there for that vote, even though Alaska would not be admitted into the Union until 1958. It seemed that Walter and Clifton had inherited some of their Pa's restless spirit and ability to foresee potential in a newly developing pioneer region.

Walter, using his pilot's clout with a fledgling airline in Anchorage, obtained a good position for Clifton. The newly married couple packed their bags, boarded a bus to Seattle, where they took a flight to their new home.

Walter was having the time of his life, and Clifton tagged along. The war over, the airlines began buying up government surplus planes. Walter was amazed and thrilled that three of the planes were ones he had worked on in California. The airline was chartered to transport certain Jews to Israel, flights from New York to Germany, and returning war brides to the States where they could be with their husbands. Soon the airline had become the largest non-scheduled airline in the world, and Walter and Clifton were in the thick of it. Walter flew the planes, and Clifton kept them in the air!

The phone jarred Farmer and Emile out of a sound sleep in March of 1947. When Farmer finally got to the telephone, he heard Clifton's excited voice on the other end.

"Pa, we had a baby boy! Thought he would be born on Janee's birthday, but he waited 'til after midnight."

"Rachel an' Clifton have a little boy!" Farmer called to Emile. She joined him at the phone.

"Well, Son, I reckon this ta be a powerful big praise to the Lord."

"What did they name him? Is the baby and Rachel healthy and well?" Emile was waiting impatiently. Farmer was fully awake now. Emile could hardly contain herself!

"We named him David Lee after a brave man I served with in the Air Corps. Rachel was in labor a long time. The delivery was most painful, but the baby and Rachel are both fine - and exhausted - sleeping now."

Emile had her ear close to the receiver, trying to hear what Clifton was saying.

"Ya best tell yer Ma," interrupted Farmer handing the phone to his anxious wife. As she began to listen, Farmer saw joy and exhilaration expressed in her face. Several times she exclaimed, "Oh! Yes! Oh, my!"

Then her expression changed to one of longing. "I so wish we could be there for you all, and to see and hold the baby," she repeated over and over.

Walter made that possible. As soon as it warmed up, he provided a flight for Farmer and Emile from Portland to Anchorage where they spent two weeks thoroughly spoiling their new grandbaby. Farmer was also able to explore a tiny piece of some of the roughest territory he had ever seen in his life.

Technology was on the rise. New and modern appliances were showing up in stores across the United States. In 1948, nearly one million homes owned a new form of entertainment called television. By 1950 that number would increase to over seven million although, Farmer knew it would still be years before Douglas Landing would be able to view a show in a box.

In the five years after the war, travel skyrocketed across the country. Folks had the urge to travel, and the Mother Road exploded with vibrant life. Restaurants, service stations and places to spend a night mushroomed along the road. New hope and happiness came with a boom in the economy.

Andrew and Susan made two trips to spend time with Farmer and Emile. Hirum and Vivian yearned to make the journey once more, but his health would not permit. Vivian refused to leave him, against his persistence for her to go. Emile and Susan especially cherished those precious few moments together. Andrew was getting better at leaving work in Texas and learning to relax.

To Farmer's and Emile's elated surprise, a profitable wheat and cotton crop made it possible for Jacob and Dorothy, along with their son, Sidney, to bring Ma Allison for a visit to

Oregon. When Walter and Clifton heard that Grandma was coming, they made travel plans, and Walter, Clifton, Rachel and little David Lee arrived in Douglas Landing two days before the Texas guests drove in. Words fail in any attempt to describe that family gathering. It would seem there is great joy and happiness in seeing a loved one who has been gone a long time, and that was certainly the case for Walter and Clifton. Then there was baby David to be seen by his great grandmother for the first time.

They also asked to see the old ranch, but Farmer made excuses and let the others go out. They made little comment when they all came back in, only that it was beautiful and run-down.

All these travels had taken place by the end of 1948. In addition, Farmer and Emile made three short runs down to Southern California to stay with Harold, Leah and Janee. They also enjoyed a second visit to Alaska. David was walking, no running by then!

"Leah called this morning!" Emile announced happily one cold - blistery day in January of 1949. Farmer stomped snow off his boots on the front porch. He had just gotten home from work.

"You should have heard her! She was so excited! They had their first snow ever in Los Angeles," Emile laughed.

"Not surprised as cold as it be. She can have all the white stuff from here she wants," Farmer spoke with dry humor as he hung up his coat.

"She told me that Harold got a big bonus at Christmas time. She also said that Janee just got a contract for a new role in a movie. She said her part was extensive through most all of it, and the shooting would begin in February. The best part, though, Farmer, is that she thought Janee would be old enough to spend part of the summer with us."

Janee indeed livened up the summers of 1949 and 1950 for her grandparents.

A peace and calmness enveloped the whole nation after the war. Farmer and Emile felt a contentment that had been a long time coming, and although there were many warm smiles and days of laughter, dark clouds formed at times, and there were certainly moments of sadness and sorrow. Parting with the children and grandchildren always pulled at everyone's hearts. It seemed each time got harder, and all of the family was so far away. Farmer wondered if they should pull up stakes and move, but where? It looked to him that he and Emile were mid-way between the children. So they grew to live from one visit to the next.

One quiet morning, Farmer lost track of time as he laid Wind to rest in the grove of trees next to Sunset's grave. He sat there a long time, remembering the two horses. What faithful servants and companions they had been. For a moment he saw Walter, Clifton and Leah on the backs of Sunset, Wind and Dusty, yelling - laughing - racing through the trees. He wished that those days could be relived.

Later, during a bitter winter's night, Farmer was awakened by a noise in the small barn behind the house and sensed that something was wrong. He threw on clothes, turned on the barn lights and found Dusty lying on his side. Farmer recognized the signs of pain and impending death. Old age and cold had taken its toll on the little mustang. Dusty was down and couldn't get up. Farmer covered the struggling animal with a blanket, knelt down and stroked the horse's face and mane. He talked to Dusty about the great trip they made from Texas, and the times on the ranch, and Janee riding on him the last two summers, and how disappointed she would be next year if Dusty wasn't there waiting for her.

Emile came through the barn door all bundled up. She had gotten worried; Farmer was gone for so long. She took one look at Farmer, then Dusty. She covered her mouth, retreating hurriedly back to the house.

Farmer could tell that Dusty was suffering and knew what he must do. He ran to the house, got his rifle and slipped a cartridge into the chamber. In a few minutes it was all over.

Farmer put on a pot of coffee. The icy air had cut to the bone, and the act of putting down his last horse left him numb. Sleep was out of the question, and in an attempt to occupy his mind he switched on the radio while the coffee was brewing. He heard the voice of Charles E. Fuller on the "Old Fashioned Revival Hour" speaking.

"Last week on this broadcast I announced that my topic for this week would be on 'Heaven.' God willing I intend to do that very thing, but first I want to read a letter from an aging gentleman who has been quite ill. He wrote: 'Next week you are to talk about Heaven. I am interested in that place because I have held a clear title to a piece of property there for over 55 years. I didn't buy it 'cause it was given me, but my donor purchased it for me at a tremendous sacrifice. I am not holding it for speculation since the title is non-transferable. Yet it is not a vacant lot. You see, for more than a half-century I have been sending material out of which the greatest architect and builder of the universe has been building a home for me, which will never need repair. It will suit me perfectly, and will never grow old. Termites cannot undermine its foundation, fire cannot destroy it, and it will never be repossessed!

"There is a valley of deep shadow between the place where I now live and that to which I shall journey in a very short time. I cannot reach my home in the City of God without passing through this dark valley, but I am not afraid, because my Best Friend, Jesus, went through the same valley alone, a long, long time ago, and He made it.

"I hope to hear your sermon on 'Heaven,' from my home here, but have no assurance that I shall be able to do so. My ticket to Heaven has no date that I can see. So I may not be here while you are talking on the radio next broadcast, but I shall meet you in Heaven someday!'"

"I can't take all this talk o' death and Heaven and property bein' repossessed!" Farmer griped as he clicked the radio off and went to pour a cup of coffee.

"Not today!"

Chapter 42

IS IT POSSIBLE?

Have you ever been restless and unsettled, but had no clear reason to be? Without knowing why, a darkness that is black as a starless night seeks to cover your life. Storm clouds may form even though it's a clear day. It seems that bad news is coming; yet there's no evidence to support our fears.

That's the way Farmer felt early one October morning in 1951. It came strong on him the evening before. He arrived home from work; he was finished for the week. Tomorrow was Saturday and the opening day of deer season. Douglas Landing was crowded, overflowing with hunters, many of whom were from out of state. The lodge, constructed in the late '40's, had been booked up months in advance. Rooms in Applegate were taken, the campgrounds were full, and Farmer spoke to one hunter in passing at the post office who was planning on sleeping in the woods in his car so he could be ready as soon as the sun came up.

That evening, after an enjoyable supper with Emile, was when these uneasy, unsettling feelings suddenly darkened his thoughts. He tried to brush them aside, but they persisted. It made no sense to him. Everything seemed to be going well.

He felt good! All the family was in good health and prospering! He and Emile were secure - maybe too secure? Had he sinned? He searched his heart. He asked God to look also, but felt the love and closeness between him and his Father met the test.

"You are very thoughtful and quiet tonight," Emile ventured after sitting in the living room a long time without uttering any words.

"Somethin's a troublin' me, Emile," Farmer replied after a period of more silence.

"What?"

"Don't reckon I can figure it out. It came sudden-like as I was on the back porch watchin the sunset.. Was like a voice or somethin' tellin' me a part o' our life was closin' - jus' like the settin' o' the sun."

Emile took notice and the softness of her face and smile took on a serious tone.

"What do you think it means, Farmer?"

"Don't rightly know, but it seems a darkness has come ta my head. Been prayin' - been prayin' a lot, and lookin' at my heart. Don't reckon thet ta be the problem. More - like - well - like maybe there's somethin' the Good Lord is a wantin' us ta do. Reckon He will be showin' us in due time."

Farmer could not sleep. Restlessness came over him that felt akin to how he felt as a youth wanting to go west. Was it possible the Lord had another move in Farmer and Emile's future? The minutes clicked by at a pace that drug the hours along so slowly Farmer found himself pleading with God for the morning to hurry and arrive.

As soon as the bedroom grew light enough to make his way around, Farmer got up. He sat on the side of the bed for a long time watching Emile. He recalled when they first married and how passionate and intoxicating their love was. The passing years had not diminished their love, only deepened it, and formed and molded it into something more beautiful, powerful and enduring. Farmer studied Emile's face as she slept. The years had not faded her beauty, only enhanced it - defining it more clearly. He could still see little features of the young woman he remembered on their wedding night.

Farmer quietly gathered his clothes and wobbled to the bathroom to wash his sleepless face and get dressed. He decided, rather than bang around in the kitchen, he would go down to the café for coffee. No doubt it wouldn't be long before the small eating establishment would be full. Would-be hunters who easily became discouraged at not bagging their deer in the first hour would come back in soon.

Farmer was surprised to see Rollin Graves' car among several others parked in front of the café. He had remained friends with the banker over the years, but didn't go out of his way to spend time with him. Farmer spied the aging gentleman seated by himself at a far table. His face brightened at the sight of Farmer, and he gestured an invitation to join him at his table.

"Well, howdy, Mr. Graves, ya be a mite outa yer weekend territory. What brings ya in from Applegate? Ya come ta see the hunters' parade?" Farmer drawled with a chuckle.

"Believe it or not, I'm in town to see you, Farmer, and another family."

"Can't take my house, ya deeded thet ta me, an' I don't owe the bank, so I'm a hopin' ya ain't tellin' me ya lost the money I put in there!" Farmer spoke coolly, half in jest, half seriously.

The banker laughed good-naturedly.

"No, Farmer, I assure you we haven't crashed. And I want you to understand that as a bank manager, it is not my only function to take away other people's property."

Farmer dropped his head, ashamed instantly for his biting remarks.

The waitress brought coffee, which defused the tension.

"You know, Farmer, that I retire in a few weeks, and before I do I wanted to speak to you."

Farmer looked into the eyes of Rollin Graves. He saw something there he had seen the day the bank repossessed his ranch. It was a mixture of kindness and compassion.

"I fought for you - and for the Brooks. Did you ever wonder why I never got promoted to a better position - a larger bank? I fought for you! To the very brink of losing my own job. I got scared! I had a family too!"

Farmer held up his hand for Rollin to stop.

"Let me finish, Farmer. I had to choose between doing what I was ordered - or lose my position. I made the choice, but I angered corporate heads. They vowed I would never leave Douglas Landing or work for another bank. They fixed my records to insure their threats. I could have changed careers, but I stayed on because I wanted to make things right for you and the Brooks."

"Ya don't owe me, Rollin. I'm yer friend, an' right proud ya kept yer job here in Douglas Landing," Farmer spoke with a sincerity that came from his heart.

"I never felt good or right about the dealings with you and your family, or Gordon and Ella May, but until recently I was helpless to do anything about it."

"And now?" Farmer's attention was suddenly focused on Graves' every word.

"You know that Cascade Mountains Lumber bought both sections and cut the best timber. The land is of no use to the mill, but as long as Uriah was at the helm, he was set against selling any of the company's property."

Rollin cleared his throat and sipped his coffee.

"But that's changed since old man Wallheim passed away," Graves continued. "I spoke to the powers that be, and they agreed to sell your ranches back, after I told them your story, and at a very reasonable price. That is if you and the

Brooks want them back. I wish to be able to loan you what you need before I retire."

Rollin waited for Farmer's reaction. They had kept firm eye contact during the conversation, but thoughts began to bombard Farmer's mind. Could it be possible? Could he have the ranch again? His mind began to spin, and he dropped his eyes.

"Don't reckon I could take a loan again," Farmer stammered. "What ifen I can't pay?" His voice trailed off into thoughts racing in his mind.

"Oh, come on, Farmer. This is a different age. You have a job, property in town. Keep working - buy a few cattle - that you can pay for."

Farmer felt that old fire and excitement surge through his soul that was once there when he was young - those old feelings that for the most part died when he lost the ranch. He hadn't realized they were gone until now. He felt strangely alive and vibrant, eager to revive a dream!

"It's yours if you want it," Rollin spoke with a smile. "All of it. I'm on my way now to see Gordon and Ella May. Coffee's on me."

Graves stepped to the counter to pay. Farmer was so stunned he stared straight ahead only vaguely aware of others in the café. He whispered a "Thank you," as Rollin made his exit from the café, but was unheard by anyone except God and Farmer.

Suddenly Farmer came to action.

"Do I want my ranch back?!" Farmer exclaimed loudly, catching the attention of everyone in the café. "Ya bet yer life I do!" Farmer shouted as he bolted out the door.

In the car he started to the house. He glanced at his watch. Still early - Emile may still be asleep - no - wake her up - no - make it a surprise! An overwhelming desire to see the old place took over and steered the car not to his house, but towards the ranch he had left years ago. The place he loved! The place he vowed never to step foot on until he could again own it - the ranch he had never been back to or had the desire to see - until now!

He pulled up to the gate that once opened to his section of land. The gate he had built years ago that still guarded the entrance to his land. Yes! His land! He could hardly believe what he was thinking, let alone doing.

He saw the gate was locked, so he shut off the car's engine and crawled through the fence. The road to the log house had small trees growing up in patches underneath where larger trees had reseeded the forest floor. Everywhere Farmer walked, he saw the stumps of once beautiful giants cut down by a lumber company only interested in board feet. He determined the first thing to accomplish was to clear the road.

Farmer came upon Cold Creek, still flowing fast and clear. Then the old log house came into view. All of the out buildings and the old chuck wagon had collapsed under many winters' heavy snows, yet the house stood firm and solid like a rock towering above the ruins of the buildings around it.

Farmer stepped onto the porch, which gave a familiar ring under his boots. He gazed around taking in a scene that had remained clearly fixed in his memory. He picked at the chinks; much was gone letting sunlight pass between the logs into the house - no it would be a home again - for Farmer and Emile. He walked inside. The door was off the hinges and propped up against a wall. Most of the glass was broken out, mice and rat droppings were scattered across the floor, and a wood rat had built a nest of sticks, pinecones and leaves in one of the bedrooms.

"All this can be repaired," Farmer thought, yet that brooding darkness nagged at him, demanding attention.

"This has ta be right!" he mumbled. Wasn't everything perfect - handed to him - just like the first time?!

"Lord, ifen this ain't yer will, then stop me," Farmer prayed as he walked out of the house. He had seen enough to be satisfied the structure of the log house was solid but in need of much repair. Neighbors would help - as before. His mind was running wild with plans. All he wanted to do now was get back home and share them with Emile. He walked down to the creek - a hundred memories - precious memories filled his mind, and for the first time in a long time he broke down and wept. He took off running!

"Is it possible?" he thought, "thet I'm getting my dream back?"

He came to a patch of brush that was higher than his head. He slowed down, working his way through it. As he reached the end of the brush and stepped out into an open area in the trees, he heard a loud crack, a thud as something hit his body, knocking him to the ground!

Chapter 43

THROUGH THE VEIL

Farmer was aware of a horrendous pain in his chest. He was in darkness and wondered how long he had been in the woods. Emile would be frantic with worry, and he must get to her right away!

It seemed to get light, and he opened his eyes to see a man standing over him whom he didn't recognize. The man was apologizing and telling Farmer how sorry he was. Farmer was confused as to what was happening. The man kept saying over again how sorry he was, and he thought Farmer was a deer. Farmer reckoned that to be foolishness, as he certainly didn't resemble a deer, and Farmer wished this fellow would stop fretting over him.

Farmer looked past the man and could make out the brush and trees. For an instant he thought he saw figures in the shadows. The pain in his chest became unbearable, and everything went dark, only to have the light come back. He opened his eyes again. The man was shouting for help as loudly as he could. His shouts turned into a pleading scream that hurt Farmer's ears. He tried to talk - his mouth moved - but no sound came forth. His chest burned with a pain that racked his whole body. It rose until he blacked out.

Farmer had no idea how long he had been lying on the ground when he opened his eyes. He could make out the forest, but the light was dim like when the sun has gone down and twilight has fallen, casting long shadows.

"Gosh!" Farmer thought, "Reckon I been here all day - gotta get home. Emile will be worried fer sure!"

He sat up, realizing the terrible pain had passed. Suddenly, he was aware of a strange glow coming from behind him. He turned and was startled to see what appeared to be a woman in a flowing gown standing there.

He started to speak, but could see she was not looking at him but was intent on something in the trees. He turned his head towards a noise he now heard. From the shadows emerged the most hideous creature he had ever seen! Its frame was twisted, and it walked haltingly with a limp. Red, bloodshot eyes turned its gaze upon him, and each breath the creature took expelled a foul-smelling smoke. Farmer choked, the stench was suffocating!

Its skin looked like rawhide covered with hairy patches and open wounds, and sores oozed a slimy green-looking puss that coursed down its body.

A step - another - then another - it headed straight towards Farmer - belting out stagnant vapor with labored effort. Razor sharp fingernails now clearly exposed, it took a giant leap, landing directly in front of Farmer. Farmer cried out in terror and scrambled to his feet. The woman stepped quickly in between Farmer and the monster.

"Be gone! Give him to me! Be gone!" the hideous figure snarled.

"You have no claim, Zoogot. This is a redeemed one!" the woman retorted.

"Proof!" the one called Zoogot challenged. "I must - see - proof."

"See!" the woman moved to the side and gestured towards the trembling man standing behind her.

Zoogot took a halted step towards Farmer, raising its claw-like hand, peering intently, searching Farmer's forehead. The evil smirk Zoogot had on his face suddenly dissolved, and the creature hurtled backwards to the ground as if struck by some unseen force.

"See!" the woman exclaimed again, "he has the seal of the Holy One."

Zoogot leapt to his feet, vile cursing and cutting accusations belched from his mouth that were mixed with deep guttural growls.

"Then I'll have his body," Zoogot looked off to the side. Farmer followed his gaze and was shocked to see himself lying there. A man on his knees, face in his hands, was huddled over - his body.

Farmer discerned that the man was distraught and sobbing. He saw the man's rifle where he apparently dropped it - or thrown it. He also now observed another glowing figure hovering near the man, and several hideous creatures, much like Zoogot, attempting to strike firey darts into the man's body. The guardian tried to ward them off, but some of the darts got through, jolting the man.

"I will have and defile his body!" Zoogot made his demand clear as flaming drops were spitting from his mouth.

"You have no authority here!" the woman stood firm with grim resolve.

Zoogot rose from the ground and moved towards Farmer's still body. The woman confronted him!

"Be gone! You have no power here," Zoogot snarled, as fire and smoke continued blasting from his mouth with each word.

"I stand against you in the Name of the Lord of Hosts!" the woman shouted.

Zoogot drew a jagged sword. Before Farmer's eyes the two beings began to grow taller. The woman drew a glistening blade that shone brightly. They circled each other growing taller until their heads were as high as the treetops. Wings snapped and unfurled. Zoogot's were deformed and torn, but the woman's - magnificent. The clash of the swords sent forth what appeared to be lightning strikes. Farmer was gripped with a horror he had never known! He cowered on the ground covering his head, trembling and crying out in fear. The struggle for his body was fierce. These two giants were engaged in a combat like none Farmer had ever witnessed. The clang when their swords hit was deafening, but not a sound of steel hitting cold steel - something else - a sound unheard by mortal ears.

Strangely, as the battle waged on, Farmer felt a calmness come over him. He looked up to see these two towering creatures locked in conflict. Blow upon blow, lighting the whole sky with showers of brilliant sparks, Zoogot growling and cursing, the woman fighting in silence.

Farmer stood up, and as he watched the battle, words his grandmother spoke to him when he was a little boy came back.

"If the devil bothers you, Farmer, you just tell that ol' meanie to go away in the Name of Jesus."

Renewed courage flowed through Farmer, and a strange and different boldness gripped him until he was moved to the point of uttering, "Go away in the Name of Jesus!"

Instantly, the fighting stopped, and there was total silence. Both creatures shrunk to the size they were before the battle began. Zoogot seemed in a state of disorientation.

"What spoke ye?" Zoogot questioned with a gasp.

Courage took hold of Farmer that he had never experienced nor did he understand. He moved closer to Zoogot and stood firmly before him. He spoke louder this time.

"I said, go away in the Name of Jesus Christ!"

Zoogot covered his ears with his hands. He gagged and coughed, flame and smoke spitting from his mouth. Finally, he bellowed a tirade of profanity. Then an evil of even greater proportions seemed to possess him.

"I hate that Name!" he whined, "and I curse the day you believed on it!" He hissed at Farmer, and with that he vanished.

Farmer stood stunned for a moment. He wasn't quite sure what to make of it all, but sensed that a growing knowledge was beginning to form in his mind. The other man had left and the creatures with him. He slumped down on the ground, looking at himself. Something like this should traumatize a person, but instead Farmer seemed to have a sad understanding.

"It is time for you to go," the woman spoke gently.

"Am I..." Farmer started to ask, not taking his eyes off the still form on the ground. His body's chest was covered in blood.

"Yes. It was your appointed time," the woman replied.

Farmer turned his head to look up at her, tears now streaking his face.

"But I wasn't ready to die!"

"Humans never are - until they see the other side."

"Who will take care o' Emile? She's gonna be hurtin' a powerful lot an' grievin'."

"The Master will comfort and provide for her. Come! We must go!"

Farmer stood up to go with this creature.

"Who air ya? What air ya?" Farmer wanted to know.

"I am Adreen. I am your Guardian Angel."

"How long...." Farmer hesitated. He wasn't quite sure what to ask, "hev ya been - thet?"

"I was created for that purpose. I was sent the night you were conceived. I have been near you since that moment."

"Ya was there when I was born?"

"Yes," Adreen replied quietly.

"When I married Emile?"

"Yes."

"Ya was there when we made - "

"I was always near - to guard you."

The two walked through the forest in silence. Farmer's feet were moving, but as he looked down he was floating and not touching the ground. He marvelled at this but said nothing.

Here the forest changed, and they walked in places unfamiliar to his recollection.

The sky grew darker, and the shadows deeper. He could see figures move in amongst the trees and bushes. This was a creepy place, yet Farmer was surprised that he was not afraid.

"Where are we?" he inquired of Adreen.

"This is the valley of the shadow of death."

"Zoogot was -?"

"A fallen angel."

"The Bible calls them demons."

"Yes," the angel nodded.

"What do I see in the - shadows?"

"More of them."

They made their way deeper into the woods without conversation. It got so dark that Farmer could barely see where to walk. Soon, Adreen's glow was the only light they had. Farmer's thoughts went to Emile, and he began to cry.

"I miss her already. She will be terrible hurt an' alone. We has always been together, me a carin' fer her." Then a thought came to Farmer.

"Does - Emile hev a angel like ya?"

"Yes."

"What it be named?"

"Her Guardian Angel is called Froton."

"Is she a woman like you?"

"Angels are neither male nor female, but have characteristics of one or the other. Emile needed a strong angel, so the Master sent Froton."

"Then why did I need a woman angel?"

Adreen smiled. "I reckon to soften your rough side."

Farmer laughed, then the sobering reality hit him. "Does she - have a - like Zoogot?" he shivered at the thought of a horrible monster trying to harm Emile - or his children - or grandchildren. He wanted to pray for them! Adreen seemed to read his thoughts.

"Your time for prayer is over," she spoke with sadness. "Every person born is given a Guardian Angel. There is also a fallen angel that comes to oppose all that the Master would do in that person's life. Sometimes, many demons attack one person in an attempt to foil the Creator's plan. Zoogot fought hard against you. He struck you with bitter blows - when you lost your ranch - when Leah got pregnant. He danced every time you went to your knees in despair."

Farmer dropped his head. "An' my Emile has a demon ta fight her?" he was admitting to himself.

"Yes, a wicked, evil one of death named Gaamog. He tried to take her life and Leah's while you traveled. Froton and Gaamog fought long and fiercely for many days. I aided Froton in that battle, and Zoogot tried to get you into trouble while I fought. Gaamog wanted to bring death to all of you in that flash flood."

"Something - someone warned me?"

"The Holy Spirit spoke to your heart. I pushed you to move your family," Adreen smiled knowingly.

"Did Gaamog or Zoogot cause my death?" Farmer asked.

"They cannot interfere with your appointed time."

As they continued their journey, Farmer tried to imagine all these creatures, angels and demons - his, Emile's, their children's in their home. He shuddered and was thankful they couldn't be seen. Farmer noticed a faint light at a far distance in the darkness. "Soon you will see Him who purchased you with a great price," Adreen spoke gently.

Farmer's heart leaped inside him at the thought. Strange! He didn't have a heart, yet he did. He wasn't breathing - yet he was. He could feel, taste, smell - then again - did he really?

The light became brighter and larger the closer they came. Farmer became curious, "Is that Heaven?"

"No," Adreen answered, "that is the Veil."

"The Veil?"

"Yes. You must pass through it."

"Will you go with me?"

"I will be your Guardian Angel for eternity."

Concept of time was lost. Farmer had no idea how long it took to reach the Veil, nor did it matter. He was surprised at the enormity of it. It shown with a blinding brilliance and had the appearance of flowing water, except the ground at the base was dry.

Farmer halted in front of the Veil. It rose many stories above them and spread out a great distance to either side. It was a bright light in the midst of darkness. All around the Veil was blackness - so thick it would seem to want to devour and swallow up any and all light thrust upon it - but it could not! The Veil emanated light so powerful - so strong the blackness was helpless before it.

"Come. Let us pass through," Adreen took his arm.

Farmer closed his eyes, but he was not afraid. As he walked into the Veil, he had the sensation of streams of fine sand flowing over his head, his body, to his feet. He opened his eyes on the other side to a place so beautiful and wonderful that no words in any language could fully or accurately describe what he now beheld.

Chapter 44

FACE TO FACE

Farmer was experiencing so much emotion. One moment he wanted to laugh and sing, the next he was fearful. Then he felt like dancing down the path on which they were walking, and Farmer had never been much of a dancer. His emotion swung from pure joy to weeping. He was surprised he still had tears and wondered about it.

"Adreen, I thought there were no tears in Heaven."

"Heaven is where the Almighty is on His Throne. This place is called Paradise, which the Master has been filling with his people ever since His glorious return from earth as the Risen Lord. He brought many with Him who were captive from the beginning of mankind.

"You mean such as Adam and Eve, Moses, Noah, Abraham and Sarah?"

"They are here...and many others."

All the Old Testament saints had always seemed rather distant - ancient I guess Farmer thought of them. The reality that he could meet them - talk to them - seemed beyond his comprehension.

"Man still sheds tears here. You will soon understand," Adreen went on to answer the rest of Farmer's question.

"The Master will wipe away all tears, but that will not happen until the end of all things and you have been received into the new Heaven."

The path they walked upon was like clear crystal that changed color in the light. The most beautiful trees and plants that Farmer had ever seen surrounded them. From his farm background he soon noticed that there was a definite absence of weeds and thorns. He also observed there were no leaves on the ground - or whatever it was the plants were growing in. He stopped to look with wonder. There were trees with leaves of vivid colors mixed among the trees of green.

"That one has fruit!" Farmer pointed excitedly.

"Are you hungry? You can eat, but not yet. You must first meet the Lord," Adreen instructed.

The path wound among the trees descending a steep hillside. Soon it emerged out of the trees and bushes onto the bank of a clear flowing stream. The water sparkled in the light as it ran cool and deep.

"You must cross the stream of living water," Adreen's voice took on a reverent tone. "Your Savior waits to greet you."

Farmer looked across the water into a gentle slope filled with green luscious grass and flowers of countless brilliant colors scattered everywhere. Farther up the hill a man could be seen walking among the flowers. His countenance shone brightly. Farmer could not see Him clearly, but his heart quickened for he knew it was the Lord!

Adreen took Farmer's hand. "Come," she urged.

"Should I take off my clothes?"

"No. Go as you are."

"Will you come with me?"

"I cannot follow you in this. I will be near you again after you meet the Master."

Farmer stepped into the water. It felt clean and refreshing. He sank up to his knees, then chest. He attempted to swim, but felt as though he had lead weights for feet. The current pulled him in over his head. He thrashed around trying to reach the surface, but his feet were stuck on the bottom!

"I reckon I'm a goner fer sure," Farmer thought. "I'm gonna drown! No - wait! I'm already dead!"

Farmer opened his eyes and began walking along the floor of the stream. He could feel a transformation taking place, but what that involved, he wasn't sure. All he knew was when he climbed out of the water on the other side he had a sense of being alive far surpassing anything he ever experienced on earth. The rags he once wore were now shed for glorious new raiment.

Coming up on to the grass, all he could think of was meeting his Lord, Jesus Christ. He began to run, and as he did, Christ ran towards him. The faster he ran, the faster the Lord ran, now with outstretched arms.

The closer Farmer got to the Lord; wave after wave of God's love washed over him growing in intensity to the point Farmer could stand no more. He was submerged; he grew faint from the love emanating from the Lord. He never experienced in his mortal life the resulting, exploding capacity to be able to love in an undiluted way. He collapsed in a heap at his Savior's feet. "I don't deserve to be here!" Farmer cried out. All he could think, "This is the Lamb that was slain - for me!" He reached out and lay hold of that Lamb and pleaded for mercy. Through blurred vision he could see the nail prints in the Lord's feet. He wept even louder. He was overwhelmed with a sense of failure and shame. "I made such a mess of things, my Lord! I failed Ya; I lost the ranch; I made bad decisions; I got angry; I reckon I let Ya down terrible bad! Ya gave me a beautiful chance, an' I went an' lost it! I'm powerful sorry!"

Christ knelt down and tenderly lifted the broken man from the ground. When Farmer looked into the eyes of his Lord, he saw only love, acceptance and kindness. Without a word spoken, Farmer knew in that instant that every sin he had ever committed was paid for and forgiven. "It's not about the ranch, my son. It never was about the ranch."

"I don't understand," Farmer stammered.

"I needed you there," the Lord spoke with a gentleness that rang of authority.

"Lord, I don't understand atall! Don't understand the way I died. Adreen says thet demons can't interfere with a man's appointed time. Did ya hev me shot? I wasn't ready ta die like thet - I mean, ifen ya wanted, it be alright - an' I fear fer my Emile - what will -?"

Jesus silenced Farmer with a smile. He wrapped Farmer in His Arms and held him. Farmer felt his knees weaken and his heart melt. Then the Lord held him at arms' length and looked into his eyes with a gaze that searched every part of Farmer's soul and spirit.

"My child, you cannot understand it all now. The story of your life is still unfolding. It will all be revealed in due time, but not yet."

"You are here because I bought you with a great price, and you believed. Welcome, Farmer Trevor, into your rest. Well done, my good and faithful servant. I have long awaited your coming. Come, let us walk together."

The two turned from the river and started back up the slope. Farmer felt the grass and flowers against his feet and legs. Looking down he saw that he was touching the ground walking, not floating as he had done with his Guardian Angel. He was surprised to see sandals on his feet in place of his logging boots. His jeans and flannel shirt had also been transformed into new bright shining garments.

Jesus and Farmer walked in silence, almost as if the Lord were waiting for Farmer to say something. A thousand thoughts and questions flew through Farmer's mind, yet he was so in awe of the Lord he was at a loss for words. He just felt a reverent silence before his King. As they approached the top of the hill, Farmer could no longer hold back!

"Lord, can we stop a minute?"

"Of course, my friend."

Farmer dropped to his knees. He looked into the face of Him who loved him.

"Lord, I feel so foolish an' ashamed. The first thing I seen Ya, I'm a goin' on 'bout stuff thet don't count thet much an' fussin' 'bout how an' when I died - like I knowed a better way fer Ya ta do it!"

"Farmer, you have always been one to speak what came to your mind," the Lord spoke with such love and compassion that Farmer felt consumed by it.

"But, Lord, I was a hopin' thet comin' here would fix thet problem." Farmer immediately gasped and covered his mouth. How could he be so bold and presume he knew Jesus so well as to joke - even if he was serious. How dare he should take such liberty! The thought crossed his mind that if he wasn't careful he was going to get kicked out of Heaven.

The Lord Jesus laughed, as He took Farmer's arm and lifted him up.

"My child," He said smiling, "when I walked on the earth with my disciples, how do you think they spoke? How do you suppose they acted or thought? Peter was a fisherman! What came out of his mouth when I first called him was unthinkable. Matthew the tax collector didn't have a civil tongue in his head - a social outcast - but he could remember with great detail. James and John, now there was a pair. They could burn with anger and wanted to call fire down on those who upset them."

He gazed off into the distance, and it seemed that the thoughts of Christ drifted to another time and place as He recalled something precious.

"I love them all," He murmured, turning His attention back to Farmer, He went on. "You should have heard some of our conversations around the night fires. They questioned, they argued, complained, fussed, doubted, told Me I was wrong, I didn't know what I was doing. Still, I love them just as I do you, my son."

By now, Farmer was weeping and falling back to his knees, bowing before the Son of God.

"Lord, Jesus, I wasn't mindin' my manners. Stedda frettin' 'bout those things I said, I shoulda been thankin' Ya fer savin' me and lettin' me come to this beautiful place. Lord, I ain't never been much count with words. I jus' feel things powerful strong, but when I try ta express what I'm a feelin', it jus' don't seem ta come out very good. I'm jus' a wantin' ta tell Ya how grateful I be fer payin' the price an' lovin' me an' - an' thet I love You a powerful lot!"

Jesus looked on Farmer raising his face with His Hand until their eyes met.

"Farmer, you were saved by the Father's Grace through your faith."

"An' by yer sacrifice," Farmer added.

"Yes… I shed My Blood on the cross that you might be washed whiter than snow," the Lord spoke softly.

"I can never thank Ya enough," Farmer whispered. Suddenly, feelings vaguely recalled in life on earth and barely understood, started growing inside of Farmer. He did not know what was happening to him nor could he control it. Those feelings just touched on in mortal life now were welling up inside of him in an overwhelming flood. He raised his hands to his Savior, and out of his mouth came the most amazing and lovely song. The words were new to him in a language he did not know; yet he seemed to have clear knowledge. Farmer sang praises to the King of Kings and Lord of Lords. Joy so filled Farmer's heart he jumped up and began dancing in circles around Jesus who was laughing and clapping His Hands!

When Farmer finished, he walked to the Lord and bowed his head in silence.

"I have looked into your heart all of your life, my son, and I am pleased with you. Come, let's walk."

As they continued up the hill, Jesus spoke.

"I remember how I loved to walk with Adam and Eve in the Garden. We would walk and talk like you and I are now."

"Sure wish Emile was here 'bout now. Lord, I miss her a powerful lot! She would sure nuff take in these flowers an' be pickin' a few," Farmer longed for his wife. He couldn't help worrying over her and wondered how she would fare.

The Lord knew Farmer's thoughts. "Her appointed time will come. I am with her, and she has friends and your children."

"Lord, I saw me a movie once 'bout a fella who died an' Saint Peter let him go back ta his life on earth ta make right mistakes he had done. Does thet ever happen?" Farmer asked.

Jesus smiled, and then grew solemn. "That kind of story comes from the imagination of those who do not know me nor understand my Word. It comes from a desire to live apart from me and still have a second chance. Once you cross the Veil there is no going back."

Farmer stopped to take in the magnificent view around him. He held his arms wide, slowly turning, trying to take it all in. He dropped his arms, looking at Jesus.

"This be different then I had pictured!" Farmer exclaimed.

"Eden looked like this when I created it," the Lord explained.

"I reckoned thet God created everthing," Farmer was puzzled.

"I and the Father are One," Jesus replied, and then continued. "Earth is an image of Heaven made in its likeness.

When sin entered the world and its curse took hold, the image was distorted. It won't be restored until I return."

"Will thet be soon?" Farmer asked.

"Only the Father knows the exact time, Farmer, besides, you just want to see Emile," there was a twinkle in the Master's eyes.

The pair continued their walk up the slope of the hill. Not only did Farmer feel like he had known Jesus all his life, he had a new and complete understanding of what the Lord meant in the scripture when He said, "Ye are my friends."

The top of the hill yielded to a long, wide valley spread out below. The stream of living water cut across the valley with gentle bends and stretched through groves of trees. It disappeared to the left, obscured by the hill that Farmer had just climbed with the Good Shepherd. The view before Farmer was breathtaking! A whisper of a breeze sent rippling waves over the grass and flowers. Leaves fluttered on the trees, and the river shimmered in the light. In one meadow by the river was a sizeable gathering of people. Farmer felt his heart quicken!

"Who air those?" Farmer pointed.

"In church you sang a hymn, 'Shall we gather at the river.' Do you remember the words?" Jesus asked.

Words came instantly into Farmer's mind. 'Shall we gather at the river, where bright angel feet have trod, with its crystal tide forever flowing by the Throne of God? Yes, we'll gather at the river, the beautiful, the beautiful - river. Gather with the saints at the river that flows by the Throne of God.'

"Should I?"

"Yes, Farmer, they are your loved ones who have been eagerly awaiting your arrival! You must go to them now!"

Farmer turned to Jesus, but He had vanished.

Chapter 45

GATHERING AT THE RIVER

Farmer started running down the long slope towards his loved ones waiting for him by the river. Suddenly Adreen was hovering beside him. The distance that would have taken near thirty minutes of an earthly walk was covered in an instant. The first person Farmer saw and recognized was his Pa, Franklin.

"Pa!" Farmer shouted and ran into his father's outstretched arms. Franklin held his son, as a loving parent would enfold his child and hold him close. Other relatives gathered around, patting Farmer and saying words of welcome, but he hardly heard. The love, kindness and acceptance Farmer longed for from his Pa his whole life was now extending to him, and he never wanted it to end. He began to weep and wail, as he never did on earth. His body convulsed as a lifetime of hurt and pain poured out in his cries and tears.

After a time, Farmer was spent. He had no idea how long he stood there in his Pa's embrace. Minutes? Hours? Maybe days! Farmer had lost all concept of time. Franklin stepped back holding Farmer's arms with a strong grip.

"Son, I sure am proud to see ya!" Franklin spoke with sincerity and love. Gone was his rough harshness. It had been replaced with a gentle nature.

Franklin held onto Farmer tightly as though he was afraid his son would run away.

"I was wrong, Farmer, terrible wrong the way I treated ya an' Emile, an', an' my grandchildren!"

Farmer had never seen his Pa cry before, but tears were streaming down his face. Farmer tried to stop him from saying anymore, but his father would not hear of it.

"No, son, I'm a sayin' things I shoulda said while I was alive! I was a fool an' not honest with ya or myself, an' I been waitin' a spell ta get this out!"

Farmer stood stunned at what his Pa was saying.

"I thought I could make ya stay in Texas on the farm. I tol' myself it was for yer own betterment. I thought yer respect -."

Farmer started to speak to confirm his respect for his Pa, but Franklin held up his hand, "Let me finish, son! I thought yer respect an' wantin' ta obey yer Pa was strong enough ta make ya stay. I thought forcin' ya ta choose, between' our love and leavin' fer Oregon would make up yer mind ta stay on the farm. When I saw ya was determined ta go, I got even madder! I figured the trip an ignorant move on yer part an' ya was impetuous an' bullheaded.   The morning ya left -!" Franklin's emotions overtook him, and he had to stop.

"Ya have no idea how bad I wanted ta come see ya all off, but stubborn pride kept me away, an' I refused ta face myself 'til I got here an' came face ta face with our Lord. He asked me if I didn't get sore tired a fightin' Him. I asked Him when was I fightin' against Him. He tol' me it was His will fer ya an' yer family ta make that trip ta Oregon.

"I tried ta convince myself I wanted ya ta stay so I could give ya the farm, but the truth was - I was plumb scared! Scared ya an' Emile an' the boys would be so far away, an', an' - " Franklin broke down again and spoke between sobs. "My pride done robbed me a holdin' an' seein' my grand-daughter, Leah. But the thing I was most scared of was not havin' ya there ta help with the plantin' an' harvestin'. That was mostly why I wanted ya ta stay, an' I was selfish in it. Jesus tol' me it wasn't 'bout the farm at all! Farmer will ya forgive me fer all I did ta ya?"

"Pa, I fergave ya long before I got here!"

"I need ta hear ya say so. I need ta hear those words I've longed ta hear - ta know yer forgiveness as I have found the Lord's."

Farmer looked his Pa square in the eyes and experienced depth of love for his father, which exceeded any human capacity for love he had ever held during his earthly life.

"Pa, I do forgive ya, an' it's forgotten. I jus' be thankful thet we both made it here."

"Yes," Franklin agreed, and his face broke into a bright smile. "Tell me about yer Ma!"

"Oh, Pa, the last time I saw her she looked - so - old - an' thin - an' -."

"I miss her terrible!" Franklin spoke with a longing to see and hold his lifelong mate.

"An' I hev a powerful hurt fer Emile," Farmer spoke with sadness.

"Did ya die o' a heart attack like me? Was yer Emile by yer side?"

"Lands, no! I was shot dead by some trigger-happy outa state hunter!" Farmer flashed hot - then dropped his head. "I don't reckon I know how long fer the bad news got ta her. Worry fer her was the worse part o' dyin'!"

"Did yer Ma - ?" Franklin hesitated as if afraid to ask the question for fear of the answer.

"What?"

"Did - she - remarry?"

Farmer laughed!

"No, Pa, her love fer ya never died."

Franklin smiled in relief.

"Now tell me all the news 'bout everbody!"

"Well, Walter an' Clifton grew ta be strong and handsome," Farmer began. "Leah was born soon after we got ta Oregon an' is a right fine-lookin' woman. She married a part Indian man, Harold. They hev the sweetest lil' gal, Janee, an' Clifton what married his childhood sweetheart, Rachel, an' hev a son, David Lee. Now Rachel was with second child ta be a comin' next spring, so's by then ya will hev three great-grandchildren."

As Farmer began recounting details of the family and events that had taken place since he left Texas his relatives drew close, eager to capture every word. He became aware of the multitude of angels around them, no doubt guardian angels, and several times noticed their expressions of curiosity. Out of the corner of his eye he caught sight of several other groups gathering at different locations on the riverbanks. Without being told, he sensed they were there awaiting a loved one.

Farmer described the difficulties and dangers he, Emile and the children faced on the long journey from Texas to Oregon. He told of the raising of their log house, the birth of Leah, and the terrible Depression, and the horrible war to follow.

"Jacob married Dorothy Shipley."

"Hot dang! I knew those two would get hitched!" Franklin shouted gleefully. All the relatives cheered.

"They hev a son, Sidney Dean, all growed up now," Farmer went on. "Jacob stayed on the farm, but William was called ta war."

"He didn't get -?" A look of panic crossed Franklin's face.

"No, Pa, but he lost a arm an' leg in the Africa Campaign, an' Clifton was in the Air Corp in the Pacific. He also survived the fightin'."

Farmer explained what each of his children were doing with their lives and all about his granddaughter, Janee's movie career - an' what movies were. The sad news of Stella's slip into a dark and rebellious life caused great concern in all the family and some began to moan. It was then Farmer recognized his grandma and grandpa Trevor, and grandmother and grandfather Carter. He reached out to them! They had been waiting patiently along with all the others, and tremendous happiness filled Farmer to see the grandparents he loved dearly. They pulled him close to them, just as he remembered them doing when he was a little boy! He had always been afraid of his grandfather Trevor, but even that now disappeared. All Farmer knew was that this gathering at the river left him with a satisfying sense of fulfilling resolution.

Chapter 46

HEAVEN AND ANGELS

Farmer had no idea how long he was with his relatives by the river. The group consisted of family three generations back. Each one told the story of their lives, and all were full of questions for Farmer. Numerous times as they laughed, talked and cried together he caught a glimpse of the Master at the top of the hill with someone - directing them to their loved ones who were gathered in groups at various points along the river.

Farmer's family was anxious to show him more of Paradise, and for the first time since his arrival was he able to take in the beauty and grandeur that once had been only a hazy dream seen on the spiritual screen of his mind.

The River of Living Water flowed across a small valley emerging from the mountains in the distance. The floor of the valley was filled with trees and flowers arranged in multiple clean and crisp colors. Everything was in perfect coordination and inviting to the eye.

The group followed the bends and stretches of the river through the valley. A canyon in the mountains provided a passageway for the stream of water that came tumbling in rapidly over rocks. The family moved swiftly through the canyon. Farmer had no idea what to expect next, but nothing could have prepared him for what he was about to see.

The canyon opened into a huge valley of hills and dales that reached beyond sight to far distant mountains. This valley was teaming with life. He saw multitudes of people, plus all manner of animals and birds. A ladybug lit on his arm, playfully fluttered its wings, and then took off.

Trees, shrubs and flowers were everywhere, and scattered throughout the valley were villages and cities stunning in their brilliance. The buildings appeared not to have been constructed by any human hands and were made of precious gems and metals. The light shining on the cities reflected rich colors to blend in harmony with the colors of the plants. The greatest accomplishment of architecture on earth paled miserably in comparison to what Farmer gazed upon.

"The light comes from the Throne of God," grandmother Carter pointed out.

"There's no night here," Franklin added.

Suddenly it dawned on Farmer that he was not tired, or hungry. As he thought about it, he remembered he was spirit and wouldn't have need of sleep or food. Rest seemed associated with peace.

The family made its way into the valley and stepped onto a road that resembled gold. Farmer bent down to look more closely.

"It is gold!" A distant cousin answered Farmer's unasked question.

Farmer was amazed, and as they continued on the road he became fascinated that the birds and animals had no fear of humans. Some of the species he recognized - others he had never seen before. As they walked, it was not uncommon for groups of animals to join them and run alongside. Beasts that resembled lions and oxen were gentle and playful. Horses were in plentiful supply. A small herd ran up to the road and stopped - eyeing the crowd coming down the road. Farmer spied one horse that reminded him of Dusty.

"Do animals come ta - this place? Ya know - like pets we had?" Farmer asked the question which now had surfaced in his thoughts.

"Don't think so," grandfather Trevor answered. "The Good Book tells us that animals don't have spirits like we does."

"Still, we sure have seen animals that looked like our pets," his wife chimed in.

The horses mingled with the humans and the other animals for a ways then wandered off into a grove of trees. An eagle gave its shrill cry from high above. Farmer looked into the sky, but it wasn't blue sky, as he had known on earth. This seemed like a huge dome that covered all of Heaven with a vibrant light. Sometimes it glowed, other times it grew bright – always coming from God's Throne – always lighting all of heaven. Farmer noticed as he watched the sky that it would change hews. Not always a brilliant blue, but sometimes-softer color tones. The color changes would also change the appearance of Paradise.

"Have you figured out there's no shadow cast here?" his great grandfather asked with obvious amusement.

As Farmer looked he saw it was true, and when he looked down, he saw again that even though their legs and feet were moving, they were not touching the road – or anything for that matter. It seemed they could go slow or super fast by just their thoughts and words.

The group moved in silence for a while now. Farmer became aware of the guardian angels that seemed to be ever present. Sometimes they were by the side of their humans, others times they hovered overhead.

"What interesting creatures!" Farmer thought.

When he smiled at Adreen and she smiled back Farmer sensed a look of curiosity. He did not know what the angels understood of love as he knew and felt it, but he had no doubt of their devotion and allegiance to Jesus Christ. He had noticed Adreen when the Lord was mentioned. Her wings folded, her head bowed, reverant. Farmer knew for certain were he to attempt to get Adreen to go against God's will, or command her to do something that would bring reproach on the Son of God; she would instantly draw her sword against him. No! The angels' beauty came from being unsoiled by sin. Then Farmer shuddered when he thought of how the fall had deformed Zoogot into a hidious monster.

"Oh, look!" someone in the group exclaimed. "It's an archangel!" Farmer's gaze moved in the direction of the pointing finger until he saw a brilliant spot of light moving along the horizon towards a city. He could barely make out a figure in the light.

"I never thought much about angels 'til I got here," Franklin spoke with a far-away look. "I asked my angel, Terzon, a wagonload of questions.

"An' I reckon ya got an earful," Farmer smiled.

"Yep, got a good education on it. Most beautiful an' powerful are the cherubim. They are about the worship an' glory of God. Next is the seraphim that be concerned about devotion to God. These all are around the throne an' we ain't seen 'em yet," Franklin paused, but one could tell he delighted in sharing this information with his son. It was like he wanted to make up for time lost in his earthly days.

"There's destroyin' angels like what brought destruction on the Sodom and Gomorrah cities or the terrible plagues that fell on Egypt," Franklin continued. "Ain't seen them either that we know of. An' there's the gathering angels like what will gather up the believers when Christ goes back to earth. Like the one who gathered us up to meet you today - er - whenever that was."

They both laughed and other relatives joined in as they all agreed they had no concept of time in Heaven. There was no night, no passing of days, no clocks. All they knew was that Farmer died in 1951 and arrived in Heaven sometime after that.

"Anyways, there's also archangels who deliver messages from God. Special messages it seems. That angel we just seen musta been a tendin' ta that. There's other angels a doin' different kinds of work, and our guardian angels, of course."

The angels hovering with Farmer's gathering broke out in song, their wings unfurled. Heaven and angels! Farmer could scarcely take it all in! No wonder the scripture writers could not find words to describe what they had seen.

Chapter 47

NEW ARRIVALS

Farmer's family led him a great distance to a village that was nestled in a grove of lush trees and vegetation near the base of a large outcropping of what appeared to be rock. The light glistened on the face of the rock giving the whole area a slight appearance of a western setting, only much more grand. The rock cliff jutting up from the ground reminded Farmer of one he had seen in the Arizona landscape, reflecting shades of reds, oranges and golds.

"The Master gave us instruction to bring you here as this be your dwelling place," Franklin told his son. "Some of the rest of us live here too."

Two angelic creatures met the arriving party at the entrance to the city.

"Welcome, Farmer Trevor, to the village called Passage. Your abode awaits you!" One of the angels addressed Farmer in a bold voice, yet with a tone of utmost respect. Both angels bowed to Farmer and commenced to lead him and his loved ones through cobblestone streets except the stones were all precious gems.

"We never laid eyes on rubies an' emeralds the likes o' these, eh, Farmer," grandpa Carter pointed out in mirth.

Farmer was speechless! The village was incredible, with beautiful buildings lining the broad streets. People were everywhere, smiling, laughing, and giving hellos and welcomes to the new arrival. There wasn't any sense of fear here, nor of envy or jealousy. There was no concern about making an impression or wrong impression, or speaking that cutting remark hurting another's feelings. Farmer knew without being told those things were absent from Heaven. There were no sinful thoughts or ways - no dark secrets here. Heaven was full of God's light and love and every person reflected it!

Farmer was flooded with well-wishers. They shook his hands - hugged him - others had eager questions and wanted to talk later. For the first time Farmer realized why Heaven would last forever.

As Farmer made his way down one of the streets, all of a sudden he was face to face with a beautiful young woman. She seemed familiar, but Farmer wasn't sure. She stood firm staring him in the eye, her face beaming. The noisy crowd grew still as they sensed the importance and reverence of the moment.

"Farmer Trevor, it's me, Ruth Riggs -."

"From Hurricane!" Farmer interrupted. He hugged and kissed her then stepped back to look at her.

"I - I reckon ya look a lot younger then I remember ya an' - an' -."

"And a lot thinner!" Ruth laughed. You look a pretty picture yourself, Farmer. I learned two things the time I been here. One is that everyone is about thirty years old in looks. I asked about that and one fella told me he heard it's that way because our Savior was crucified at age 33. Now the second thing I learned is to take folks' word about how I look, 'cause there ain't no reflections in Heaven. Not in the jewels, not in the water, an' there ain't no mirrors here."

316

"That means we don't have to fix our hair - ever - again. Praise the Lord," one of Farmer's cousins, he had met for the first time at the river gathering, laughed jokingly.

"Don't need no make-up neither!" another relative added.

Everyone laughed and began praising God for saving them and the beauty He had bestowed upon each person. Farmer looked at his Pa and realized how young he looked. Then he eyed his grandparents - how handsome his grandfathers - how young and pretty his grandmothers. His great-grandparents? They were the same! Farmer turned back to Ruth. She grew serious.

"Farmer," she said with deep emotion, "I have thanked the Good Lord a thousand times if not a million fer sendin' you to my doorstep that hot June day, and fer you tellin' me about Jesus and prayin' fer me. I can't thank you enough, my dear brother!"

"I'm - jus' -," Farmer choked up. "Reckon I'm jus' right proud yer here."

"Thank you, Farmer, and bless you!" Ruth kissed him gratefully on the cheek, and Farmer wondered if he turned red.

"You remember when you had coffee that morning how full of questions you were?"

"Yes'm, the first led ya ta accept Christ as yer Savior."

"Right, and I will be eternally glad you asked it. You had three questions, Farmer Trevor, and I have three questions for you."

"What be they?"

"How did you die? How are Emile and the boys? And what did you have born in Oregon? A boy or a girl? I been dyin' to know - but that ain't what killed me!" With that Ruth broke into a jovial laugh that swelled in volume - the same laugh which Farmer remembered hearing often in Riggs little makeshift hospital.

As Farmer began to speak, the crowd drew closer to hear his answers. Ruth, who was always one to command a situation, and still a bit of a tease, held up her hand to stop Farmer.

"You're a new arrival here, Farmer. You get yourself settled an' we can hook-up later. I'll be anxious to get your answers. Have we got a lot of catchin' up to do!"

Everyone groaned, and then laughed together heartily as Farmer moved on down the street.

Chapter 48

A SUMMONS

The angels led Farmer to a sizeable building with many doors. It reminded him of a plush hotel like he had seen in Hollywood - only better. The walls were made of a material unfamiliar to him. It gave out a silvery blue cast and appeared transparent, like you could see into it but not through it.

His door was a most beautiful wood with a solid gold knob, and above it was gold lettering, "Farmer Trevor." The angels passed through the door without opening it. Farmer hesitated!

"Go on," Franklin urged.

Farmer was unsure. One angel came back out and motioned for him to follow. Farmer took a breath, and to his amazement he stepped through the wood as though it wasn't even there!

He gasped in surprise as he looked around. His room glowed from the light coming through the walls. Thick over-stuffed sofas surrounded the wall space providing ample seating for many guests. In the center was a long low table with many rich colored pillows placed on the floor on all four sides. Silver bowls of delicious looking fruit had been set on the table awaiting the arrival of Farmer and his guests.

The walls were graced with pictures in beautiful and rich-looking frames. Farmer was shocked in closer examination that the pictures depicted various episodes of his life and people he knew! He sobbed uncontrollably upon seeing Emile and his children. God had taken snapshots.

Later, Farmer walked into a side room that contained a most comfortable-looking bed, far too large for him alone. His curiosity was peaked as to why a bed. He hadn't slept since his death nor had he experienced tiredness. He also noted there was no bathroom, as the need for one had been eliminated. Farmer chuckled, and then realized he was alone except for the two angels and Adreen. They saw the puzzled look on his face.

"Your family awaits your invitation to come in," one angel informed him.

"Yes, yes. I reckon I'm a fergettin' my manners! Does this door open? I want it ta be open ta everone!"

Farmer grabbed the door and swung it wide open. He had an overpowering compulsion to welcome everyone. He was thrilled with the place the Lord had prepared for him!

Every person who was waiting outside entered the room, and the strangest thing happened. The room and the table and seating kept expanding to accommodate every last guest.

Immediately, ministering angels were among them serving food and drink. Farmer had never tasted such delicacies in mortal life.

The mood was light and happy. As they ate, the conversation shifted to more questions directed towards Farmer. He told in detail of the long trip from Texas to Oregon - of the flash flood and how God spared them.

"Adreen warned us!" Farmer smiled as he glanced at his guardian angel that stood nearby.

"Emile got terrible ill with the baby an' was near death. Thet's when we run across Ruth Riggs."

"Okay, what did ya have Farmer? Boy or girl?" queried the woman just mentioned. "Been years wonderin'!"

"Had us a beautiful lil' girl we named Leah."

"Did she have her Pa's restless spirit and movin' feet?" came a question from one side of the room. Farmer did not recognize the woman, but the voice sounded familiar. He stepped closer for a better look; then recognition came.

"Margaret! Margaret Hatchet!" Farmer shouted, reaching for this old friend.

"You look terrible pretty!" He exclaimed, breaking their embrace.

"Terrible, might fit. I hoped the Dear Lord woulda taken a few pounds off me when I got here," Margaret joked, "Guess it would be uninteresting in Heaven if everyone was thin. You didn't answer my question, lad."

Farmer dropped his head, "Yes'm, 'fraid she did - an' more so. She was headstrong - got pregnant young and married the man. His name is Harold. They hev a little girl - Janee."

"Got another question, Farmer. Did those automobiles ever catch on?"

Farmer shook his head suppressing the urge to laugh out loud.

"Did they ever catch on? Margaret, they be everwhere! Even in Holt, goin' faster then anything - well, not as fast as we can go now - but powerful fast - and big too!"

Then everyone greeted Margaret and her husband, and all wanted to know about automobiles as none of them had seen one in their lives, except for Margaret, Farmer and Ruth.

Farmer described cars, trucks and airplanes. He went on to paint a mental image of the beautiful ranch they had in Oregon, and of losing it in the Great Depression.

A somber mood came over the room when Farmer relayed news of the awful war.

"Many came here from that war," a man remarked quietly. Some nodded their heads, and a tear trickled down Farmer's cheek as thoughts of Little Gordie came to mind. He determined to search for the young man later.

"You didn't answer my other questions, Mr. Trevor," Ruth broke the mood.

Farmer went on to tell about his children and grandchildren after the war. He worked his way backwards through Ruth's questions as he relived his and Emile's life together, the trips they made, Janee's acting in the movies. He had to explain for most of them what movies were - moving pictures on a screen showing a story.

Farmer ended with his death.

"Looked favorable to get my ranch back an' me bein' so eager went out there ta check on the land an' house. Some young green hunter thought I was a deer an' shot me dead!"

The room was quiet.

"How 'bout ya, Ruth? I reckon ya kept on doctorin' in Hurricane?"

"Not in Hurricane! The conditions grew less favorable there so I moved south into Nevada to a little town and set up a place to deliver babies. Discovered a small church there and joined up. Met an older widower who also attended, an' we married. Work took us to Montana. I doctored some there, and my mister and me started a church in the town 'cause there wasn't one. Oh, we weren't the preacher or anything - just helped get it going."

"You have children?" someone asked.

"Did I have children? Honey, I had kids scattered from Utah to Nevada to the western part of Montana and eastern Idaho. Kids I brought into the world - with my heart and hands. Did I give birth to my own?"

Ruth grew sad. "No, but I suppose that's one of those aches the Lord will take away someday."

The group sat quietly - lost in thought - remembering. Farmer noticed a man he had not met.

"Air ya part o' my family?" Farmer directed his question to the man.

The man looked up startled, seeing Farmer was speaking to him.

"No," he replied looking around the room. "I live in Passage, and when I heard you coming down my street, I joined in. I came from a country distant from yours where my people worshipped idols. I heard of Master Jesus from a tourist, and I believed. My mother and father disowned me when they heard of my decision and threw me out. I traveled many miles to a village where there was a church, and they took me in. One night our village was raided; I was stabbed in the dark. I long to see my mother, father, sister and brothers, but, I - don't know... I have no family here so I thought..."

Cries were uttered, and the family took this young man in with an incredible display of love and acceptance. The thought of anyone, anywhere in Heaven being excluded for any reason seemed utterly unthinkable.

While this was taking place, a gathering angel appeared in the room with a summons. He called out names, Farmer's included.

"Come! You have a loved one arriving," the angel instructed.

The group, following the angel, arrived in the small valley by the river in the blink of an eye. Others joined them swelling in numbers. Each person was excited, wondering who was coming. Farmer's heart began to race, or at least it felt like it. Farmer knew he had no heart, but there was a place inside that felt and loved even more now. How he hoped it was Emile! He longed for his mate, and found himself pacing back and forth as he had done in life.

"There's Jesus!" A shout arose, and all eyes looked to the top of the hill. It was Jesus, and He had his arm around a woman. Farmer's hand covered his mouth. It looked like Emile! He wanted to fly up the hill, but the gathering angel stopped him.

"You must wait!" the angel spoke with great kindness.

The Lord seemed to be in deep conversation with the woman, and then pointing her towards the gathering, He disappeared. The woman started down the hill.

"Oh! Oh! Oh!" Franklin gasped. "Merciful God, it's Allison Jane!"

Farmer joined in his Pa's joy as he watched his Ma fly into his Pa's arms.

"Welcome home, Ma," Farmer breathed softly.

Chapter 49

I SEARCHED HEAVEN OVER

Eventually, Farmer's friends and family scattered to their own dwellings. He decided to lie down on his bed. It gave him a great sense of relaxation and peace. He stared at the ceiling, then at Adreen who stood at the foot of the bed.

"Do ya ever lie down or sleep, Adreen?" Farmer instantly felt the question silly.

"No," she answered. "I was not created to tire."

Farmer thought for a while, then suddenly remembered a quest he had meant to make. He sat up!

"Adreen, how can I find others I might know - I reckon Heaven is a big place, but there must be some sorta directory?"

"I will ask."

"Ya will?! How?!"

Adreen looked deep into Farmer's eyes. Then she began to sing a lovely song that rose and swelled until the room was full of the melody. Then she grew still as if listening for a far distant reply.

After what seemed a long time she looked at Farmer. Her face revealed a heavy sadness he had never seen on her.

"He is not here," she said sadly. "But there is another who seeks your face."

"Who? Wait! How did you know who I was wanting ta find?"

Adreen went to a picture in the main room and pointed. Farmer walked to the picture. It was taken of Gordie outside the Church in the Woods.

"That was taken the Sunday before Little Gordie left for the Marines." A terrible ache stabbed through Farmer's heart. How could this be? Gordie grew up in the church, he was a good kid; he gave his life for his country. He had to be here – somewhere - in Heaven!

"Come, Farmer, I shall take you to see the one who seeks you."

Farmer followed Adreen to a village of small cottages in a more remote part of the great valley. The town reminded Farmer of a storybook land. Adreen stopped in front of a quaint, interesting-looking house. It was one that invited you to peek inside. Splashes of brilliant colored flowers and exotic orchids overflowed from planters that hung below each window. People were walking in the street, some spoke to a woman sitting on the front porch of the cottage. Her guardian angel nodded to Adreen.

"Hello," the woman smiled at Farmer as he passed through her gate.

"Howdy yerself." Farmer looked into a pretty face. The woman seemed more concerned, than happy.

"I don't believe I knew you," her eyes searched his face.

"Don't recollect ever meetin' ya either. My name is Farmer Trevor."

"Oh, Farmer!" the woman rose to come to him. She gently took his face in her hands. "I'm Betty Jean Harrison, Benjamin's wife. I've searched Heaven over and can't find him anywhere. I hoped against hope that you have seen him."

Farmer shook his head - Betty Jean burst into tears and fell heavy against his chest. Farmer held her for a long time - his own heart torn apart. When she was spent, she motioned for Farmer to sit with her on the porch. She wanted to tell her story.

"Benjamin fell in with bad company. We would drink and dance 'til all hours. I didn't like where our life was leading, but felt helpless to get out of it. I read your letters where you wrote to Benjamin about Christ. I could tell it bothered him, but he never uttered a mean word about you. Oh, Farmer, how he loved and admired you! He planned to take a trip to Oregon - so I could..." Betty's voice trailed off. "Then those evil men murdered him! He always said your religion wasn't suited for him. Oh, dear God! If only he hada listened - believed!"

"Well, yer here," Farmer attempted to console this woman who seemed near frantic with grief.

"When he got shot, I thought I was going to die along with him; I loved him so much! At the funeral, I got to thinking about some of the things you wrote in your letters, and the preacher talked about Heaven an' Benjamin being here, so I wanted to be here too. I found me a church to attend, and that's where I accepted the Lord."

"Did ya die old?" Farmer asked.

"I got very ill and died in a Texas hospital. Farmer, if Benjamin isn't here in Heaven, then - " the sudden shock of where Benjamin might be hit her hard!

"Farmer, he has to be here - somewhere!"

Farmer looked to Adreen as if to say, "Will ya try again?"

Together, Adreen and Betty Jean's angel raised their voices until the melody filled all of Paradise. Their wings lifted them up until the sound was full and complete, then they set back down, their feet touching the ground, their wings folded. They listened, then with downcast eyes, shook their heads - no.

"Benjamin used to joke about all his friends and him being together and drinking and enjoying wild parties in hell," Betty wailed.

"Won't be good fellowship or fun parties there," a man passing by on the street had heard the conversation. He stepped through the small fence and joined Farmer and the distraught Betty.

"In my life I had a near death vision of hell," the man ventured on. Farmer started to object to further discussion of the subject.

"No. We have to face it!" The man raised his hand to silence Farmer. "God knows we all have to face it once we arrive here. Christ made it clear in His Word there are only two places, Heaven and hell! No other - no second chances - it's forever - no end!

"Our eternal destination is sealed when we draw our last breath. We see the wonder and glory of this place, people on earth dream of it, yet think little of hell, even deny its existence. But I caught a glimpse of its horror one day.

"I was near death, and in my vision I was forced into some kind of elevator with a group of other folks. Not any of us wanted to go, but had no choice. We were lowered into a dreadful canyon where everything was steamy and dead. Terrible odors came up from the bottom, choking the very breath out of us. The elevator opened to staggering heat. We stepped onto ground that was alive with worms. We tried to brush them off - beat them off. I'll never forget the screams!

"Then I saw it. Tables and chairs set up for us. On the tables were ice-cold glasses of water. The thirst was more than I could stand! I ran to grab a glass - I drank! The liquid burned like fire. I cried out, the drink left me with greater thirst. I tried to leave it alone, but couldn't. No amount of determination or willpower could keep any of us from taking up the glass that would never run dry. The burning! The insatiable thirst! Then it dawned on me; this is forever. It will never end. There is no trusting Christ now, though I repent 10 million times 10 million, I will still be here, to relive my regrets - over and over. No forgiveness for sins!

"Well, that vision scared the hell out of me! When I came to, I gave my heart to Jesus Christ and believed on His atoning work on the cross. I dedicated my life to win as many as I could, so they wouldn't go to that awful place that I saw in my vision."

The man put his arm around Betty's shoulder to try and comfort her.

"I grieve with you for your husband," he said.

Betty covered her face in her hands. "Poor Benjamin," she sobbed.

Farmer's heart broke for a friend he never reached.

Chapter 50

A LIFE UNFOLDING

Farmer returned in silence to his own dwelling, his mind full of questions. It wasn't confusion he was experiencing, none of that occupied Heaven. It was a grief and sorrow of proportions he had never known in life on earth. He studied the pictures on the walls of his home. There were many of Little Gordie growing up with his and Emile's two sons. Farmer had complete trust and confidence in God's love and justice, but wondered where the lad missed Christ.

Then there were a dozen pictures of Benjamin. Pictures of when they were boys, playing, in school together, one taken the last time Farmer saw Benjamin - the day he brought the maps for the trip. Farmer looked at each picture a long time and remembered. Finally, grief overcame him, and he could find no comfort. He cried out to the Lord!

In an instant, the Lord Jesus stood in the room. Farmer was startled and dropped to his knees. He could not speak! The Lord placed His Hand on Farmer's shoulder. Love and peace flowed into Farmer's being, and he was comforted with the knowledge that the Son of God shared in his grief. Farmer gazed with questioning eyes into the face of his Savior as He raised him to his feet.

Jesus led Farmer to a picture of Little Gordie, Walter and Clifton.

"Gordie came the closest to faith in Me right there," the Master spoke softly. "Walter and Clifton spoke words and testimonies. He was almost persuaded."

"Then why didn't he?" Farmer questioned.

"Where were you the Sunday of Pearl Harbor?"

Farmer was taken back by the Master's question.

"Why - er - I was in church!" he stammered.

"Where was Gordie?"

Farmer had to recall.

"I reckon he was outside in his car. He heard the news on the radio."

"Yes," the Savior's tone took on a deep sorrow. "His heart was not with Me. He made the mistake of having faith in his mother and father's relationship with Me to save him. His whole life he attended fellowship because his parents made him. He never trusted in Me for himself. I tried every way possible to reach Gordie Brooks. Message after message was preached at the Church in the Woods, but Gordie preferred to remain outside. When he was in church, he made jokes and thought of other things. Before the end, I even sent a Marine Chaplain to speak to him, but Gordie was only concerned about what his friends thought."

Farmer dropped his head. It was clear that Little Gordie condemned himself, yet the thought of burning in an endless hell left Farmer with a sense of dread and horror for his two friends.

"You gave My message to Benjamin many times," the Lord pointed to numerous pictures. "Here - here - and here. This time when you were both fishing, you testified of Me. When you wrote this letter," Jesus touched a picture of Farmer in the log house sitting at the kitchen table writing a letter.

"When we was in Oregon," Farmer murmured sadly. "The last time I was able ta write ta my friend…"

"You were like two brothers who took different paths. Benjamin's heart was choked with cares of the world. He never stopped blaming Me for coming between yours and his friendship."

"Ya didn't, Lord!"

"I know, but he was blinded by jealousy he never knew he had."

Farmer began to weep for his friends, and felt guilt. If he had only tried harder, been more concerned, exerted diligence, maybe it would have turned out differently. Jesus, knowing his thoughts and feelings stood Farmer in the center of the room and held out His arms.

"Behold." He spoke of all the pictures.

"I don't understand - the meanings!" Farmer exclaimed.

"Do you remember when we met on the hill a moment ago when you arrived?" Jesus asked.

"Yes, my Lord. It seems years ago now."

"In earth time it has been, but in light of eternity, an instant. You remember I told you that the story of your life is still unfolding. Well, some of it has, and I will reveal it to you now."

Jesus stepped to a wall and removed a picture showing it to Farmer. It was a smiling man standing by a horse.

"Thet's Preacher Tunnell," Farmer grinned.

"He was ready to resign the church and leave his calling. You spoke words of encouragement that day which changed his mind and the course of his life."

Jesus replaced the picture and took another. It was of a happy couple walking hand in hand.

"Words you spoke to Timothy about his unfaithful wife, Karen, helped them save their marriage."

The Lord pointed to a picture of a man and woman and their children. They were seated in a church.

"Remember George and Debra Apperson? You gave them water and towed their car to Glen Rio? You made them give their word that they would go to church. Well, Farmer, they did keep their word, and the Holy Spirit touched their hearts. They and the children who followed were saved in that church."

Farmer wanted to beg the Lord to stop!

"You saved the lives of Bob and Kathleen Buchwald along with their children. They all were Mine, and I used you and Emile to warn them of danger."

Farmer looked at a picture of a frightened and grateful family, the same faces he saw when he first reached the Buchwalds' car after the raging creek had subsided.

"You saved the lives of a family stranded in the desert and gave them water. They never forgot, and neither have I."

Farmer was humbled and only wanted to give God the praise and glory, then he wished to seek the Lord's forgiveness for not doing more!

"Remember this fellow?" Jesus asked, taking another picture from a sidewall. It was of a red-haired, freckle-faced man holding a Bible. On either side and behind him were vast multitudes of people.

Farmer looked. The face looked familiar, but he connected nothing else.

"It's Peter." The Lord smiled knowingly, "You were sent to the hotel lobby to bear witness of Me. I planted those words deep within him and didn't let go. My hand was upon that young man and my call to preach. He finally surrendered to me, and I delivered him from strong drink. All these are the ones who have believed on Me by Peter's ministry." Jesus replaced the photo and took another.

"Praise be unta ya, Lord!" Farmer declared.

"And I brought this family to you, Farmer."

"Oh!" Farmer cried aloud upon seeing the Wild Eagles. But there were only three in the picture.

"I spoke to them through you, Farmer, and My Word does not return to Me void. They could not escape the story you told around the campfire that night nor My Word you gave them to read. Henry trusted Me first, after a long battle within himself and with his old ways. Hettie followed him, then Omney and finally after running away, Curtis accepted me. I took them on to California where they built a home and later became a vital part of a church. Curtis was killed in the war, and soon after Henry and Hettie succumbed to sickness. Omney still lives and serves Me faithfully. Her picture is over there." Farmer's heart ached for them as he looked at the three, but Jesus did not take Omney's picture from the wall.

"This was one of my favorite times." The Lord took another life photo from its place on the wall.

Farmer looked but only saw a whole bunch of people he didn't recognize.

"These are all the ones you gave your cattle away to, so they had food to eat."

Farmer shook his head!

"How could thet be a favorite time, Lord?" Farmer questioned. "I was goin' bankrupt an' doin' a foolhardy thing!"

"In the eyes of the world, yes, My child, but not in My eyes."

"But Lord, Ya blessed me with those cattle, an' I was givin' them away!"

"Farmer Trevor, do you think I gave you those cattle just so you could make money and support your family?" Jesus spoke sternly.

"No," Farmer whimpered. His lip quivered, and he tried to hold back tears.

"More than at any other time your heart displayed true love and generosity." The Master held the picture up in front of Farmer.

"Because of your kindness and words, every one of these are Mine, beginning with Mitchell and Grace, whom you gave your first steer to." Jesus replaced the picture and led Farmer to the door.

"Come, Farmer! Come into the joy of your labor."

Jesus opened Farmer's door to a great throng of people waiting outside. When Farmer came into view there arose a loud cheer accompanied with applause! There was Henry Wild Eagle, Hettie and Curtis was near them. Farmer saw Mitchell and Grace - others he didn't know. Peter waved - there were the Appersons, and he recognized the Buchwalds! Pastor Tunnell, who baptized him, stood with his wife - beaming. The crowd rushed in upon Farmer, each eager with a story to share - each with words they had waited a partial lifetime to express.

Chapter 51

PILGRIMS THREE

Farmer learned one thing from the Master's visit. The only pictures that Jesus took from the wall were of those deceased. Each time Farmer studied the pictures that graced his walls he was puzzled. In many of them, he was viewing people and places in which he had no clue as to their meaning.

"Your life is still unfolding," was the Lord's only comment.

Farmer was filled with astounding joy, yet an ever present longing to see ones he knew on earth and hear any news - especially of Emile and his family. His wish was about to come true with the appearing of three pilgrims.

The first came when he received word that someone new was coming to dwell in Passage. He waited eagerly in the street with the rest of the crowd to welcome a new neighbor. Soon he could make out the sounds of talking and laughter. The commotion grew louder as the throng drew closer. Farmer was excited, hoping it was someone he knew.

When the new resident arrived, ushered along by family, Farmer caught a glimpse of a man, but couldn't see his face clearly. He rose up off the ground a ways to get a good look - then recognition came!

"Joe Baltman! Joe!" Farmer yelled.

The man stopped and looked. He peered long into Farmer's face.

"Farmer! Bless God in Heaven, it is you. I figured as mean as you was, you might not make it!"

The two men gripped each other in a display of brotherly love that had moved from a strong friendship on earth to a stronger one in Heaven.

"My family is getting me settled, an' soon as they do I'll come calling. Where you stayin'?"

Farmer laughed! "Ya ain't changed a bit, Joe. I'm right here," Farmer pointed to the door behind him.

"See you as soon as I can. Have we got some talkin' to do!"

Joe and his family disappeared down the street around a corner. Soon their sound faded. Farmer walked slowly down a side street towards the large rock outcropping that stood above the city. He had discovered a beautiful garden in a courtyard. Multi-colored roses and other flowers grew in perfect squares surrounded by walkways. Trees lined the walk, and there were many benches on which to sit.

"Emile would love this place..." Farmer thought and knew one day he would show it to her. Farmer was not impatient; that was one thing absent in Heaven. One felt excitement, eagerness, but no impatience. He had all the time in the world.

"Will I know when Joe comes to my dwelling?" Farmer asked Adreen.

"I will know," she responded. "I will alert you."

Others were walking and sitting in the garden, but a man standing on the far side under a tree captured Farmer's attention. Farmer took note that the man was large in build and had a powerful-looking guardian angel. The angel pointed to Farmer, and the two approached. The angels bowed their heads in greeting.

"You Farmer Trevor?" the man asked gruffly.

"Yeh, thet's me, but I don't reckon I know who ya be."

"You knew me, or of me, by the name of Gardner Grubb."

Farmer was floored! Gardner Grubb was the last person he expected to see in Heaven. Immediately, a picture in his dwelling came to mind.

"Thet's it!" he thought. It was a picture of a path through the trees. It reminded him of his ranch, but it was the path Farmer had walked on to Gardner's place.

"You look surprised, Farmer," Gardner growled a course laugh.

"I - I - what can I say? Ya be here ta the praise o' God!"

"You had a part, and I came to thank you and tell you how it happened.

"My real name was Luigi Giavonni. I was called Lu, The Shadow. I could be places and never seen. I was a hit man for the mob. Came the day I wanted out, but the boss wouldn't hear of it. I decided to cooperate with the D.A. an' turn state's evidence. The mob hated my guts when I helped put some of them away. A contract was out on me, so the Feds had a place fixed for me on a plot of ground in Oregon, and I became Gardner Grubb."

"But ya were killed?" Farmer questioned.

"Not me. I died an old man in Cleveland."

"But - how - where?" Farmer stammered.

"Didn't call me the Shadow for nothin'," Gardner chuckled. "I fixed an alarm system to warn me of intruders. That's how I knew you were on my property that day.

"Anyway, the mob found me and sent two of their henchmen to whack me, but I got 'em both."

"But the body?"

"One of them. I took their car and disposed of the other body where it was never found. I burned the whole place down, called the boss with my disguised voice and told him it was finished, and slipped away. By the time they figured it out, I was long gone - never to be found."

"Well, I don't reckon ta understand how I hed anythin' ta do with ya bein' here. We hardly spoke, an' ya scared the livin' daylights outa me!"

"You made me so mad I wanted to kill you, comin' 'round my place with a Bible like some preacher. But it troubled me the more I thought about it. Either you was the dumbest man alive or you had something. I was raised to respect the church, but it always seemed separate from my life. One day I found a little Bible someone left on a windowsill. I thought of the one you carried that day, so I slipped the Bible in my pocket. In the solitude of my apartment, I read it through. That's how I believed and got saved."

Gardner's tone and demeanor softened, and Farmer felt genuine love and gratitude flowing from this coarse man. He gripped Farmer's hand.

"Thank you for coming that day!" tears streamed down his cheeks. His face broke into a broad smile. "Jesus forgave me of all my crime and murders. You pointed me to Him."

Farmer reflected on the meeting later as he sat on his porch. He would never have guessed the encounter with Gardner Grubb on his place in Oregon would have produced any results at all - yet now he saw how God had orchestrated the whole thing - to the very end.

By and by Joe Baltman joined Farmer on the porch.

"Sorry I'm late," he teased.

"Reckon there ain't no early - or late here," Farmer smiled. "But I am all eat'n up wantin' ta hear any news ya might bring."

"Well, Farmer, it sure was bad news you getting killed. We all took it right hard, especially Emile and the children. I was told she and little Janee hung onto your casket and wouldn't let go 'til your boys helped 'em. She couldn't walk."

"Oh, dear God, I don't know if I can take this!" Farmer cried out.

Joe, sensing Farmer's grief, took the conversation another direction.

"People came from all over to your funeral. Your children and grandchildren were there. Most all of Douglas Landing - both mills shut down. Lots of people from Applegate, and some of your family from Texas. Emile's sister and her husband, your two brothers and their families were there. Your Ma was too sickly to come. She passed away shortly after."

"Yes, she's here. So are Emile's parents." Farmer added. "I've been with them for many visits."

"The accident shore hit everyone hard, especially the young fella who shot you. He was broken bad at the funeral. Donald an' the preacher led him to Christ that night. An' Farmer, would you believe that the Lord called that young man into ministry down in California. He started a church that has reached thousands! Why, even Rachel, Clifton and their children visited there and reported how fine a preacher he was. That was right hard on them seeing as how he shot you for a deer."

"Praise God!" Farmer breathed a prayer. "You said children?"

"Farmer, if you could see our kids! Clifton is so handsome and a good worker. I couldn't have asked for a better husband for Rachel. Their love has grown, and Rachel has blossomed like a lovely flower. A year after you died, they had a beautiful girl they named Morgan."

Sadness came over Joe.

"I won't get to be at David's high school graduation."

"When is that?"

"Two months."

"What! How old is he?" Farmer gasped.

"Eighteen. Morgan is thirteen."

"What year is it?"

"1965."

"Dear Lord, Emile is sixty-five!" Farmer dropped his face in his hands.

"And as pretty as ever," Joe added brightly.

Farmer looked up, almost afraid to ask the next question.

"Did - did she - did she - remarry?"

Joe Baltman studied Farmer for a long time before he answered.

"Would you be terribly hurt an' upset if she did?"

Farmer looked deep inside himself. There was no jealousy or need to protect a man's territorial rights in Heaven. He knew the scripture, and it said that death freed the living to remarry. He thought of how difficult the loneliness would have been for her, how needed companionship would have been. Still, a part of him was sad to think of her being wife to another. He was nonetheless prepared for whatever answer Joe gave him.

"No, Joe, I'd be right proud an' happy fer her."

"I don't have to tell you, Farmer, that wife of yours was a looker an' a fine woman. Many a man came around to court her as they saw her a prize to be won. She went to dinner with a few, attended church with others, caught a movie with some, most she turned away. After awhile, she just said no to all advances. She told Sally one day that she gave her heart away a long time ago to Farmer Trevor, an' she didn't have anything else to give to any other man."

Farmer broke down and wept! His heart was overflowing with love and longing for his mate.

Farmer sat in silent thought for a long time. Joe waited.

"What news of Walter, Leah, Harold an' Janee?" Farmer ventured, looking up at his friend.

"Walter an' Clifton transferred with their company to Seattle. Walter flies an airliner; Clifton is over maintenance. Harold an' Leah are still in Hollywood." Joe grew solemn as he relayed the next bit of news. "Janee's a movie star, you know. She's a wild one, and that concerns her Ma an' Pa. Emile told me an' Sally that she was more than a handful, but she is a mighty pretty girl, Farmer. You'd be proud of her."

Farmer tried to absorb everything Joe had told him. He felt unsettled over Janee - the same feeling he had about little Gordie, and that scared him to think his granddaughter might be lost, and he was helpless to do anything about it!

Farmer got up and paced back and forth on his porch. After awhile he stopped, turning towards Joe.

"How did - ya die, Joe?"

"Guess my ticker just quit. I was out in the trees cuttin' firewood. Don't know how long it took before Sally found me. I had to leave before that. I sure worried over Sally grievin' - you know she is..."

Farmer nodded. He understood Joe's feelings perfectly.

"Was there a demon waitin' ta attack ya?"

"Lord yes! Farmer, I was frightened out of my wits. I've never seen such a monster!"

Before further comment could be made, a gathering angel came for Farmer.

"Who do ya think it could be?" Farmer asked excitedly.

Joe shrugged his shoulders.

In an instant, Farmer travelled the distance to a spot by the river. His Ma and Pa were there, along with other family members. Many were still arriving.

"Oh, let it be Emile!" Farmer hoped with all that was in him. He could hardly contain himself! Then the voice of the Lord whispered to his heart.

"Each person has an appointed time."

Suddenly, the Master appeared at the top of the hill with a man. Everyone strained to try and figure out who it was.

Jesus talked to this person for a long time, and then He held him in His arms. Finally, the Lord sent him down the hill.

"Who is it?" Franklin was as puzzled as the rest of the family.

"It's William!" Allison screamed for joy.

"Look! He's whole!" Farmer shouted. "He has his arm an' leg back!"

Everyone rushed to William, but was taken back by his words of desperation.

"A terrible thing happened!" he blurted out. "Phyllis and I were ridin' in the car with Sidney Dean. He was drivin' too fast. Had a couple of beers. Should never a gone with him, but he talked us inta it. He lost control, an' we flipped over an' over!"

William looked over the whole group as if searching. His eyes were wild!

"We were put in ambulances, goin' to a hospital, when I had to leave. It was terrible - a demon fightin' fer me in the ambulance. I don't know if Phyllis an' Sidney made it. They ain't here, are they?"

The family shook their heads, and then tried to comfort a broken-hearted man who had gone on a simple evening ride that turned into a nightmare.

Later, as the conversations waned, William, without warning, had a look of shock on his face. He looked like he had been stabbed, if that were possible.

"Stella's not here?" he questioned.

"No, should she be?" Franklin answered.

"God have mercy! She died two years ago!"

The families' first reaction was to their guardian angels who searched Heaven with their voices. It was a desperate hope, for they knew in their hearts that if Stella were in Heaven, she would have been gathered with the rest of the family.

"Your sister is not here," Adreen spoke to Farmer quietly.

Soon a moan of sorrow and grief rose from the lips of the family that could be heard all over the valley. The angels joined in with downcast wings.

Chapter 52

A SPECIAL PLACE

Farmer and Joe went back and forth between their dwellings in Passage. As they had been good friends and neighbors in Douglas Landing, so they were in Heaven.

Once, when Joe was at Farmer's place, he took him over to a picture. He tried to remove the frame from the wall as the Lord Jesus had done, but to his surprise found it would not budge.

"I already tried that," Joe laughed. "Can't take 'em off their hook."

"Hmmmph," Farmer mused. "Anyway, look at this one. Can't fer the life o' me figure out its importance. Jus' ya an' me talkin' in church."

Joe studied the picture, and his eyes grew misty.

"I can tell you what it was, even what we said."

Farmer looked at him with a blank stare.

"You gave the message that morning," Joe went on. "You told your feelin's about losin' your ranch an' how God was workin' a plan - even in bad times".

Suddenly, Jesus was in their midst.

"You speak the truth, Joe. Farmer, you were like Joseph. I dealt harshly with you so you could help others. You were faithful in good works.

"Joe asked you for prayer that morning. He and his family were hungry. You gave your brother all the money you had. You unselfishly asked about other families, and you declared to Joe, 'As long as I'm a workin' an' money comin' in, I swear we will be bringin' ya all food - 'til better times come!' I know, I was there. I even retold it with your Texas accent," the Lord laughed, and then became gentle and serious.

"I saw, and you kept your word, Farmer."

Both men bowed humbly before the Son of God as they gave Him praise and glory for sustaining them in those dark times.

"Farmer, follow Me," Jesus commanded.

They both disappeared through the wall of Farmer's house and were instantly in another part of Heaven.

Farmer had been in numerous cities since his arrival, all of them beautiful beyond compare, but this place displayed a strange wonder, almost mystical. There were high cliffs with incredible cascading waterfalls everywhere, creating a soft mist that glistened rainbows of brilliant colors. Dwellings were embedded throughout the cliffs. As Farmer followed Jesus through this city it began to sink into his consciousness how massive this place was. It also struck Farmer how childish these men and women acted when they gleefully ran out to greet and kiss the Master. The further they went into the city, the more people poured out of their houses. It bottled up inside until Farmer could no longer hold back what he felt.

"Lord, there be - thousands - no, millions here. They act like children! What's wrong with them?"

"Child," Jesus replied sternly, "there is nothing wrong in Heaven. This is a special place. It is called, 'The Heart of the Father.'"

"I'm sorry, Lord. Ya be right. Heaven is without sin or blemish. I reckon I stuck my foot in my mouth."

Jesus put His arm around Farmer. No sin had been committed, and no forgiveness needed - only instruction.

"Come with me," the Lord spoke gently. Soon they entered into a magnificent dwelling nestled at the base of a waterfall. A sad-looking young man jumped up, upon seeing Jesus. The man dropped to his knees and wrapped his arms around Jesus' legs.

"Rise," Jesus lifted the man to his feet.

"Farmer, this is Janee's son."

"What!" Farmer was flabbergasted. "How? When?" he stuttered.

A different kind of sadness appeared in the Lord's face.

"Janee gave herself to a man who only wanted her body," Jesus explained. "When she discovered she was pregnant, she became afraid and had an abortion. She never knew whether she carried a boy or a girl. I searched Janee's heart for a name for her child. When she was little playing dolls one day, she called her baby, 'Seth.'"

Farmer sat hard into a sofa. He was astounded! These people - by the millions - covered by the precious blood of the Lamb, had no history. They knew nothing! No wonder they acted like little children! What had Janee done? What madness drove her to have her own baby ripped from her body. Farmer's mind was reeling when the Master's soft voice broke into his thoughts.

"Farmer, you can help your great-grandson now," and Jesus disappeared.

Farmer sat staring at this young man who stood trembling before him.

"I don't understand," Seth began to cry. "Didn't my mother and father want me? I don't even know them! I'm alone! I have no family!"

"Seth, I reckon thet ain't true."

Then the understanding of what the Lord meant when He said, "All things will be made right," came crashing down on him and love for Seth filled his heart.

"I'm yer family, Seth. Come. Sit with me, 'cause we got a powerful lot o' talkin' ta do. Ya got a family, an' ya got a history, an' a Ma an' Grandma an' Grandpa an' a Great Grandma still livin' an' me - here in Heaven, an' I mean ta tell ya all about them an' what yer family came through!"

Chapter 53

CLOSE OF A JOURNEY

Seth was so full of questions, Farmer decided to bring him to his dwelling. He obviously was hungry to become part of the family he never knew. He followed at Farmer's heels everywhere he went.

When Farmer was in Seth's dwelling, he realized there were no pictures on his walls. As they made their way through the streets of "The Heart of the Father," Farmer was mobbed by young men and women. They acted like orphans longing and hoping someone would adopt them.

Farmer observed that of the times he was in the city, Jesus Christ frequented the streets and houses as well. He became aware that a sudden influx of new inhabitants was continually flooding this huge community. It also seemed the number of people arriving, whom he had known on earth increased.

Shortly, after William's homecoming, Sidney arrived. Farmer could only imagine his brother Jacob and sister-in-law Dorothy's shock and pain over the loss of their son.

A little longer and Phyllis was greeted in Heaven by the family. She had succumbed to the physical damage inflicted by the car accident, but she told William as he held her in his arms that she lost the will to live when she heard he was dead.

Each time they were gathered to the river, Farmer made sure to take Seth with him. The young man basked in the love and acceptance bestowed upon him by the family. He exhibited a childlike exuberance when meeting someone new.

Farmer's time in Paradise had brought him to a greater understanding of two major discoveries.

The first began to occur to him every time he walked the streets of Passage, or visited other cities and villages. No one was a stranger in Heaven, and everyone had this strong and holy desire to testify about what God had done in their lives. Every person telling their life story and all who listened ended up praising God and giving Him the Glory. No one ever tired of the telling or the hearing, and Farmer experienced that the excitement level never diminished.

Farmer thought of the millions of people in Heaven and all there was to tell. He suddenly began to understand eternity. There could never be an end to it all! Once you had met and spoken to every person here - you could start all over again - and so what if just one conversation took a hundred years!

His second greater understanding came to him on those occasions when he sat quietly alone. He remembered! He found himself reviewing his life in vivid detail - days and events when he was a little boy - services in church. He thought of the Sunday he accepted Christ as his Savior, and later when he was baptized. He once again was at the Pioneer campsite with his Pa. He saw himself running away from home. School days with his friend, Benjamin brought feelings of horror for where this man was now!

Farmer relived days on his father's farm and his struggle with it. He realized again his hopes and dreams, and made that great trip from Texas in their chuck wagon over and over. He thought of their brief time on the ranch, and the little house in Douglas Landing, and all the precious memories molded and formed in that place they called home.

His heart overflowed with love when he recalled the birth of each of his children. Once again he saw them grow up before his eyes. He wept as he saw Leah sitting on her bed, broken and afraid, the day he learned she was pregnant. Then he thought of young Janee, laughing and playing in their house. How she would come at night with a book in her little hands wanting him to read.

It seemed yesterday - only a moment ago a golden-haired child was flying across the field on Dusty's back.

He reviewed wondrous days in the great Alaskan Territory with Walter, Clifton, Rachel and his grandson David. Farmer would smile and his face shone when he remembered happy, precious memories.

Other times, faces, encounters, some by chance that were only for a moment, came into his thoughts. He would wonder - "I could have witnessed to that person, or I should have been more kind and loving." He saw times he should have spoken and other occasions it would have been better to remain still. Missed opportunities blared in his face. These thoughts loaded him up with sorrow, giving him, for the first time, an understanding of what it meant in the scripture that Lazarus, who died and went to Paradise, was comforted. Farmer had always thought there was no grief or sorrow in Heaven, but some memories were too heavy! There were times of weeping, grieving and the pain of loss. These feelings were intensified in the spirit; however, deep in Farmer's heart he knew there would come a day that the Lord, Jesus Christ, would do what none of them could manage on their own. He would wipe away all tears and remove every sorrow - grief never to be experienced again. Until that time he would remember.

Every time a gathering angel came for him, he hoped it was Emile. Each time he was thrilled to see a loved one, but disappointed it was not his life's mate.

He thought a lot about her in those alone moments. He recalled the first time he saw Emile, a skinny schoolgirl. He felt a boyish crush turn to something richer. He could picture her the night he confessed his love for her - what she wore - how beautiful she looked - her face shining in the moonlight - hair blowing softly in the night air. He lived again their wedding night and times of lovemaking. He saw it now for its sacredness.

A thousand little memories of his lifelong companion made their way through the chambers of his mind. He longed to have her there.

Once he panicked! He got to thinking, "What if Emile wasn't saved? What if she just thought she was? Maybe she has already died and isn't here." He cried out to the Master for some reassurance, but Jesus simply said, "All those who have repented and believed on Me will be here."

Farmer had not seen his parents or the Holts for a while, but didn't think much about it. He visited brothers and sisters non-stop, partially because something in his spirit compelled him, and partially to keep from remembering so much. But now he wanted to be alone. He dropped Seth by his dwelling in "The Heart of the Father." He decided to walk a fern-lined path by the city's many waterfalls. It was there it happened.

Farmer felt a wave of loneliness and longing pass over him. A very faint tug in his heart ever so slight, but he noticed. It made him feel that something was happening, like Emile was trying to reach out to him. He dismissed the notion until a gathering angel appeared before him later.

"Come. We must go to the river," the angel held out his hand.

Farmer stood stunned.

"Oh, dear God!" he whispered. "Could this be the time? Please let it be!"

Excitement surged through Farmer! He flew to the river, arriving ahead of the angel and Adreen. He had to stop for the gathering angel to show him the location. Farmer was the first one to arrive. He began to pace. He stopped!

"I forgot to get Seth," he told the angel.

"Another will gather him," the angel answered with a smile.

"Who is it? Do you know who is coming?" Farmer asked.

"My work is to gather," the angel answered.

"Do ya know, Adreen?"

His guardian angel dropped her eyes and was silent.

Other members began arriving. Farmer paced back and forth. He kept his eyes on the hill - waiting to catch a glimpse of the Lord. He talked with family members! He paced some more - back and forth.

"Oh, hurry, Lord!" Farmer was having trouble containing himself. He wanted to fly up the hill.

"Look!" Jacob shouted as he joined Farmer.

Farmer jumped. He saw the Lord with someone. It was a woman! He bolted to run up the hill, but Adreen blocked him.

"You must wait until the Master is ready," she said firmly.

Farmer paced, keeping his eyes steadily on the Lord and the new arrival. He could not be sure if it was Emile.

Jesus walked slowly with his arm around the woman's shoulder. He was talking to her, and it looked like he wiped away her tears - it was hard to tell.

"Oh, please hurry, Lord Jesus," Farmer breathed. It seemed like an eternity was passing. Then the Savior lovingly held out His arms to her. The woman fell at His feet, and Jesus lifted her up and held her.

Farmer began jumping up and down. Another eternity seemed to pass before the Lamb of God pointed the woman to her family.

Was it her? Farmer still was uncertain until he saw her walk. He saw that same walk coming down the aisle of the church on their wedding day, a familiar walk coming out of their house a zillion times!

"It's Emile!" he screamed and took off running up the hill.

"Emile! Emile! It's me!" Farmer was yelling and waving his arms.

Emile recognized him and came running, laughing.

"Farmer, oh, Farmer! I'm here!" she answered.

They ran into each other's arms, never to be separated again.

Chapter 54

A PLACE FOR FARMER AND EMILE

What a reunion it was! Farmer and Emile together after so many years. Hirum and Vivian Holt were waiting there as well as Emile's brother-in-law, Andrew, who was hoping the new arrival would be Emile's sister, Susan, who was still living on earth.

There was Farmer's side of the family who were also eager to welcome Emile home. It was anybody's guess how long they all remained at the river; there was so much exuberance in the conversations. Eventually, the family escorted Emile to her dwelling in Passage not far from where Farmer was staying.

Her place was gorgeous! In looking around, Farmer was impressed at the large number of beautiful pictures that graced her wall - probably more than he had. He noted that he was in many of them. He had no interest in making a comparison count of his and Emile's pictures - he was only pleased and proud at how wonderfully the Lord had blessed and used Emile in witness and ministry.

"Hey, Emile, I reckon I know what this picture be. It's ya fixin' Thanksgiving dinner. The one where Harold showed up!"

Emile came to look.

"You are right, Farmer, but why would that be in here?"

"You'll see," Farmer smiled.

After much visiting and eating, family members began to depart to their own places. Joe Baltman stopped by and he too had left. Only Seth remained. Emile sat with him holding his hand in hers.

"You look like your mother," she told him.

Later, Farmer took Emile to show her his dwelling. They left Seth at Emile's place.

"I can't tell ya how terrible glad I am ta have ya here, Emile. I missed ya powerful!" Farmer told her as they walked to his place.

"Oh, Farmer, I died a thousand deaths. Once I even considered taking my life to be with you; I missed you so much!"

"Why didn't ya marry again, Emile?"

"I thought about it, but realized I could never love anyone like I loved you. You were mine from the time we were children - the only man for me."

"I worried 'bout ya, Emile, who would care fer ya. The Lord said He would."

"And He certainly did, Farmer."

They arrived at Farmer's dwelling.

"I can open the door or we can pass through it," Farmer laughed.

Emile looked puzzled.

"We can, Emile, an' we can go through walls easy as pie! But I want ta carry ya in - like when we first married," Farmer swooped her up.

"Silly!" she giggled, and Farmer walked through the door.

"Oh!" she exclaimed. "That was - so - incredible!"

"How beautiful," she said in awe as she looked around. She went in every room and studied Farmer's pictures. Her expression changed when she came to one that had Janee in it. Farmer saw the troubled look.

"Is Janee a Christian?" Farmer asked bluntly.

Emile turned to him, pain written all over her face. She shook her head, no.

"Janee has become a star," Emile explained. "She has the world at her feet, but the fame and money, I'm afraid, has ruined her.

"She is a foolish, pigheaded, young woman, not the sweet little girl you knew. She has embraced different beliefs learned from her associates - all of them false. It became impossible to talk to her about Godly things - God knows I tried. Farmer, I had no idea - she - had an abortion! Seth!"

Emile dropped her head in her hands, and Farmer tried to console her.

They talked for a long time, perhaps months. There was so much to share - years of Emile's life. Farmer wanted to know about every minute. Then there were all the heavenly events Farmer had experienced.

"I better take ya ta yer place, Emile," Farmer got up from the sofa.

"But I want to be with you. My place is with you," she spoke with determination.

"Then I'll go with ya ta yer house," Farmer smiled.

That's what the two of them did. They stayed at Farmer's dwelling awhile, then at Emile's - but always together.

One day when they were at Farmer's place, the Lord Jesus appeared before them.

"I knew you would be here," Jesus greeted the couple warmly. "Are you comfortable with your dwellings?" He asked with a twinkle in His eyes.

"Oh, yes, Master," Farmer and Emile quickly responded.

"But you are always together in one or the other," He laughed.

"Yes, Lord," Farmer answered, embarrassed.

"Come with Me," He spoke with a great love.

Jesus took them across the reaches of Heaven to a place neither Farmer nor Emile had been. They came to thick woods in the mountains. Trees were tall and majestic, all kinds of animals roamed amongst the bushes and the timber. Jesus led them to a mountain stream running clean, clear living water. Nestled nearby in the trees was the best and biggest log house Farmer had ever seen.

"Ahhh!" Farmer caught his breath. Emile covered her mouth with her hand as she cried out in surprise.

"I don't reckon I know what ta say, Lord Jesus," Farmer shook his head in amazement. "But I thought we had our places?"

"Those are only temporary. Don't you recall the scripture where I promised to go and prepare a place for you - that where I am you would be there also. This is what you asked for, Farmer".

"I don't - I asked?"

"Don't you remember? The night Leah was born. You stood by the corral under my stars looking around, and prayed for a place like that when you got to Heaven. I heard your prayer, so this is the mansion I have prepared for you. And Emile, I have searched your heart and its desire is to be with your husband. The privilege of sharing an abode in Heaven is reserved for those who shared a special kind of love in their lives on earth. As you were one in life, so shall you be together in Heaven, forever. This is yours, a place for Farmer and Emile!"

"A place for Farmer and Emile!" Emile bubbled over in sheer joy. "Can we go inside? I want to see!"

Printed in the United States
64548LVS00001B/85-270